Misplaced Fortune

"Luck is not chance, it's toil;
Fortune's expensive smile is earned."
Emily Dickinson

love from
Mary x

First published 2021

Published under licence by Brown Dog Books and
The Self-Publishing Partnership Ltd, 10b Greenway Farm, Bath Rd, Wick,
nr. Bath BS30 5RL

www.selfpublishingpartnership.co.uk

ISBN printed book: 978-1-83952-326-7

Cover image by Denise Di Battista
Cover design by Kevin Rylands
Internal design by Andrew Easton

Printed and bound in the UK

This book is printed on FSC certified paper

FSC www.fsc.org
MIX
Paper from responsible sources
FSC® C013604

Misplaced Fortune

MARY POWLES

BROWN DOG BOOKS

Previous books by Mary Powles:

The Accidental Stalker

Moving Times

Available in paperback or e-book format from Amazon.

About the author

Mary Powles was born and brought up in Suffolk and trained as an English and Drama teacher at Homerton College, Cambridge. She moved to South Wales with her husband, Simon, where they settled in a place very like Pontardeilo. She taught at a nearby school, wrote in her spare time and brought up two boys and two dogs within sight of the sea.

Dedication

To Griffith Arthur Powles,
remembering those who have gone before.

Thanks

My thanks go to Simon for his unwavering support and technical help.

I am grateful to Denise Di Battista for the generous use of her image, "Green Meadows", for the front cover (www.artofwales.com).

I am indebted to Alex and Greg for reading the text and giving me feedback.

I am also grateful to everyone at The SPP who has assisted me in my endeavours.

Prologue

1983

Grace Palmer stopped to rub soot from her eyes before skipping past the smouldering remains of a bonfire. She was venturing into the grounds of a property named Long Acres and knew what it was called because she had read the sign at the bottom of the drive where the car was parked. Accompanying her was Richard, Grace's elder brother, not forgetting a rugby ball that had taken on the status of Richard's best friend, and their father, an estate agent, who was talking.

"Long Acres was rumoured to have been built by an English industrialist who became an iron and coal master in the eighteenth century when he made the bold step of crossing the border to Wales. His meteoric rise was tempered by a catastrophic fall and crippling debts."

Richard chased off after his ball and Grace had stopped to pick up a pretty feather from the gravel on the drive.

Undeterred, the history lesson continued. "The son inherited the house but he did not inherit the father's hard-working ethos; Long Acres was lost in a high-stakes gamble at the card table. I believe it was once known by the Welsh name *Pen y Banc* but the winner of the game had little time to enjoy his winnings: the thatched roof caught fire and it was burned to the ground."

By now, he had realised that neither of his children was listening so kept to himself the last gem of knowledge, that it was thought the current property had been built at the end of the nineteenth century.

Hitching up his high-waisted trousers, he stared down at the highly polished brogues worn on his feet. It was an inconvenience for him to drag Richard and Grace around a property evaluation, especially when he could have been playing golf. His wife had gone off to visit her family in Felixstowe. It was a mercy dash. Something to do with women's troubles. He didn't like to ask about it. Fixing his mouth into a professional smile, he strode towards the front of the house and rang the bell.

Watching her father's retreat, Grace flicked blonde plaits behind her shoulders, then switched attention to her elder brother. Arms wrapped round herself for comfort, she waited for his next move. He and his rugby ball were imagining glory at Stradey Parc in an up-and-under manoeuvre. He was either not particularly skilful or was accidentally-on-purpose throwing the ball in the vicinity of his sister's head. She dodged out of his way so that he was unable to barge into her, another favourite trick. He caught the ball and ran ahead, disturbing a couple of noisy pheasants that erupted from the hedge with a burst of indignant clucking.

Richard had no interest in the house on the outskirts of town with distant views towards Gower; the assumption that he would eventually join the partnership of Pughes and Palmer, Estate Agents, troubled him like an itch. Truth be told, he wanted to get the hell out of South Wales and make his fortune somewhere bigger and more exciting than his home town. Why would he want to work with his father, whose charming persona could be far less charming with members of his own family? Houses bored him. What did it matter about proportions, aspects and views? Who cared? He booted the rugby ball with great force down the field at the front of the house, imagining that all his woes were contained within it. Baritone and soprano laughter emanated from the porch as their father disappeared, welcomed by the couple who were selling the house. He popped his head out to issue instructions to the children to behave before leaving: they were expected to amuse themselves.

Grace sat on a picnic bench and drank in the view before her as her brother ran up and down the field. She could imagine living in this tidily square house with windows in the place where she might draw them. And how lovely to gaze at the sea every day. The tide was out but the sand glittered in grey strips, to contrast with fields the colours of autumn, on Gower, beyond the estuary.

She shouldn't have taken her eyes from Richard. At the last moment she saw its shadow as the ball flew towards her and was lucky to raise her arms instinctively to catch the ball.

"Well done, Gracie! You're getting better!" Richard sounded disappointed.

Grace shifted herself from where she was sitting and started running, anger fuelling her every step as she hurled the rugby ball towards her brother.

She heard her father's voice. "At last! You're playing nicely together!"

September

Chapter 1

He was as good as dead, he knew he was. His wheezing would make a useful contribution to an avant-garde concerto and he could barely move. But it had been a good life, a fortunate one, Rex never having to think of anyone but himself. No wife. No children. Plenty of money in latter years, oddly when his handsome face had become more lined, as if he had endured and understood life's difficulties, when in actual fact he had simply smoked and drunk too much and had limited knowledge of skincare. To Rex's delight, the roles had come thick and fast and he had a quick brain, a good memory for learning lines and was never happier than when in front of a camera or treading the boards.

There had been no shortage of women. His youthful self began by keeping a tally but there were too many names to be recalled now. Few women stayed for long but there would always be an eager replacement. He was never deliberately unkind but any girlfriend soon realised that they would never be the sun, always a planet. He would entertain with stories of actors he had known – Maggie or Joan, Michael or Alan. He was a shameless name-dropper but those in his orbit seemed to like it, their youthful shiny faces smiling up at him.

The only problem was that in his twilight years, he lived alone. His house was on a hill and he could look out to sea but if he wanted to get a pint of milk he had to get in the car and drive.

There was a television attached to the bedroom wall, between the two sash windows and he often caught some of his performances on

ITV3. He had been a detective, a politician, a surgeon, an assassin, a psychopath, a judge and even a vet, but never a timelord or 007. During his heyday, he had lived in London when property was more affordable, but he had sold up in the capital and told his friends he was going home to die. Nobody took him seriously: where Rex was concerned, melodrama was as necessary as breathing. Now he was in a place far too big for him, one which had been bought years ago when he got a wodge of money from landing a long-running role in a soap opera. The décor was stuck in the eighties but he didn't really mind because, to a certain extent, so was he. His bedroom had a blue, nautical repeat-patterned wallpaper, boats and seagulls drawing the coast indoors. A contrasting border ran round the top of the walls, giving the impression that the room was held together by a piece of rope.

He closed his eyes and snuggled under the bedclothes, a fistful of turquoise Welsh blanket in his right hand. It had belonged to his grandmother and featured the Portcullis design. Could he remember snuggling under it when he had gone to stay with her or was he creating a memory that soothed him? Before he had time to answer that question, he was aware of a presence beside him in the room and cautiously opened his eyes.

"You really shouldn't still be in bed, you know. It's past nine. You need to get up, have a shower and breakfast before I get here. It's not a pretty sight, I can tell you! And I want to change the sheets and hoover round."

Rex hauled himself up, reaching for his cigarettes, but the woman was too quick for him.

"And you don't need one of those to get you going!" She grabbed the packet, tucking it into the pocket of her apron. "Anyway, what about health and safety in the workplace? I shouldn't have to inhale all that rubbish! You must have heard about passive smoking? Why don't you try the nicotine patches like the doctor suggested?"

Rex glowered up into the pleasant, if somewhat weathered face of Maxine. She had started out doing a spot of cleaning but her role had extended to housekeeper and general helper. He refused to use the word *carer* and now he regretted asking her to drive him to the hospital appointment to see the consultant.

"If you must smoke, I could pop into the market and get you one of those vaping things. My neighbour says you can get all sorts of flavours."

"Why don't you bugger off, Maxine? This is my home. I'll do what I want." In spite of his protestations, he didn't like to go against her and made a mental note to conceal some cigarettes in the shed.

Maxine laughed, an unforced chuckle that momentarily melted Rex's frown. "Now have you got to the stage where I have to undress and bath you?"

"No, I bloody well haven't." Rex rose up to lean on the headboard, spluttering and coughing with the effort. He insisted on sleeping shirtless, wearing only a pair of boxer shorts. His concave chest heaved at the effort. He had lost so much weight.

Maxine knew that her goading would motivate him. She pinned a smile to her face to disguise her distress at Rex's decline. "Spit spot!" She pummelled the pillow behind him.

"Maxine, you are *not* Julie Effing Andrews. Good God! I've met the woman! And very charming she was too. Mary Poppins might have been a tyrant with those children but you, with your puffed-up hair and icy glare, remind me more of Margaret Thatcher." Maxine, a dyed-in-the-wool Labour supporter, winced. "A hit, a very palpable hit!" muttered Rex.

"Half the time, I've no idea what you're on about. I suppose that's a quotation, but I'm not interested so don't bother telling me." She helped to get her employer to his feet and eased his arms into an ancient Paisley dressing gown.

"Surely you know that it's from *Hamlet*, Maxine. Act five, scene two. Hamlet is fencing with Laertes. Now Laertes has good reason for the fight as Hamlet has killed Laertes' father Polonius. He's stabbed him through the arras. And before you ask, that's not something rude, although schoolboys always titter. An arras is simply a tapestry and Polonius is hiding behind it. Hamlet has also been responsible for the death of Laertes' sister, Ophelia, who drowned herself as a result of Hamlet's cruelty and rejection."

Maxine levered Rex to his feet and jabbed each one into a leather slipper. "Ouch! Have a care! But I digress. 'A very palpable hit' is spoken by Osric, a courtier, who is trying to suck up to Hamlet and is saying that Hamlet has scored a point, fighting Laertes. You know, all things considered, you should really be paying me for furthering your education."

By now, Maxine had manoeuvred Rex into the bathroom. Resisting the urge to drop him unceremoniously on the floral-patterned chair beside the shower, she lowered him on to it. "You do try my patience, you know. You are far and away the most patronising bastard I've ever had the misfortune to work for. If you must know, I went to see *Hamlet* at The Grand, many years ago on a school trip. I thought that the so-called hero was so self-obsessed, he deserved to die. And all his long speeches, trying to work out what he should think or do, I was nearly dead myself by the end." She patted her hair, to ensure that the lacquer had held firm and then bobbed down to kiss the top of Rex's head, as she might a child. Taking a step back, she did her best to disguise astonishment at having administered the kiss and said, "Now be a good boy and I'll make your breakfast. See you in, shall we say, thirty minutes?"

"I don't know when you thought it was acceptable to kiss me. These lips have kissed only the most beautiful of women. You used to be so timid. Who'd have thought?"

"I wasn't kissing your lips and have absolutely no intention of doing so. I imagine that your breath is quite disgusting. Now do you need me to pop up to help you downstairs or are you okay?"

Sulkily, Rex grumbled, "I'm fine. It just takes me a little longer to get going. Stop fussing, woman!"

"Hang on to the handrail, then!" With that, Maxine strode towards the windows in the bedroom, heaved up the sash windows to dispel the fug of stale breathing and left the room. Rex could hear her blowing her nose as she descended the stairs.

How did he become so decrepit? Maxine wondered. Whatever

had come over her? Some sort of long-buried maternal instinct must have kicked in when she realised how vulnerable he had become. She moved with some speed towards the kitchen, to remind herself that at least *she* was still full of what her mother would have called "vim and vigour". When she had first worked for Rex, Maxine had been overwhelmed by his handsome appearance and aura of sophistication and fame.

She used to stutter when he asked her a question, on the rare occasions when he came to Long Acres, usually with fancy London types, leaping around in the garden, reciting lines from plays in which they had performed. But as recent years had brought poorer health, he spent more time in Wales, often on his own. "Are you here for any particular event?" she asked him once.

"Recuperation," was the defiant reply.

The awful truth now, was that Rex's health could never be restored.

Maxine took out a Pyrex bowl from one of the pine kitchen cupboards. She selected two eggs nestling under the rigid wings of the ceramic chicken that lived on the worktop. Smashing them expertly into the bowl, she cast aside the shells and beat the yolks and whites with especial energy until they were smooth.

She had thought that Rex was invincible until that terrible day when he froze on stage at the Wolsey Theatre in Ipswich, when he was performing the title role of *The Master Builder*. Rex told her that the actor playing Hilda stared wide-eyed at him, thinking that the silly fool had forgotten his lines, when in actual fact he was having a minor stroke. He couldn't see properly and it felt to Rex that he had somehow blundered into the wrong play. She didn't make any sense to him. He had blushed when recalling the unexpected *Dead Black Out* followed by the heavy thud of red curtain falling as he was propelled offstage by a stagehand.

The role of Hilda demanded that the younger actor should be in awe of the eponymous hero, but she made no secret of the fact that she despised Rex. He knew that he shouldn't have plonked a good-luck kiss on her smooth cheek before the performance but was it really necessary to rub the spot so vigorously that the make-up woman had to touch up with more foundation? When the play came to an abrupt conclusion, she didn't wait to see if Rex was all right but fled from the stage, a look of revulsion distorting her pretty features. Maxine had been surprised when Rex had been so honest about what had happened. Apparently the actress was all for reporting him for sexual harassment until she was persuaded by her agent that the publicity might in fact damage her own reputation, given that the poor man had collapsed on stage.

The headlines in the paper the next day suggested that Rex, who had a reputation for drinking, had been sozzled. Some of the tabloids issued an apology when the truth emerged, but Rex's reputation had been irreparably damaged. There followed roles in repertory theatre and pantomime tours followed by humiliating so-called celebrity appearances. But it stretched all credibility, given his distinct lack of interest in home-making, to be cutting a ribbon at the opening of a new IKEA superstore. It hadn't helped that he had overheard someone say, "Who's he, then?"

Maxine added a splash of milk to the eggs and put the bowl in the microwave. She would have to ring Auntie's Angels, the local independent carers. Perhaps someone could come in three times a day or maybe just overnight. She hadn't signed up to attend to Rex's personal needs. She didn't mind cleaning, even a spot of cooking, but Rex needed further help and she didn't want to have to try and sort it all out after a crisis, like a fall from bed. But who on earth would put up with him? And who could be trusted not to sell their story, to Rex's total humiliation, to the *Daily Mail*?

The telephone rang, interrupting Maxine's anxious thoughts. She answered it. She found that she was tightening her grip on the receiver as she realised who it was.

"No, he's in the shower at the moment. I'll tell him you rang, shall I?" Maxine debated whether or not to pass on the message. "No, he's not any better, but he's not any worse. He's certainly got his wits about him and we've just had a very interesting discussion about Hamlet."

Chapter 2

Tiffany, Rex's niece, slung her mobile phone on to the kitchen counter. It was like being caught up in some sort of computer game – that bitch, Maxine, being a guardian at the gates to the castle. She rarely got past the woman to speak to her uncle. He had a mobile phone but the old fart never seemed to look at it.

Moving into the lounge, she hurled a faux fur cushion from one sofa to the other in her mother's flat, which overlooked North Beach and beyond it, Tenby harbour. It was a 1960s construction that she shared with her brother. The rooms were spacious and the advantage of being inside the flat was that you didn't have to look at the boxy construction from outside.

Uncle Rex had been a glamorous uncle – not especially generous with his time, but always generous with his gifts. She remembered one Christmas when he swooped in, exactly as you might imagine the arrival of a film star, all air kisses and laughter, tailored clothes and expensive aftershave, to interrupt a particularly tedious game of cards. Of course he had missed the Christmas dinner and a walk on the beach, but who cared when he had beautifully gift-wrapped presents? (His girlfriend at the time had been busy.) There was a PlayStation, Tracy Island, a Lego train set and a Cabbage Patch doll.

Tiffany understood why her mother no longer had any contact with him. To be fair to her uncle, it hadn't helped that his sister had asked for frequent handouts but it wasn't as if he couldn't afford it. According to Tiffany's mum, Rex had always been the family favourite. Money had been provided for auditions and trips to London and it only got worse the more successful he became. Once he had landed the part of Oliver, he never looked back and his infant sister grew up learning to make sacrifices to secure his future. Their mother's most frequently repeated story was of the child actor being invited to a party in Bexley Hill, Kent, where he met Dorothy Squires, who was born a stone's throw from Rex's home town, and her younger husband, Roger Moore. When Roger Moore later became James Bond, the anecdote was daily spilled from their mother's lips.

Rex had disappointed his sister too many times, was either horribly late or completely missed family meals, birthdays and important events and yet expected her to be totally up to date with the minutiae of his daily existence and completely sympathetic about his latest ailment. Hypochondria inspired many of his phone conversations. Tiffany could visualise her mother with a phone tucked beside her ear, while she got on with stirring a stew or typing a letter, but making the appropriate responses. "Really? That does sound nasty; should you get that seen to? Has it got any worse? Perhaps you should go back to the doctor." But now, it looked as though his worst fears had become reality. No matter what Maxine said, the truth was that this time there really was something wrong with him.

The jungle drums had been banging. A friend of a friend was related to Maxine's mother and as Tiffany sipped her appletini in a Tenby bar, she listened attentively as the litany of woes were described and possibly exaggerated.

Marilyn, Tiffany's mother, was keen that her children wouldn't miss out when the time came to divide his spoils. She ran a restaurant in Funchal but Tiffany FaceTimed her most days so she didn't really miss her. Before she had tried ringing her Uncle Rex, the suggestion had been made that Tiffany should renew contact. And if he wouldn't speak to her on the phone, then she would have to make the short journey from Pembrokeshire to Carmarthenshire and make a planned *impromptu* visit.

Tiffany wedged herself into an end of one of the sofas, shut her eyes and cradled the cushion that she had just manhandled. The thought of visiting him didn't appeal. It was ages since she had seen him. In fact, she couldn't really remember when she had actually visited. He lived in London for years. She had a brief memory of being in the back of a taxi while he pointed out various landmarks. Westminster Bridge, Big Ben and the Houses of Parliament shot past, transitory images as if the pages of a history book had been hurriedly turned. And there was a boat trip on the Thames but she had been cold then, having left her coat behind in the taxi. Marilyn, her mother, had been furious when she returned home without the coat and there had been an angry telephone conversation, demanding money to replace it.

Illness and death were as alien as witchcraft and alchemy. What if he was too ill to speak or didn't recognise her? Perhaps he would be rambling and incoherent or running with sores. She opened her eyes and giggled a little at feeling so ridiculously anxious. If he was that ill, she just needed to say her little speech and leave. She would take his hand as they did in films, squeeze it and walk with sad determination to the door where she would turn and blow a kiss. Her mother always said that she had inherited her uncle's acting talent. She had an A* for GCSE Drama to show for it. She wasn't a bad person, she just needed to persuade Uncle Rex that she was a really good person, deserving of a substantial legacy.

The tide was out, boats leaning at crazy angles in the sand. Most of them had been lifted from the harbour to overwinter by the yacht club. It was unusually still, the wind had dropped and Tiffany felt a little flutter of excitement as if she were on the brink of something important.

Her brother, Joshua, might come with her. There would be safety in numbers. He was a practical sort of person, fixing problems with holiday lets, replacing broken toilet seats or curtain poles if guests got carried away. He was always astonished by what people got up to in their vacation, but benefited financially whenever anything got destroyed or damaged. He never seemed to have any free time, but she'd surely manage to persuade him.

Chapter 3

Rex was having his breakfast. He scuppered Maxine's plan to boost his immune system by rejecting the bowl of yogurt, augmented with berries, nuts and drizzled with honey, heaped attractively, like something that should be posted online. Not wanting to waste it, Maxine sat opposite him and ate the contents of the rejected bowl herself. It was a fairly recent development that she should join her employer at meal times. One morning, Rex had barked at her, "Will you stop fussing about and just come and sit down and eat?" He had settled for the scrambled eggs, insisting on smothering them with tomato sauce and mixing everything together. Maxine tried not to think about blood and guts.

She had her back to the window overlooking the drive, but could tell that the florist's van had arrived by the change in expression on Rex's face. Since Rex had returned from London, he had decided that the house needed a regular change of fresh flowers. Naturally, Maxine had offered to pick some up in town, but no, Rex had spotted a new florist's shop that had opened and decided that he should support it. Such philanthropy was of course admirable. Rex talked with animation about the decline of the high street and the importance of boosting the local economy, but when Maxine first met the florist, her suspicions proved to be correct. Olivia Garland was a stunner, with a pleasing smile. Of course she wore make-up but if Maxine had to choose one word to sum her up it would have been *wholesome*. She could have appeared in a pastoral scene and blended into the cornfield with Tess of the D'Urbervilles. She was naturally pretty. Dark curls reached beyond her shoulders and luxuriant lashes framed hazel eyes.

Cutlery clattered on Rex's plate as he struggled to his feet. Maxine rolled her eyes. "There's no need for you to get up. Your eggs will go cold."

"Bugger the eggs!" Rex was off, ardour working like fuel in an engine. Even the coughing had subsided.

Maxine got up from the table and watched as her employer accepted the bouquet of lilies, eyes locked into those of the pretty girl and then he looked down. In an odd sort of way, Maxine was reminded of a ballerina accepting her tribute at the end of a performance and half expected him to bow. You could tell that Rex was attempting to extend the conversation, but clearly the florist had little time for chatting. When the cold air got to Rex's lungs and he started to cough again, she took her cue and slammed shut the doors at the back of the van, gave a sweet wave and moments later was accelerating down the drive, gravel spraying behind her.

Rex tried his best to retain an upright posture until the van had rounded the corner but he was struggling. Making his way back to the warmth of the house, he had one last look behind him, in case, by some miracle, Olivia Garland had returned.

Maxine was giving the mess of eggs another quick spin in the microwave by the time he returned. She decided that it was probably best if she didn't comment on his infatuation. It was a weekly ritual and her observations on his foolhardy behaviour hadn't gone down well previously.

Wordlessly, she plonked down his breakfast in front of him and resumed eating her yogurt and fruit.

"Charming girl!" Rex mused.

Silence.

"The quality of the flowers is excellent, you know." He gestured to the white lilies, lying in state at the end of the table. "And really, it's not bad value when you think that you get them delivered."

Maxine glared. *How many people can afford to have flowers delivered every week? Good value?*

"I haven't spent much on renovations. It's a nice little luxury."

Maxine gazed around the room. It was certainly true that there had been few alterations since the immediate renovations decades ago. A new owner would knock down the partition between the kitchen and the dining area. There was an arch, connecting them and she could glimpse the units, trimmed with pale blonde wood, now weathered to a shade of orange that had been all the rage in the 1980s. If it were her kitchen, she would paint all the wood in a pastel colour, blue maybe.

"Well, aren't you a stimulating companion? You aren't usually this quiet."

"I haven't got anything to say on the subject of pretty florists and expensive flowers."

"Aha! Spite! There's jealous you are!" Very occasionally Rex would revert to his native Welsh accent, usually when he'd had too much to drink or was excitable, as now.

"I'm not jealous, Rex. But I don't want to see you make an idiot of yourself." She scooped up his abandoned plate, placing her bowl on the top, and marched through the archway to the sink.

Squirting washing-up liquid into the sink, she clattered about with the china and cutlery, knowing that the noise would annoy Rex. She expected him to follow her and continue the argument, but she had dried up and put everything away before she registered that he was still sitting, staring out of the window at the autumn leaves swirling outside.

He was wearing jeans that had become too big for him and a favourite brushed cotton shirt with a blue check, which she had ironed so many times that she knew the cuffs were beginning to wear a bit thin. Quietly she walked behind him.

"I was thinking," he said, not turning away from his view down the drive.

"Don't do that. It doesn't do you any good."

"I don't suppose I'll see autumn again. You know, I don't think I've ever seen such golden gold and 'mellow fruitfulness'. Too busy to really gaze at the colours properly before. See those leaves!" He pointed at a *prunus*, shedding its foliage. "Red and gold, green and brown."

Maxine tried to look as he might, for a last time.

"I think I ought to put things in order. Could you contact the estate agent's for me? I ought to get the house valued. And I'd like to have a chat with a solicitor. Perhaps that tall, slender woman who wrote my Will for me. I'd like to update it."

"Now don't go all maudlin on me. Cheer up. You won't be wanting someone else, then? The numerous solicitors who happen to be male?"

He turned and she gazed at the man before her. Illness had not diminished the power of those expressive eyes.

"Yes, okay, I'll do it. Which estate agent's do you want?"

"I really don't care." He turned his back on her. "Might as well use the ones who were selling the place when I bought it, if they're still going. What were they called? Pughes and Palmer."

Chapter 4

Maxine was ushered out of Pughes and Palmer, the local estate agent's. She regretted crying as she explained why they needed a valuation for Long Acres. Grace Palmer, the proprietor, was used to dealing with a range of emotions from the people she met daily. Sometimes anger exploded into the room when a wronged wife or husband responded to a request from the ex-partner. Only the previous day, a young man had shouted, "No, I won't bloody well agree to that offer. It's too low. She might want to get shot of the place, but I don't!" And there was a box of tissues on her desk, especially for those who sobbed.

Luckily, there were moments of euphoria to counterbalance the darker days. A young couple getting the keys to their first home was always a triumph. People fell in love with property, almost as they might with a real person. She once heard someone describe how she had felt a flutter in her stomach at the exact moment of stepping over the threshold of the house that she had decided to make her home. "I knew, I just knew it was the one for me!"

Perhaps a valuation would lead to a sale. That would be a boost to their monthly income. It was a substantial house, although it sounded as if any new owner would have to spend quite a bit on it. Rex Glyn was a fading star but she remembered her father's enthusiasm when Rex bought the property in the eighties. In the back of a drawer somewhere was a signed photograph of him, which her father had procured for her. At that time, the actor's face seemed to be everywhere. Rex's agent knew how to market her handsome product.

Grace had been a child at the time when the focus had been on her brother, the expectation being that he would take over the business. Richard had bucked the trend and lived in a substantial house in St Albans, having had variable success as a banker in London. Grace smiled. The expectation had also been that she would marry happily ever after. She was happy, certainly, but divorced many years previously, currently content to be unmarried to Paul, a teacher from Suffolk.

At first, few would have said that the stars had been in alignment. They had met when Paul's father had disappeared from home to attend the funeral of his first love, Grace's mother. Decades previously she had moved west and married a Welshman. Grief had teetered on the edge of madness but Paul's father had eventually returned home and Paul had decided to stay.

Grace's business partner, Byron, bored by the lack of clients visiting him, came and sat on the edge of Grace's desk. In his sixties, he was twenty years older than Grace. What he lacked in youth, he made up for in style. He was delighted that waistcoats had had a bit of a comeback as they had never gone out of favour with him. A follower of rugby, not soccer, Byron had nevertheless admired Gareth Southgate's elegance beside the football field. The England manager's figure was quite different from the estate agent's but Byron found that a waistcoat could keep him warm and also disguise his expanding waistline. On this particular autumn day, he was wearing a grey suit and a rather surprising orange velvet waistcoat that exactly matched the coloured stripe on his white shirt.

Byron cast a critical eye over Grace. She didn't look too bad. Her blonde hair was brushed, make-up had been applied and the grey sweater she wore toned with the pastel colours of her needle cord skirt.

Grace looked up from her computer. "What do you want?"

"Nothing. Just wondered if we should rearrange the desks.

Perhaps I should be nearer the door."

"What? You used to be nearer to the door. You complained of a draught."

"That was years ago. Before we got double-glazing."

Grace laughed. "I have news."

"Yes?"

"Remember Long Acres? I'm going up there to do a valuation."

"Is that the place we sold to Rex Glyn?"

Grace nodded. Byron's face lit from within. "Rex Glyn. I used to adore him. Remember *Pirates We Might Have Known*? He was fantastic in that. Funny, athletic and ridiculously good-looking."

"I preferred his version of Mr de Winter in *Rebecca*."

Nancy, their employee, appeared with mugs of tea. "Who's Rex Glyn?"

Byron rolled his eyes. "You do make me feel old, Nancy. Ask your mother."

Nancy tossed her hair prettily over her shoulders and tripped across to the window to rearrange the houses displayed in the window. "Okay then, who is he?"

"He is an actor of some renown, currently residing in a property on the outskirts of Pontardeilo. He met all the stars in his day. I remember being told that he once met Roger Moore."

"And who's Roger Moore?"

"He was James Bond years before Daniel Craig and all the rest of them."

"Oh." Nancy sounded unimpressed. "What's this Rex Glyn been in, then? Any films in the last five years?"

Byron had to admit that he couldn't think of any.

"So, has he been in *I'm a Celebrity* or one of the other shows to revive his career? What about Instagram? What's he done on social media?"

Byron had no idea. Nancy lost interest and turned away from her colleagues to finish the task in hand. She waved to a friend who was walking past. She longed to update the offices of Pughes and Palmer but was stymied by the restrictions imposed by Byron and Grace. They were generous employers but as Byron had carefully explained, the interior decoration of the estate agent's had been deliberately frozen in time. Any obvious improvements would make the punters question the amount of money they were handing over and would lead to disagreements about the payment of fees. A similar approach had been adopted by a number of solicitors in town whose stark waiting rooms lacked the cheapest of IKEA improvements.

Byron suddenly became energised and trotted to his own desk to open the filing cabinet nearby. "Aha! Here it is!" Byron waved aloft a scrapbook that he placed in front of him. Grace joined him. Byron flicked through the pages, which contained newspaper cuttings of prominent properties that they had sold. There was an extract from the *Western Mail* that described Rex Glyn's favourite room. The article was ostensibly about Long Acres, which he had recently purchased, but it was also a means of advertising his latest film. "I remember this piece. In it, he explains that he was named after Rex Harrison, and his sister after Marilyn Monroe. His mother was a great fan of the movies."

From the window, Nancy called, "I've heard of Marilyn Monroe but who was Rex Harrison?"

Byron enjoyed imparting information. "An actor, of course! Marvellous! I get the chance to tell one of my favourite anecdotes. Rex Harrison had a reputation for being intolerant and off-hand, particularly with fans. The story goes that one night, after a performance of *My Fair Lady*, an old woman was waiting at the stage door. It was cold and raining and Rex Harrison had no patience with her and refused to give his autograph. She rolled up her programme and hit him with it. It was said that for the first time in stage history, the fan hit the shit!"

Grace laughed but Nancy remained unmoved. "Now, let's get back to our Rex – Rex Glyn," Byron continued. "In this article, I remember feeling quite sorry for the couple who sold Long Acres to him. I seem to recall that he was ruthless, bargaining for a reduction in price, having listed all the improvements he would have to make. It wasn't as if he couldn't afford the asking price."

He cleared his throat, a preliminary to reading aloud. "Listen to this: *The property was in a dreadful state when I bought it. There was a lean-to kitchen at the back that was worse than useless, the décor was stuck in the fifties and the owners had a distinct lack of imagination. Everything was painted magnolia. The doors were in the wrong places, there were howling draughts everywhere and there was a whiff of damp, dogs and fried food on entering the place.*"

"Not exactly sensitive."

Nancy walked across the room and took the scrapbook from Byron. "That's so harsh! How did the vendors take it?"

"Badly. The wife in particular, who wasn't very well, felt that they were portrayed as people who were dirty somehow. She kept saying, 'It was spotless when we left it. Really, it was spotless.'" He turned to Grace. "So why does Rex Glyn want a valuation?"

"I think he's dying and wants to get his affairs in order."

"There is such a thing as karma, then," said Nancy.

Chapter 5

Grace Palmer held her nerve as she swung right and left along the narrow lane that rose steeply to the house on the hill – Long Acres. Mature trees created tunnels above as branches met from either side of the road.

Property valuation wasn't an exact science but she had been in the business long enough to be confident in her assessment. The difficulty was that greed had a nasty way of creating conflict if the owners of the property thought that she had come up with a figure that was too low. She had quite literally had a cup and saucer snatched from her grasp as a smiling, pleasant middle-aged woman transformed into a malevolent witch whose disappointment manifested itself as unrestrained fury. Sometimes, if it were a probate valuation, the owners were hoping for a lower-than-market valuation, to avoid paying excessive capital gains tax.

It must have been decades since she had been on this lane. A boyfriend in her youth had driven her up here once and parked expectantly in a quiet passing place. He was supposed to be taking her home but clearly had other ideas. She remembered that she had been tasked with picking up some sausages from the market that day and had kept her shopping bag balanced on her knees as he reached for her. She had fancied him but hadn't fancied having sex in broad daylight on a country lane and had made that quite clear. She remembered her mother complaining about the sausages being quite squashed by the time she returned home. No explanation had been given but she had told Byron the next day and for many months squashed sausages became a euphemism for something else altogether. When she thought about it now, it wasn't funny. Her formative years were spent in a pre-*Me too* era and she supposed she had been lucky enough to escape harm.

She wondered if she would meet Rex Glyn or if Maxine the housekeeper would be dealing with the business side of things. The sound of gravel beneath the tyres as she drove in took her back to the visit with her father all those years ago, especially when a pheasant splashed colour across her peripheral vision as it flapped its way to the sky, cackling indignantly.

It was a surprise that the man himself was standing in the doorway by the time that she had retrieved her work bag from the back seat. Grace walked towards him and tried not to do a double-take as she registered the contrast between the glossy pictures of the film star and the emaciated man before her. She wondered what was wrong with him – he looked like an end-stage cancer patient, but that was until he started speaking.

"Hello! Welcome! I believe I dealt with your father when I bought this place." In one sentence he managed to convey an equal measure of confidence and charm.

"Yes, that's right. I was a child at the time."

"Now don't." His voice was authoritative, pretending to be serious. "That ages me." He grasped her hand with both of his. He had the most seductive smile; she almost forgot to smile herself and then he started coughing as he turned to enter the house. She found that she was still holding one of his hands as he led the way.

"Ms Palmer!" It was Maxine. Grace dropped Rex's hand and extended her own to the housekeeper, waiting in the hall. By contrast, the second handshake was brisk and over in seconds. "Come in. Sit down. I've made coffee for you."

In the kitchen, Rex's charm seemed to evaporate as Maxine took control of the situation. Grace thought it wise to accept the mug of coffee and take it with her on her tour of the rest of the house, relieved to escape the strained atmosphere.

It was a desirable property. There was much to be done to

bring it up to modern requirements but the position and outlook would sell it to an interested buyer. It was a spacious home without being intimidating. She admired the numerous film posters hanging in the sitting room, leading from the kitchen. They all featured Rex the action man or Rex the lover; in short, Rex the hero, whatever the role. She would have liked to spend more time looking at them, but she wasn't there to gape, she was there to perform a task. She noted the drinks cabinet in the corner. Hadn't Rex got a reputation for following one of the other Welsh greats, Richard Burton? There was another room, with a wood-burning stove, furnished in a traditional style, dark wood dominating. On one of the walls, more photographs of Rex were displayed. She made her way to the garden room at the back, an addition to the original footprint, which extended across the width of the house and afforded the view she remembered from sitting on a bench outside.

Grace wondered who would inherit it. Didn't he have a sister? As far as she knew there were no heirs. Perhaps he would leave it to the nation or a charity. He had a reputation for flamboyance but wasn't noted for his philanthropy.

As she made her way around, notes were scribbled in her workbook. She made her way to the bottom of the stairs and found Rex waiting for her, with his arm slung round the newel post, as he leaned against it, striking a youthful pose. He looked very much like his painted self on one of the posters for *Rebecca*, when he played the part of Mr de Winter, although the staircase at Long Acres was, of course, much more modest than that at Manderley. Grace wondered if he was in fact clinging to the stairs for support but she could see the ghost of the young man he used to be and was sensible enough to realise that he had taken many young women on the tour upstairs.

"Shall I lead the way?" he asked.

Maxine appeared with a brown brogue in one hand and a shoe brush in the other. "Rex! The woman's trying to do her job. Can I have a word?"

Rex shrugged his shoulders. "She gets a bit jealous when other women stray into her territory. I do apologise."

Maxine raised her eyes to the ceiling. Grace tried to remain impassive, not wishing to conspire with either party. She tried to ignore Rex's wink as he passed her *en route* to the kitchen.

Grace wasted no time and ran up the stairs to put distance between herself and the actor. She breezed in and out of the family bathroom, a single bedroom and three other bedrooms, all with dual-aspect views, and finally arrived in the master bedroom with its blue colour scheme and dated border round the top of the wall. It was a good size with plenty of room for a wardrobe and chest of drawers. She walked into the *en-suite* bathroom and dressing room, which were clean and serviceable. There was a full-length mirror in the dressing room and she could imagine Rex admiring his reflection before joining his guests downstairs.

As she returned to the bedroom, a silver-framed black and white photograph caught her eye on the chest of drawers by the window. It was of Rex (no surprises there) but also of a young woman who was smiling up at him. It must have been taken some years previously because Rex looked about thirty, maybe forty. They were in Edwardian costume. Grace supposed that the unknown woman must have been acting in the same production as him. Rex was smiling straight at the camera with a confidence that only very attractive individuals possess, in the knowledge that it would be almost impossible to capture an unflattering image, as long as he knew that the photograph was being taken. He had his arm round his co-star, gathering her to him so that she looked as though she were in danger of losing her balance. Grace found that she was smiling with them. Their happiness radiated from the picture.

"How are you getting on?" It was Maxine, whose carefully neutral expression suggested that she had been observing Grace for some moments. Had the woman tiptoed upstairs, hoping to catch her out? Grace found that she was blushing, aware that she had become distracted by Rex's personal possessions. She hoped she wasn't suspected of looking inside the wardrobe. She was no deranged fan, breathing in the scent of the adored, burying her nose in a tweed sleeve or cotton collar.

She had always taken the view that it was best to admit to one's transgressions. "Sorry, I was looking at this photograph here. I didn't mean to pry. It caught my attention. They look very happy together."

"Yes, I dare say. They starred in a production of *The Importance of Being Earnest*." Maxine adjusted the photograph. Grace had moved it slightly from its original position. "A long time ago now. Would you like to go out on to the balcony? I've got the key for the door."

They stood on the balcony for a moment, exchanged pleasantries about the view and then they both returned downstairs. Grace got the impression that Maxine was keen to usher her out but she managed to break free to pop her head into the kitchen to say goodbye to Rex. He was sunk into a corner of a battered-looking brown leather sofa, reading the paper, but whipped off his glasses to wave to Grace.

"It was a pleasure to meet you," he called.

"Likewise. I'll send you the valuation. I've got the details."

Grace turned to go and almost walked into a slim, dark-haired young woman, whom Grace recognised as being a lawyer in town.

Rex got to his feet. "Hello! Welcome!"

Grace was ushered out by Maxine with less ceremony than when she arrived. As she drove off, she caught a glimpse of Rex kissing the hand of the attractive lawyer.

Chapter 6

Rex was sitting in Maxine's car, which was parked near the lifeboat station. Maxine had decreed that a change of scene was what was required and she had driven him to the coast. The tide was up and they were gazing across the harbour to the other side, where autumnal sun illuminated an array of attractive houses and a promontory that led to an endearingly squat stone lighthouse, topped with a black gallery and red lantern.

"Of course, it might have been rather nice to live in one of those houses." Rex gestured towards the properties opposite. "But it would have been no use as I would never have got any peace, back in the day, when I had quite a fan base."

Maxine snorted unattractively. "Get over yourself, you with your *fan base*! Luckily our presence seems to have gone under the radar today." A lone dog-walker strolled past with a fat black Labrador, neither dog nor man registering the existence of the ageing film star and his companion sitting side by side in the car.

"It does me good, sitting here, looking out at this familiar scene." Rex had taken to ignoring Maxine's sarcasm, especially when he couldn't think of an immediate put-down. "I find it humbling to think of all those in the past who toiled here, creating the dock to export Welsh coal. I wonder what those men would make of the fact that there is a marina here now. I don't suppose they got much leisure time."

Maxine considered their plight and then imagined the unnamed wives and daughters mired in domestic servitude. "Nor the women. I wouldn't have fancied running a home with limited money, somewhere cold and draughty with no washing machine or radiators, having to boil water in front of the fire."

Silence ensued. Phantom figures from the past hauled coal or wrestled with a washboard. Maxine, sensing that Rex might be becoming maudlin, sought a change of subject matter. "How did you get on with the lawyer? You never said." As Maxine predicted, Rex rallied.

"Marvellously. She was really on my wavelength, understood my predicament, not having an heir. I had to disclose my estrangement from certain family members, which was slightly awkward, but she was incredibly sensitive. I got the impression that nothing would surprise or shock her. Lovely young woman. Most professional."

Maxine had become aware that Rex never mentioned his sister's name if he could help it. "Have you rewritten your Will, then?"

Rex turned towards his companion, smiling in a way that Maxine found intensely irritating: there was an indulgence, an expression of superiority, conveying that somehow or other Maxine had been caught out. "It's a work in progress. Wondering if you got a mention, is that it?"

"Don't be ridiculous. What do I care what you do with your money? You've paid me enough over the years. Leave it to the cats' home, for all I care!"

Archly, Rex replied, "*The lady doth protest too much, methinks.*"

"Oh, do shut up, Rex."

"Shall I enlighten you as to where that quote comes from? Shakespeare again."

"Please don't. I think I'll just go and get some air. You'd better stay here. You'll only start coughing if you come with me." She slammed the car door, having taken the keys with her. "I hate him!" she muttered to herself as she stamped towards the footbridge, rejoicing in every step that took her further away from Rex.

Chapter 7

Olivia Garland was topping up the water in the buckets of flowers in her shop. She wore a lilac-coloured tabard, her long dark hair pinned up in a haphazard sort of way. This was her kingdom, surrounded by individual blooms that she tended carefully. Wilting foliage was removed, the odd drooping rose or tired chrysanthemum reluctantly discarded into a large black plastic bin. "Another one bites the dust," she said to herself and then started to hum the song by Queen. Every flower she threw away ate into her profit margin.

The shop was small, on a side street, not far from the estate agent's, Pughes and Palmer. It had previously been a bric-a-brac shop that had mainly been used for storage, because it never seemed to be open. Olivia had been renting it for a year and her mum and dad had helped her paint the walls an off-white colour, selecting the shade on the basis of a name that amused her: Natural Hints Violet White. It seemed an auspicious choice, referencing one of her favourites: white violets for innocence. Olivia knew the meaning of all the different flowers.

Just about making enough money to keep the flowers and herself from going under, Olivia was giving herself three years, if she could manage it. New customers were complimentary about her hand-tied bouquets and interesting selection of colours and textures, but who could blame them for being seduced by the cheaper prices of the supermarkets? One of her regulars, an elderly woman, blushed when she was caught coming out of Asda, clutching to her chest a bunch of something, the garish orange cellophane surrounding it, obscuring the identity of the flowers. Only a couple of sprigs of gypsophila escaped as if waving two fingers in Olivia's direction.

Today she wondered what it would be like to no longer have to worry about money. Her thoughts kept returning to the evening that she had spent with her boyfriend, Stephen Samson. Could she even call him a boyfriend? He was so self-assured and capable, not a boy at all. She had never actually seen him click his fingers to demand attention, but she suspected that he was capable of it.

The previous night, while consuming a bottle of champagne, he surprised her by producing a generously sized diamond ring and had proposed. Samson, a self-made man, was newly released from his second marriage. He had wanted to show her the latest project, a former piano factory on the seafront in Pontardeilo, which was being turned into a restaurant and bar with an industrial vibe.

The diamond gleamed enticingly in the candlelight; Olivia looked away to see the shadows of herself and Stephen momentously frozen, stretching up cavernous walls to the ceiling above. She had played for time, prattling on; now, in the solitude of her shop, she found it hard to recall exactly what she had said. She did say something about only knowing him for six months, that of course she was enjoying his company and it was enormously flattering that he should want to marry her. She didn't want to mention the age disparity but he had had the opportunity to travel the world, whereas she had hardly left Pontardeilo. Olivia had been brought up to believe that you shouldn't have to rely on someone else to shape the future. She wasn't ready for commitment and maybe it might be sensible if Stephen didn't tie himself down so soon after his divorce.

The ring box had been snapped shut and there was a tightness to the smile that accompanied the dismissal. Stephen had got to his feet. The poor man had been crouching on one knee on the polished concrete floor of the empty bar of his newest acquisition.

Brushing dust from his mustard-coloured chinos, he had said, "At least you're being honest. Best if you go now. You've got work in the morning."

Honesty was important to Stephen. He had confided in Olivia that his former wife had lied about his wealth to secure a bigger settlement. No wonder he was bitter. But it was a bit of a shock to be wordlessly escorted to the front door as if she had sneaked into one of his clubs without paying and he was a weary bouncer. Olivia's high heels had echoed through the empty building and all attempts to give a conciliatory hug were defeated. Stumbling on to the pavement, she heard a gull crying, buffeted by the wind. It was a starless sky. Olivia was unable to see the waves breaking on shore but the scraping of shingle was a sound she knew well, fading with each step as she tottered home.

Usually Stephen sent a cheery morning text. Olivia checked her mobile. No message. Putting the phone to one side, she grabbed a broom and distracted herself by cleaning the floor with unusual force, so much so that she was unaware when the bell rang to signal that she had a customer.

Maxine had taken Rex back to Long Acres after their trip to the harbour. She stood on the threshold of the flower shop and watched the young woman as she worked. She felt as if she had seen this girl before she started calling at the house to deliver flowers. Rex seemed to go for a particular type of woman, perhaps that was it. Rod Stewart went for leggy blondes and Rex went for pretty brunettes.

"Excuse me!" Maxine's voice sounded louder than she'd intended. Olivia almost dropped the broom as she turned round. "Sorry," Maxine continued. "I just thought I'd save you a job by collecting the flowers. I was in town anyway." She tried to sound nonchalant. "I had to get some stamps from the post office."

Olivia was flustered. "But I'm not due to deliver them till tomorrow morning. I haven't prepared them yet."

"I'll wait! Perhaps I could sit on this?" She gestured towards a painted wooden stool.

Olivia grabbed a cloth and wiped it. Frowning, she considered her stock. She was due to get fresh flowers the following day. It was important that she didn't lose this customer. The lilies were already opening, their pollen-laden stamens protruding from the petals. Maybe white roses and Lisianthus with some eucalyptus foliage would do it. She gestured to the flowers. "Do you think these would be nice?"

Maxine barely glanced at the selected flowers. "Yes, fine. As long as it's not chrysanths. He hates them. Associates them with death."

Olivia arranged them on a sheet of cellophane. "I expect you know what one another likes. Have you been married long?"

Maxine toyed with the idea of masquerading as the film star's wife but found that she was laughing. "God! I'm not married to Rex. He's impossible! I work for him."

It was when she was in the post office that she'd conceived a plan to thwart him. How dare he suggest that she was after his money? Rex worked himself up whenever the florist arrived and then there would be a descent into adolescent melancholy when she had gone. It seemed like a good idea to prevent the nonsense, if only for one week.

Olivia looked up from what she was doing. "Sorry, didn't mean to pry."

Maxine could see that the young woman felt uncomfortable about her mistake. Maxine could lengthen the silence or break it by continuing the conversation. She asked her if she was married. The answer was *no*, accompanied by a shake of the head. She didn't immediately expand on the subject.

Maxine added. "I've never married. Didn't meet anyone who seemed to fit the bill." She was used to trotting out the cliché. There was no need to explain but somehow she felt obliged to do so.

When Olivia gave her the flowers, she smiled, grateful to the woman for smoothing over the blunder and not enquiring further about her relationship status. It was then that Maxine saw the resemblance to the woman in the photo frame in Rex's bedroom. Her skin was paler than Rex's co-star but Olivia would be ideal for playing the part of Cecily Cardew in *The Importance of Being Earnest.*

Chapter 8

Although Tiffany shared the flat with her brother, she rarely saw him. He tended to work during the day and then he went over to see his girlfriend who lived in Saundersfoot. Tiffany was helping out a friend and was working most nights in a pub, where she laughed at the unfunny jokes the punters made and was usually patient when older folk spent an age making up their mind about ordering a bar snack. She did nearly lose it when one old dear, who always appeared on a Tuesday and ordered the same thing from the menu, kept her waiting for what seemed like an age as if, for once, she was going to branch out and have something different. "Let me see now... so much choice... the specials look interesting... perhaps I'll try the fish pie." Tiffany wrote down *fish pie* on her notebook, smiled and turned away, only to be recalled. "You know what? I think I'll have cod and chips!" She said it as if she had never tried such a delicacy. "Yes, I think that would be lovely!"

"Jesus! That's what you always have!" The words were out before Tiffany could stop them. It was early evening and the bar wasn't its usual noisy self. Her speech bounced around the walls and wooden floor. She hadn't intended to be so loud or so sneering.

The old lady fiddled with her wedding ring, too large on her bony finger. Her husband had died when Tiffany was a child. "I just fancied it. A bit of a treat," she whispered.

Tiffany's friend glared at her over the draught beers and Tiffany launched a charm offensive that involved offering the woman a free drink. The cost was deducted from Tiffany's wages and she was suitably contrite at the end of the evening. Nevertheless, it was noticeable that whenever the Tuesday lady arrived, she tried to attract the attention of the other staff when she wanted to order her cod and chips.

It felt like a holiday to be sitting in Joshua's van on Tiffany's day off. She had managed to persuade him that it would be fun to drive to Carmarthenshire and visit their uncle. In truth, the persuasion that the trip would be fun was less successful than the argument that it would be in their best financial interests if they reminded Uncle Rex who they were.

"I'll do the talking, you just smile and nod," Tiffany suggested.

"That would be a bloody disaster. You'd better do the smiling and nodding and I'll try and be helpful, ask if any jobs need doing while we're there. You could pull up a few weeds outside and make it look as if you were enjoying it."

Tiffany looked at her hands. She'd occasionally wondered whose hands were used to advertise nail polish and thought that hers, unblemished and slim-fingered, could successfully work their magic on the glossy pages of women's magazines. "I won't be doing that. Anyway, he's got enough money for staff."

Joshua laughed. "Your face! That's the look of horror you had when I took you paintballing as a kid." He was eleven years older than his sister. Their mother had said that it was just like herself and Rex, her older brother.

Tiffany was surprised to find that she was approaching thirty, never imagining that she would still be living in her childhood home without a partner. Failure to launch, that was what they called it. Tiffany had frequently watched the Tenby lifeboat take to the water, sliding down the slipway as the siren sounded, crash-landing in the sea, parting the waves to create a fury of foam. She had wanted to generate a glorious disturbance when she left her childhood home to share a house with a couple of friends. They thought that they would drink, laugh and console one another, riding the crest of a wave. But the excitement had diminished as squabbles, dirty washing and unpaid bills mysteriously multiplied and Tiffany fled home to her mother one wet and windy night. Marilyn was incredulous when the full amount that Tiffany had spent became apparent. Sometimes Tiffany wondered if that particular episode had prompted her mother's move to Funchal.

It started to rain as they arrived in Pontardeilo. The roads became narrower and more muddy as they followed the satnav instructions and started to climb the hill that led to Long Acres.

"What time are we due to arrive?" Joshua asked.

Tiffany shifted in her seat. "Any time," she said absently and started to rub at a dusty patch on the dashboard with her woollen glove.

Joshua, who recognised the ambiguous response to be an indication that she wasn't telling him the complete truth, pulled over into a passing place and stopped the car.

"What's up?" Tiffany said, all smiles. "It's okay, we're not too late." She made a bit of a performance out of looking at the time on her phone.

"When did you speak to Uncle Rex and arrange this little get-together?"

"Um."

"He doesn't know that we're coming, does he?"

"Of course he does!" Tiffany continued to fiddle with her phone. She started to laugh. "Okay, perhaps he doesn't."

Joshua slammed his hands on to the steering wheel. "You're telling me that we've driven for nearly an hour to visit someone who's probably out, or if he is in, chances are he won't want to see us?"

He started the car and tried to turn round but the road was too narrow. He ignored Tiffany's protests. "The next drive we come to, we're turning round."

In a temper, Joshua drove too fast up the country lane. Tiffany screamed, "Slow down!" but if anything, the noise spurred him on. A Volvo appeared at the brow of the hill. The driver wore a tweed cap, brown eyes beneath the brim, wide-eyed in shock, as he spotted the speeding van. He veered to the left as Joshua lurched towards a small verge. A collision was narrowly avoided and the Volvo driver, seemingly used to such near-misses, mouthed something inaudible but continued on his journey down the hill. Joshua got out of the car, alarmed by the scraping sound he had heard from the nearside wheel. Rain and wind assaulted him from all sides. He had slashed his tyre on a boulder placed at the corner of the verge.

Beside him was an opening to a tree-lined driveway. At the entrance was a straggly holly that had a wooden board screwed into it, containing a slate sign engraved with two words: LONG ACRES. In spite of Joshua's efforts, they had arrived at their destination.

Rex was in a sulk. He glared at the vase of flowers on the table and if he had had more strength he would have knocked it to the floor so that Maxine would have to clear it up. How dare she prevent Olivia from making the delivery! It was the highlight of his week. He thought he might ring the florist and explain that, in future, no matter what happened or who called to change the arrangements, Olivia was to deliver the weekly order.

The weather was evil, adding to his grim mood: rain thundered against the windows. Long Acres' hilltop position took the full blast of any storm. Maxine was hoovering upstairs with unnecessary vigour, the noise jangling his every sinew and nerve. He eased himself out of the armchair and prepared to try and muster the voice he had used for *King Lear*, using every Anglo Saxon curse that he could remember, to demand that the bloody woman upstairs should stop what she was doing and give him some peace.

As he made his way to the bottom of the stairs, his attention was drawn to the window and the surprising spectacle of two dishevelled young people making their way up the drive. The man was striding ahead, dressed in the sort of thing you'd expect a fisherman to wear – a waterproof coat with the hood up, but the hood didn't stay in place for long as the wind tore it down. When the man's head was exposed to the rain, he looked up into the sky as if to curse some invisible deity that was deliberately singling him out for punishment. Rex knew that feeling and was struck by a peculiar feeling of recognition. His younger self had looked very much like this person. For a terrible moment he wondered if some long-lost child had landed on his doorstep decades after one of Rex's numerous dalliances. He had read somewhere that the great Welsh painter, Augustus John, had always ruffled the hair of any passing child just in case it happened to be an unknown progeny.

Then he gave his attention to the woman in over-the-knee boots and pink puffa jacket, who followed in the man's wake. She was pretty, features arranged like that of a charming figurine, a shepherdess perhaps, rather like the one his mother used to have on her mantelpiece. He wondered if his sister still had it. Blonde hair was thrown up like a halo around her head as the wind blew. A memory stirred from the past of a girl with thin blonde curls, running to keep up with him as they raced to catch the train back to Wales. It was his niece! He hadn't seen her for years but she was instantly recognisable. What a relief! He wasn't going to have to pay for some unwanted offspring. The man must be his nephew. He would be the right age.

But why were they paying an impromptu visit? Had his sister died? Unlikely, given that she was much younger than him. Anyway, they'd know about the estrangement. It would hardly be appropriate for him to go to her funeral. In any case, if it were so, he wouldn't be long joining her on the other side, he knew that. Such a jumble of thoughts made his blood roar. Why would he want to put extra strain on his weakening heart? It would be for the best if he pretended to be out. Just as he tried to duck out of sight, the nephew raised his hand to wave. Rex had been spotted.

He opened the door and was almost knocked over. The bedraggled two had spent long enough in the rain and were eager to seek refuge in the porch. It was as if he were in the company of unruly dogs as they shook out their wet, muddy coats. Boots were removed and few words were spoken until they made their way into the sitting room.

"Please sit." Rex used a sweeping gesture towards the sofa.

Tiffany was trying hard not to stare. She wouldn't have recognised him if she had passed him on the street. His cheeks were sunken and he had an ageing, shuffling gait that was completely at odds with the memory she had of the handsome man whose arm she had linked as they strode about London. She looked around her; it was undeniably a man's room, as if a set designer had been asked to create an old-fashioned gentlemen's club. Wood panelling encircled them, Victorian clocks marked time, film posters lined the walls and he had chosen dark leather upholstery. There was a stout-looking drinks cabinet with a glass-panelled door in the corner of the room. Martini and whisky bottles jostled for attention. By the window, a box of cigars sat on a card table. No woman had been allowed a restraining hand.

Joshua broke the silence. He thought it was unlikely that the old boy would recognise them; they could sit out the rain, wait till roadside assistance came and then they could go back to Tenby. "Sorry to bother you. We've got a flat tyre. Near-miss with a Volvo driver on the lane."

Rex made an involuntary shake of his head. "Where was this?"

"At the end of the drive."

"Drive? What? My drive? What were you doing there?"

Joshua was stumped for an answer and looked across at his sister, sitting beside him on the sofa, hoping that she would come up with a plausible answer.

Tiffany smiled prettily. "We were coming to visit you, Uncle Rex. We heard you weren't well."

Joshua glared at his sister, not expecting her to tell the truth. "I wasn't going to mention our family connection. We haven't seen you for years. To be honest, I thought Tiff, here, had rung you beforehand but she hadn't. We won't stay longer than the time it takes to sort out the flat tyre. If we're bothering you, we can go back to the lane and sit in the van. It's just that we didn't have much signal on the mobile. If we could use the landline, we'll be more likely to keep in contact with roadside rescue. I wouldn't want them to ring, not get through to us and then give up."

Tiffany was incensed at being publicly humiliated by her brother. "I have rung, Uncle Rex, but your housekeeper, or whatever she is, doesn't pass on my messages." She sat with her back to the open door leading to the stairs, unaware that Maxine was descending with a Hoover grasped in her hands, seemingly raised higher than necessary, as if it might be used as a weapon. When she was visible to Rex, who sat opposite his nephew and niece, Maxine's face wore a similar expression to that of his own depicted on one of the film posters on the wall. He had starred in an epic Roman story, a spin-off from *Gladiator*, and the photographer had captured the furious expression of a battle-hardened warrior, spear raised aloft, whose prey has just been spared. The Hoover was slowly lowered to the ground and, without uttering a word, Maxine wheeled it towards the kitchen.

"Did Marilyn put you up to this?"

It was a simple enough question and Rex hoped for a simple enough answer. Joshua, mouth clamped shut, glared aggressively at his uncle. Tiffany looked as if she might cry. He changed tack.

"What I meant to say was, have you heard from my sister lately?"

"Yes, I spoke to her this morning." Tiffany dabbed at her eyes with a tissue. Rex wasn't sure if she was mopping up tears or rain.

"How is she?"

Joshua spoke up. "She's fine, thanks, but let's talk about something else. Can I use your phone? I'm happy to pay for it." He sat straight-backed beside Tiffany, in fight or flight mode, ready to spring from his seat.

Rex decided momentarily to embrace his role as uncle. "No need, my boy. Pop into the kitchen. You'll find a telephone by the French doors." He would have tapped Joshua on the shoulder but the younger man's departure was swiftly executed. He was left alone with Tiffany and wasn't sure what they would talk about. He needn't have worried. She enquired after his health, which immediately prompted a coughing fit. Tiffany leaped into action, eyes brimming with tender concern. She knelt beside him and asked if he needed a glass of water. Rex shook his head and, once the spasms subsided, asked her if she had continued with her fledgling acting career, her facial expressions being worthy of the big screen. He remembered that she had once belonged to a youth theatre.

One of Tiffany's strengths was her powerful imagination. Creative writing was one of her favourite things at school. She entertained her uncle with tales of success, treading the boards. She loved musicals and watched as many amateur or professional performances as she could afford. Instead of describing her position sitting in the stalls, she allowed herself to be taken up and transported on to the stage to take a principal role.

"Next time you're in a performance, I'll try to come and see you," Rex enthused. There followed a silence. Tiffany averted her gaze. Rex was touched by her discomfort. Of course, she was thinking that he wouldn't live long enough to see her perform on stage.

Joshua returned from the kitchen. "They're on their way. We'd better go and sit in the car."

The departure was swift. Rex watched his niece and nephew disappear down the lane. "I remembered her as being a lively sort of girl." He paused. "She's a bit like her mother. Marilyn could be quite entertaining." Before Maxine could comment, he continued. "He's a bit sullen, don't you think?" Rex's shoulders sagged when they were no longer in sight. He sighed theatrically.

Maxine stood beside him, offering a mug of coffee. "Stop it! You're brooding again!"

"Did you decide not to pass on Tiffany's phone message?"

Maxine braced herself for the temper tantrum. "I thought it was for the best."

Worryingly, Rex merely shrugged. "At least they didn't have to wait long. Remember that time when I broke down in Kent? In the Jag. Where was it? Somewhere on the M2. I was stuck on the roadside for ages."

In the kitchen, Maxine had heard one side of Joshua's conversation. "What do you mean you won't be there for over an hour?" There was no need to explain that his nephew would prefer to sit in a wet van than in the company of Rex Glyn.

Chapter 9

Grace Palmer put the phone down. The office was unusually quiet and for once she had heard every word, nobody in the vicinity chatting about en-suite bathrooms or whether properties were in a catchment area for a good school. Byron was out and about, showing a recently retired Glamorgan cricketer around a substantial place overlooking the reservoir and Nancy was having her lunch (smoked salmon and cream cheese on granary bread) in the back room.

Maxine, Rex Glyn's housekeeper, had been very odd during the call. It was as if she was saying one thing but trying to convey another. On the face of it, the valuation had been well received and Rex wanted to put the house on the market. She could hear his stage whisper in the background, directing what Maxine should say. But every dictated sentence was interspersed with her own ideas. She repeated the words, "We want you to market Long Acres." Pause. "However, now might not be the best time to sell it." There was audible harrumphing from Rex and another command that Maxine repeated. "Please come and take photographs at your earliest convenience," and then once again she strayed from the script. "There is no immediate need for you to come straight away. I'm sure you're very busy and my employer isn't too well at the moment and I don't want him to be disturbed."

There was a muffled sound, presumably because Rex had snatched at the telephone to reinforce his instructions or Maxine had put her hand over it to tell him to back off. There appeared to be a bit of a struggle until Rex emerged as victor. It was his voice she heard at the end. "Come up and take pictures and I'll sign the papers!" Then the line went dead.

Grace got up and found the old details of Long Acres, complete with a newspaper article, in the filing cabinet so that her back was to the door when it opened. The papers placed on the top of the cabinet flapped in the subsequent breeze. Grace busied herself, slapping down the palm of one hand to stop them falling to the floor, for a moment unable to see who had arrived.

Grace's mother would have said, *The apple doesn't fall far from the tree.* Unfortunately, Lucy had not lived to see Sarah, Grace's daughter, mature into a young woman. There she was, so obviously her mother's daughter and descendant of Lucy, tall and blonde, striding into the centre of the room.

"Sarah!" Grace stopped what she was doing and ran towards her, hugging her tightly. She breathed in the scent of her, liberally sprayed with Kate Spade's *Walk on air*, a hint of spearmint and possibly tobacco, none of which masked her own natural Sarahness. "But you should be at university!"

Sarah took a step back, tucking a stray blonde curl behind her ear. "Yeah, that's right."

Grace took a moment. Her immediate instinct was to ask a hundred questions but that usually resulted in defensive silence, followed by angry protestations and before she knew it the door would be swung open again with Sarah legging it down the street.

"Don't look at me like that!" Sarah muttered. "We had a reading week."

"Now, that's just silly. You've not long gone to university. They'd never give you a reading week so soon."

Sarah straightened her shoulders and Grace prepared herself for the frozen stare, followed by an avalanche of criticism. But it was not to be. Nancy emerged from the back room.

"Hiya, Sarah! How's things?"

Grace's daughter visibly thawed, grateful for Nancy's interruption. "Okay, Nance. Back for a few days. I'm just going for a wander round town." She turned back to her mother. "Want anything from the market?"

Grace shook her head.

"Cool. Catch you later. I'll be in for supper tonight." Sarah gave her mother a brief peck on the cheek, turned on her heel (rather higher than Grace thought might be wise) and turned left towards the market.

Chapter 10

Olivia Garland was reflecting on the fact that she spent half her life worrying that there was too little work and the other half worrying that she had too much. She was experiencing first hand the curse of the self-employed. A couple had appeared unexpectedly in her shop and said that they were taking advantage of a reduced offer in a local hotel. A wedding slot had suddenly become available because there had been a cancellation. It was a bit last minute but they weren't going to invite too many people, it being a second marriage for both of them. However, they did want flowers. Could she arrange it at short notice? Olivia did not hesitate, gave them her best smile, but wondered if they picked up on how her voice shook a little as their details were taken. She had been told by a teacher at school that a confident smile inspired confidence in others. It was an achievement to secure the work but now she was faced with the possibility that she would be unable to finish everything on time. There was only so much she could do with one pair of hands. Olivia hadn't lied but didn't contradict the future bride when she stressed the importance of conveying their exact requirements to "the rest of your girls". Did the woman think she had a team of florists hiding under the counter? If only that were so.

And she had work to complete for a funeral. Olivia had finished a double-ended spray for the coffin but still had two more tributes, a cross and an open heart to finalise. Freesias, spray carnations and chrysanthemums were ready, soaking in one bucket. Next to it, she had prepared foliage: eucalyptus, ivy, aucuba japonica and myrtle. She would have to stay late to wrap up everything for the following day.

As for the wedding, the roses she wanted for the posies were beginning to open up but weren't as full blown as she would have liked them to be. Then again, the last thing she would want would be for them to shed petals, unbidden confetti, during the ceremony. And then there were table arrangements. How many? She looked at her work diary. Six. God help!

One advantage of being preoccupied by work obligations was that she had no headspace left for Stephen. She had texted him earlier in the day and he had given a curt reply. She had sent him a picture of an arrangement prepared for a golden wedding: yellow roses and orange gerbera, interspersed with poppy heads and pine cones, which she had been pleased with. It was refreshingly unstuffy and she thought that he would like the sculptural form of it, maybe for one of his corporate functions. After she had pressed SEND she realised that it was a bit tactless referencing anything to do with weddings.

Olivia looked at her watch. Ten minutes past five. The gallery opposite would be closing soon. The estate agent's further away would be shutting too. The only lights left on in the street would be the ones in her shop. Her shoulders hurt from being hunched over the workbench and she was beginning to feel hungry, having been too busy to stop for lunch. She stood up, tried to relieve the crick in her neck, stretched both arms above her head and then rotated them as they used to do in gym as a warm-up. But the shop was too small for aerobics and she had unwisely looked up at the ceiling to focus on her breathing exercises: breathe in for four, hold for five and exhale for six seconds. It was supposed to disrupt the flow of mounting panic, but it would take more than poxy breathing exercises to head off the tsunami of despair threatening to engulf her. The heavy work diary on the counter connected with her left arm and spun across the room. The goddess of mischief and destruction made certain that it landed in the centre of the double-ended spray.

"Oh, shit!" Her hands flew to her mouth in horror, just like the emoji she used when she was using WhatsApp with her friends. Usually it would be a response to something trivial like a celebrity hairstyle. Motionless, she considered her options as tears threatened to spill.

The door opened, Olivia straightened up in an instant, trying to mask her distress. She recognised the girl standing in the open doorway. It was someone from school, in the year below her. Olivia did not want to look like a fool.

Sarah had forgotten that a florist had opened near the estate agent's. On an impulse she had decided that a plastic wrap of spray carnations was a worthwhile investment to placate her mother. The inevitable heavy discussion awaited her. Sarah could practically script it but she could perhaps soften the responses with the aid of a cheap bunch of flowers. She had been on nodding terms with Olivia when they were at school, circling one another in an ancient ritualised dance, pursued by the same boys.

"Hi." Olivia spoke first. "I'm closing in a minute but can I get you something?"

"I didn't know you had a shop. You didn't go to uni, then?"

Olivia was on the defensive. "I didn't want to get into debt. I just wanted to run my own business."

"Cool." Sarah pointed out the flowers she wanted. The funeral tribute blocked Olivia's access to the fresh flowers. As she navigated her way round it, she casually picked up the work diary and left it on a stool.

Sarah eyed the squashed lilies and crushed chrysanthemums in the centre of the arrangement and wondered if she should say anything. She decided to ignore the floral carnage and led with a neutral: "You're keeping busy, then?"

Olivia took the coins from Sarah's outstretched hand. "You have no idea."

Within three minutes, Sarah was ringing her mother and leaving a message. "Sorry, Mum. Won't be back for supper after all. I'm helping a friend. Don't wait up."

Mothers rarely do as they are told by their daughters. Grace had spent the evening with Paul, they had eaten at her place, but she'd dropped unsubtle hints that she'd rather he went back to his rented accommodation than spend the night with her. She had to find out what Sarah was up to. Paul was a sympathetic listener, pointing out that his own son had sometimes chosen not to confide in him.

"She'll tell you what's wrong in her own time."

"But that's no use. I want to know what's the matter with her now!"

Paul was used to hearing the urgency in her voice. Her enthusiasm was uplifting but her inability to allow the vagaries of life's ebb and flow to take her wherever, could be viewed as a flaw. She nibbled on the end of a fingernail. Gently he took the hand in his, massaging the back of it with his thumb. "Don't wait up for her. She might be really late and then you'll feel rubbish in the morning."

He kissed her, gathered up his marking, coat and a bag of groceries to make his way to the door. "I wonder if we'll ever live together," he remarked absently.

"Don't start on that now," Grace grumbled but she hugged him tightly before he disappeared into the dark. If they had had a child together it would have been different, she thought. There had been a miscarriage. They didn't talk about it. No point. It wouldn't bring the baby back to life.

It wasn't just the advice of daughters that Grace ignored – she was unused to doing what she was told by anyone. She prepared to sit and wait for her daughter's return. She sent the dog out to do the necessary. He was getting so dotty these days that she often had to remind him why he had gone out into the garden. The neighbours were getting used to hearing her entreaties, urging him on most nights. Dear old Wesley, the family golden retriever, eventually returned to the kitchen and flopped into his basket with a sigh.

Grace took her time in the shower, changed into a pretty nightie in stretchy T-shirt material, wrapped herself up in a soft white towelling robe and settled into the sofa to watch an episode of *Midsomer Murders* that was sufficiently ridiculous to dispel any anxieties she might have after witnessing a number of bizarre killings. It was the sort of thing that she and the children had watched together when they were teenagers, snuggling under a blanket. She was sitting in the same place, watching the same programme, but the memory of domestic harmony was at odds with her current circumstances.

Where on earth was Sarah? Of course, the truth was that when she was living away, Sarah would probably crawl in from a night out at all hours. The difference was that Grace didn't agonise over such behaviour because she was unaware of it.

The programme finished. It was past one o'clock in the morning. Grace rang Sarah's mobile for the third time. To her relief, Grace heard the phone ringing in the hall. Sarah was home!

Sarah was answering her mobile as she walked into the lounge. "Hello, Mum!" She spoke into her handset while smiling at her mother.

Grace wanted to launch into a spirited monologue, pointing out the error of her daughter's ways but was struck by the difference in attitude from when Sarah had been as spiky as a hedgehog earlier in the day. Now, her daughter looked tired but so much happier.

"What's going on, Sarah? Why aren't you at university? And don't give me that nonsense about a reading week."

Sarah fell into an armchair. "Any chance of a cup of tea?"

"Maybe, if you answer my question."

The frown on Sarah's face transformed into a giggle. "You know you were really proud of me because I got a place at university?"

"Of course I was. It was a real achievement."

"Let us suppose, just for a moment, that I hadn't gone to university, how would you have felt then?"

The ponderous words and professorial tones made Grace wonder if her daughter had signed up for some sort of philosophy and ethics course although she knew that she had begun a computer science degree. Grace had a feeling that she already knew what had happened but for a moment it was preferable to plead ignorance. She needed Sarah to explain. "What do you mean?"

Sarah stretched her arms above her head and yawned. "I've left,

Mum. I'm not going back. It didn't suit me."

"Didn't suit you? What do you mean, *suit you*? We're not talking a shade of lipstick here, for God's sake!"

"Funny, Mum."

"Cut the sarcasm." Grace switched to organised-mother mode. "We'll sort it out together. We'll go to bed now, get some sleep, I'll take the day off tomorrow and we'll drive back and talk to whoever is in charge and fix the problem."

Sarah looked defiant. "There is no fixing. It's over."

"That's ridiculous. You were really excited about going away. We bought new duvet covers, cutlery and all those books! And anyway, what will you do instead?"

She smiled the smile of someone in possession of a secret about to be revealed. "I'm going to be a florist, Mum."

It was only then that Grace noticed that Sarah's usually immaculate blonde hair was strewn with pieces of greenery and tied back from her face with a piece of red florist's ribbon.

Chapter 11

Maxine was making coffee for Rex and leaned on the worktop while waiting for the kettle to boil. He refused to have an electric one so she had ample time during which the Aga slowly worked its magic. The postman had called, delivering a postcard from Tiffany, a picture of Tenby harbour on the front. Maxine scanned the writing on the back. It contained a forwarding address should Rex wish to reply. The tone was upbeat and positive – it had been great seeing Rex again, his acting stories had been very entertaining, she and her brother had got back in one piece after the burst tyre and she hoped for a swift recovery for her uncle. Would it be possible to have a signed picture of him, she wondered.

Maxine hovered above the flip-top bin, the postcard awaiting its fate, but her conscience prompted the removal of her foot from the pedal and the sycophantic message was buried under the other letters on the worktop.

Flicking through the pages of the local paper, she came across a double-page-spread advertisement, extolling the virtues of Long Acres. There was a photograph of Rex in his prime, in maroon bell-bottomed trousers and a floral shirt almost open to the waist, leaning against an apple tree in the orchard, his eyes smouldering with masculine desire. Who on earth had taken the photograph all those years ago? She made a tutting noise, the sensible employee watching as if it were not her right hand that stretched towards his picture, the index finger tenderly tracing his outline. She really should have insisted on sitting with him when the estate agent called. Rex was making himself a laughing stock.

There were some carefully chosen recent photographs, including a close-up of one of his film posters, none of the bathroom or kitchen, which was understandable, given their lack of renovation. The exterior shots had been taken in the autumn sunshine, capturing the sunset and the view from the balcony, revealing a distant seascape. It occurred to her that someone might knock the whole thing down and start again. But that would be a pity. Maxine wasn't comfortable with the concept of asymmetrical, angular buildings, surround sound and wrap-around glass. For all its deficiencies, Long Acres was a house you could live, rather than pose in. After the many years she had worked for Rex, the place felt far more like home to her than her own modest flat where she lived in town. Below her there was an identical apartment inhabited by a reclusive spinster called Penelope. When she occasionally encountered her neighbour in the hall, she sometimes wondered if she were glimpsing her own future.

There also appeared to have been a rehash of the original article describing the house when he first bought it. *Everything was painted magnolia. The doors were in the wrong places, there were howling draughts everywhere and there was a whiff of damp, dogs and fried food on entering the place.*

Maxine winced. She hoped that the previous owners weren't around to read such unkindness.

The telephone rang. Rex got there first to the handset in the next room. Maxine was doing her best to protect him from the outside world but he wasn't always compliant. She proceeded to make coffee while trying to make sense of Rex's one-sided conversation. It was the estate agent, probably not Grace Palmer because he was keeping flirtation to a minimum. He broke off, coughed extravagantly and then listened. He only spoke when he finished the conversation. "I'll see you this afternoon."

They would be coming round to take some more photographs, perhaps. Maybe he'd made a mistake signing the formal documents. As she placed a tray on to the table in the kitchen,

Rex walked in and wordlessly stopped on the threshold. He had another coughing fit before collapsing into his chair. Maxine was about to ask him what was happening that afternoon but he looked so exhausted that she sat opposite, took a sip from her mug and waited for him to recover.

"We've got someone coming to look at the house this afternoon."

"What?" Maxine jumped up, spilling coffee on to her apron. "I didn't think anyone would be interested straight away. I suppose you want me to go round and clear up." She leaned towards him, her hands gripping the edges of the table.

Whenever she lost her temper, Rex often thought that she would have made a convincing Nora Helmer in *A Doll's House*. Of course, she was too old now.

"I'm not doing it, Rex! I'll have a quick tidy round like I usually do but I told you, I've got an optician's appointment this afternoon. I told you last week."

Rex looked at the agitation, written large upon her weathered face. She almost looked as if she might cry.

"You stupid bugger! The state of you! Why don't you just forget this business about selling the house? We don't say it, but you know and I know that you're never going to be able to move while you're ill." She recovered her composure and said flatly, "The consultant said you had months, not years."

"You don't have to remind me," he replied with as much dignity as he could muster. "And I'm not talking about the bloody optician's appointment."

Chapter 12

Stephen Samson was keeping busy. The engagement ring that he had offered to Olivia had been returned to the jeweller, who was kind enough not to question the lie that the ring was not to his fiancée's taste.

He had harangued several contractors for their lack of attention to detail and had started to plan the opening of the seafront wine bar, which was going to be emblazoned with massive silver curlicue letters, spelling out the word PIANO above the entrance. Inside he was going for a modern vibe – smooth concrete floors and distressed walls with a nod to the building's past. Black granite worktops would be installed at the bar and the vertical surface in front would be painted black and white to replicate a piano keyboard. Shelves would be arranged like a stave with black and white notes hanging from them to mark out a simple tune. He hadn't worked out what that would be yet.

Stephen had an idea that jazz pianists had a cool reputation. Ignorant of individual stars, although he had heard of Duke Ellington, he consulted Google and was planning to have giant black and white photographs showing the most photogenic musicians in action at the keyboard, to provide decoration. In the loos, he would use old sheet music to paper the walls and above the sinks; in between steel-framed mirrors, there would be photographs of the Pontardeilo factory workers, stilled like a pause in a song, staring out from their work stations either side of pianos. He was going to source a few uprights that were no longer playable (they were cheap as chips) and paint them grey, black and white, to line the walls in the main bar. Customers could leave their glasses on the top of the lids. Piano stools could be used for seating. They would be screwed to the floor in case things got lively on a Saturday night.

In the meantime, he was going to buy more property. His commercial investments were ticking over nicely, but he needed to find a suitable property for himself, now that he was divorced. Currently he was residing in one of the rooms in an hotel in Swansea that he owned.

He was attracted to the house he had seen in the paper that belonged to the old acting legend, Rex Glyn. Stephen's first wife had watched all the films and it was no surprise that there had been a programme from a performance she had seen at Swansea Grand Theatre, signed by the actor, among her effects, which he found after the funeral. He still had it somewhere with all his other things in storage. The devastation caused by her death was similarly locked away. He was of the opinion that no good would come of him reliving their last days together.

Olivia Garland had a similarly sweet disposition, or at least he thought so before she had refused his offer of marriage. He was persisting in radio silence. She'd sent a couple of texts, some nonsense about a flower arrangement of all things, but from experience he assumed that she would probably miss him, if not his actual sparkling personality then the tempting lifestyle that he could offer.

He had first met her when she provided the table arrangements for his thirtieth birthday bash. The evening had passed in a drunken haze. He was already separated from his second wife and numerous would-be third wives had circled him like a glittering band. Waking up the next morning with a woman whose name he couldn't recall, her make-up smeared across the pillow beside him, made him feel unsettled and foolish. He endured an awkward breakfast in the hotel, but his companion was too hungover to manage food or conversation. He got up from the table and planted a clumsy kiss on the woman's cheek. To his surprise, she suddenly became more animated.

"That's it, then? Nothing else?"

Leading her swiftly into the vacant hotel foyer to avoid attracting further attention from his staff and other guests, Stephen discovered that she wanted what she called "a memento" of their evening together. She walked with purpose towards a silver revolving display case. Inside, gleaming beneath bright lights, a local jeweller's trinkets twinkled temptingly. The woman stabbed with a lurid green talon at the glass. Stephen's mouth felt dry and his head throbbed. Wordlessly, he fetched the key to the cabinet, unlocked it and released a white gold bracelet.

She was bundled out of the door with little ceremony, the bracelet held aloft victoriously as if she had snatched the Holy Grail. Stephen sat down in an armchair beside a grandfather clock and covered his face with his hands. He did not like the man he had become.

It was at that point that Olivia Garland appeared. She walked through the entrance to the hotel, looking around with apparent interest. The first thing that Stephen noticed was her natural beauty, but her lack of affectation mesmerised him. This was not a woman who scanned the room for an audience, playing with her hair and making big eyes. She was totally unaware that anyone was watching as she paused to look at paintings in the foyer. Stephen hadn't paid much attention to them before but they were landscapes by a local artist. After a while, she made her way to the reception desk. She waited until the receptionist arrived, scrolled through messages on her phone while she was there and then handed over an envelope that contained the bill for the floral arrangements she had created for his party. She chatted pleasantly, then bought a postcard from a rack nearby. It was a replica of one of the paintings she had admired. He delighted in her voice. "*Autumn Glory!* I like the title of that picture! One day maybe I'll be able to buy more than just a postcard."

Stephen was dumbstruck but his inner voice spoke. *If ever I marry again, it will be to that young woman.* They'd always said that he was an idiot at school. But he hadn't done too badly considering his form master's assessment: *Impulsive, overestimates his abilities and lacks focus.*

On leaving school, he had rejoiced in his ability to make money, finding that success was more attractive than alcohol. His much-derided impulsiveness led him to grasp new opportunities before others had become aware of them. Quite recently, from behind the wheel of the new BMW Stephen was driving, he had taken great pleasure from cutting in front of his form master. He noted, with some satisfaction, that the older man was pootling along in an ageing Mondeo – the image Stephen saw in his rear-view mirror was of impotent rage. He told friends of this moment of triumph and everyone laughed.

He'd never been short of female company – attractive long-legged women in heels who sometimes towered over him. He had no idea what he had done wrong regarding Olivia.

The morning after his thirtieth birthday, Stephen, debilitated by self-loathing and a sore head, concocted a plan. Flowers for other occasions were ordered for the hotel and he had casually dropped by while she was working. He orchestrated a meeting over lunch to discuss floral arrangements for the foyer. Business meetings became social events. He introduced her to people who might buy her flowers. Had she found his contacts useful and merely been flattered by his attention?

As Stephen turned into the drive at Long Acres, he wondered if he would really want to live in the country. The road had been muddy as he passed farms *en route* and he would have to drive to a car wash after leaving the house. It would be different if he had a wife and children. There would be enough room for everyone and he could imagine children playing on the lawn spread out before him. The thought pained him. It would have been out of the question with his second wife, but the girl he had known from school would have made the house a home. She would have rejoiced in the mature garden, remembering how she had been delighted with the window boxes he made her when they were first married. He mourned the family that might have been.

He suppressed the thoughts that enfeebled him and took solace in practical solutions. Maybe the place would lend itself to a boutique hotel. Momentarily he lost sight of the fact that commercial property was not what he was looking for. Enormous trees outlined the plot – ash, willow, holly and oak, apple and pear, a testament to many generations that had husbanded the land. Golden leaves swirled about him as he stepped out of the car. He would sort out the trees if he bought the place. You wouldn't get very far with a standard leaf blower against that lot.

His first impression was that he liked the proportions of the building, solid and masculine. He knew from the photographs in the paper that there would be work to do inside, but that wouldn't deter him. Quite the reverse. He relished a new project.

Just as he was about to ring the bell, a van rounded the corner of the drive. Stephen paused to look. Ridiculously, he felt his heart pound. He recognised the vehicle and the driver. It was Olivia who was singing at the wheel.

She was listening to Adele playing on the radio, bemoaning her fate. Olivia knew the lyrics. "Never mind, I'll find someone like you." It troubled her that the woman in the song had dropped in, uninvited, on the ex-boyfriend and his new partner. Was that sensible? But Olivia was feeling upbeat, congratulating herself on gaining Sarah as extra help in the shop. She was good company, particularly funny about the behaviour of some of her fellow students. And she worked hard, was quick to learn and knew when silence was preferable to chatter. Olivia sang without pathos. "Don't forget me, I beg; I'll remember you said, Sometimes it lasts in love but sometimes it hurts instead." She stopped halfway through the line as she saw the BMW parked ahead of her. Stephen's car. She braked, scattering gravel in her wake, thinking for a moment that she could slam the van into reverse. Too late. He was walking towards her. No escape.

Rex watched from the kitchen window. He didn't like to class himself as a voyeur but he liked to look at Olivia. She was, as he used to say, easy on the eye. You probably couldn't say that aloud any more. Complimenting a woman could get you into all sorts of hot water. The bloke she was talking to was someone she clearly knew. Was she blushing? Surely she didn't fancy him. He was too short for her to start off with. Rex watched in horror as they embraced. He consoled himself with the knowledge that neither looked comfortable. Olivia disentangled herself and walked, head down, to the back of the van and opened the doors to retrieve Rex's bouquet. Hidden from the van doors, Stephen sagged. It looked as if he were wringing his hands.

By the time that Olivia had appeared with the flowers, Stephen was the picture of masculine confidence, shoulders back, smiling with the boldness of a man who had it all.

Olivia had spotted Rex at the window and waved. Rex responded in kind and met her at the door. He knew he mustn't snarl at the prospective buyer, but Rex's stance with feet planted apart and arms crossed, was intended to intimidate the younger man. Olivia watched as the men suddenly shook hands with an unusual ferocity. Despite Rex's weakened state, he was determined not to let go of his opponent's hand until Stephen had released his own grip, but coughing got the better of him yet again. Olivia patted his back with one hand, the flowers bouncing inside the cellophane in the other. She instructed Stephen to go and get a glass of water.

These were, on reflection, not the best circumstances for Rex to meet Stephen Samson. Sinking into the sofa, sipping his water, Rex requested that Stephen should look round the house without him. He cursed himself that he had told the estate agent's that he could manage on his own. Olivia found a vase and started to arrange the flowers, her pretty eyes darting around her. Perhaps she would sit beside him until he felt better. That would be a comfort.

"I'd like Olivia to look at the rooms with me if that's all right," Stephen said in a manner that suggested it was a command rather than a request. Olivia held Stephen's gaze but stayed where she was. "I rely on her judgement. She usually gets it right," he said more softly.

Without a backward glance, Olivia stabbed the last bloom into the vase and joined Stephen on a tour of Rex's house.

Chapter 13

Maxine needed new reading glasses. She had chosen frames from the cheaper range at the optician's. She had sat with that ridiculous contraption on her face and answered the questions, "Better or worse?" as different discs were slotted in and she stared at the letters ahead of her. The young man was newly qualified and very enthusiastic but she really would rather not have been informed that she had the beginnings of a cataract in her right eye if there was nothing that she could do to halt its progress.

It was strangely intimate sitting with someone else in the dark, his fingers brushing her face. She supposed that he considered her to be just another middle-aged woman but she wasn't so old that she didn't appreciate that he had a chiselled jaw, nice eyes and smelt rather nice.

The experience might have been more pleasurable had she not been preoccupied with her employer. Bloody Rex! She wondered how he had coped with the viewing at Long Acres. He probably didn't give her a second thought but she awoke worrying about him and she fell asleep praying for him. She didn't pray for his recovery as she was sceptical about miracles, having seen the X-ray and knowing that he had chronic obstructive pulmonary disease. She had written it down and recited the condition to herself until it was fixed in her mind. No, she wasn't going to waste God's time asking for a miracle but she prayed that he wouldn't suffer or be frightened when the end came.

The consultant had helpfully pointed out enlarged lungs and a flattened diaphragm and Maxine had been surprised when Rex's hand found its way into her own. She had squeezed it and given him her most reassuring smile, which Rex returned, but it was a distorted smirk as his teeth bit into the corner of his lower lip. She knew that he did that when he was absorbed or anxious.

As she wandered around the shopping centre after visiting the optician's, she found that she wasn't concentrating on the new anti-wrinkle products on offer at the nearby department store. Shoes, reduced in the sale, fitted but she hadn't the appetite for buying them. She took herself off to Marks and Spencer and bought herself a ready meal.

Rex lay on the sofa. He didn't even have the energy to pour himself a glass of whisky. His heart fluttered alarmingly and it had nothing to do with the fact that he had just seen the beautiful Olivia. He breathed deeply in and out as best he could, like he would have done before a big performance. He had fought off that bastard, Mr Panic, before and he would do it again. He closed his eyes and eventually drifted into a fretful slumber.

He was acting in *The Importance of Being Earnest*. This was a recurrent dream, featuring his beloved Cecily. His co-star was Amal, the woman in the photograph he cherished, kept in his bedroom. She had grown up in Tiger Bay, the daughter of a Somali immigrant, who had worked in the docks, and a woman from Carmarthenshire who had ended up working in a department store in Cardiff. Amal could carry off an impeccable cut-glass English accent but when Rex first heard her speak in a Welsh accent, his actor's smile broadened into a beaming grin.

She had been unimpressed that she was working with an established star, Amal being a virtual unknown. "What are you looking at?" she asked, immediately defensive. "You," he replied. "Marvellous you." She rolled her eyes, used to the unsought attention from confident men.

They bonded over a shared dislike of Lady Bracknell. She was played by a woman called Gladys, whose imperious ways were sustained on and off the stage. She had an unfortunate nasal delivery that they enjoyed copying.

"Never speak disrespectfully of Society, Algernon. Only people who can't get into it do that." Amal had her off to a T. They had whole conversations in Gladys-speak that made them laugh uncontrollably as they tumbled into bed.

Once, Amal had turned to him, her beautiful brown eyes blazing and in her own voice she had whispered, "I almost love you, Rex Glyn."

The dream morphed into a nightmare as Rex padded on stage naked, with only a copy of the play to cover his embarrassment. And he couldn't remember his line. It was a terrible quandary. Should he check the script to rescue the situation and risk being arrested for indecency or should he keep the slim volume where it was and ad lib?

"What on earth are you doing, lying about downstairs? If you're not well, you should get off to bed."

It was such a relief to be woken from that scene. It was a wrench to leave Amal behind but here was dear, solid, flesh and blood Maxine, standing over him with a Marks and Spencer carrier bag. He rallied, suppressing the urge to hug the woman. "When I gave you a key, I did so in order for you to let yourself in, if I am sleeping upstairs in the morning, or if I happen to be out."

"You look dreadful! Have you taken your tablets?"

"I think that's what's making my heart flutter."

"Not because you've seen me, then?" Maxine joked.

Rex deemed it wise not to mention that the same thought regarding Olivia had crossed his mind earlier – and been dismissed. "What are you doing here?"

Maxine strode through the kitchen and opened the door to the microwave. "I thought we might have a popty-ping meal."

"Your command of the Welsh language, as ever, is impressive."

"Do you want macaroni cheese or not? I'll put some garlic bread in the oven and I've selected a cheeky red. And there are nice little trifles or lemon cheesecake for pudding, if you fancy it. I shall be billing you, naturally."

Rex got up from the sofa. "Naturally. How was the optician?"

"Rather nice. Young, with a chiselled jaw."

Rex pulled a face. It was a novel idea that Maxine should fancy someone.

"Now there's just time for me to plug in the nebuliser. I'll bet you haven't done it. That'll boost your oxygen levels and for once you won't be able to interrupt me as I talk."

Maxine busied herself about the kitchen, feeling rather elated that Rex had looked so pleased to see her. It meant that she was missing yet another Pilates class but she was glad that she'd called round. He needed someone to look after him. She still hadn't rung Auntie's Angels.

During their shared meal, Rex told her about his visitors. He had had quite a time of it at the viewing. Stephen Samson had been disparaging about the state of the place, presumably a ploy to bargain his way to a cheaper offer, because if he had dismissed the possibility of buying it, he wouldn't have spent such a long time looking round. Rex had used the same trick with the previous occupants. Olivia Garland had arrived at the same time and, distressingly, it looked as if they were an item. They spent ages upstairs and – Rex gazed at the table when he told her – "She seemed quite flushed when she reappeared and that flash git looked like the bloody conquering hero." Rex asked Maxine what she knew about Stephen Samson.

"Why do you think I'd know anything about him?"

"Because you know everything about everyone."

"I don't believe in passing on information that isn't verifiable. A lot of what I might have heard I don't know to be true."

Rex laughed. "I love it when you go all prim on me." He reached over the table and for a moment she thought he was going to stroke her face. First the optician and now Rex? She held her breath as his hand moved towards hers… but he was merely reaching for the bottle in front of her. She watched as he poured himself another glass, red wine sloshing around the large globe on a slim stem. He was fussy about what he drank from – you needed space above a fine wine to absorb the smell, and the shape of the glass directed the wine to the back of the mouth to improve the drinking experience, apparently. He was always telling her things. She often pretended to be uninterested but remembered most of what he told her. He swallowed slowly, shutting his eyes to enjoy the experience. Maxine looked away when he opened them. "In the words of the rather dubious Julian Assange, 'As far as possible, facts should be verifiable.' But what if it's not possible? I mean, person A might be having sex with person B but, unless you are perched on the bedside table watching, you can't possibly know that that is the case."

"*Rex!* As if I would do that!" She was convinced that he did it deliberately to unsettle her. He might be ill but he still had his wits about him. He was always quoting from someone or other; at least it wasn't Shakespeare on this occasion.

"Not you necessarily. Just a figure of speech!" He leaned back in his chair to observe her. "Now why won't you tell me? I mean it's not as if I'm going to tell anyone, is it? I rarely see anyone these days and when I do I can't get the words out for coughing."

Maxine looked troubled, her elbows resting on the table. Rex could hear his mother's words from decades ago – *Elbows off the table!* He resisted the urge to repeat them. He would have said it ironically but Maxine would never confide in him if he continued to upset her. It was so easy to wind her up. He must stop it. Her hands were cupped together and she rested her chin in the space between. She looked as vulnerable as a child who's been accused of a crime she didn't commit.

He changed tack. "I appreciate you coming round. It was good of you to visit me. I know I don't say it very often but I don't know what I would do without you." He reflected for a moment. What he said was true. He tried to top up her wine glass but she put her hand over it.

Maxine met his gaze. "I'm driving. I must say it's a refreshing change when you say something nice." She took small sips from her glass and considered for a moment. "Do you know, I lost my voice once when I was at junior school? I was convinced that it was God punishing me for saying something nasty about my best friend. She'd upset me by sitting next to someone else in class."

"That's a bit Old Testament, isn't it?" Rex read the expression on her face and judged it sensible not to laugh.

She shrugged. "Okay, then. This is what I've heard."

She told him about Stephen's reputation as a chancer, his considerable success at making money and the fact that everyone said he worked hard. Rex wasn't interested in that. He wanted to pick over the carnage of the man's emotional life.

There had been two wives. The first was a girl he had met at school. She had died prematurely, an awful business, it was so rare these days. She had died in childbirth, pre-eclampsia and the baby had died too. There had been an enquiry at the hospital but negligence wasn't proven.

He wasn't on his own for long. The second wife was a stunner, an ardent participant of beauty pageants. Stephen had been one of the judges when she was crowned queen. She moved into his home with lightning speed, married in haste and was currently repenting at her leisure. The woman wasn't leisurely in her approach, instigating divorce proceedings, spreading muck about him around his home town. According to her he had been mean, unfaithful, emotionally detached and cruel.

Maxine paused for breath to give Rex sufficient time to reflect that all those labels could have been attached to him. She continued. Now he'd had a fling with *The Florist* (Maxine made it sound as if she had said *The Strumpet*). It was supposed that she was attracted to the size of his wallet like all the rest. Rumour had it that she wasn't making much money in that little shop.

Rex made the appropriate responses throughout the monologue, but kept his own counsel.

Olivia deserved better, of course she did. Was there anything that he could do to help?

Chapter 14

Kneeling had become painful for the elderly man lighting a fire in his semi-detached house in town. He had central heating, of course, but flames were mesmerising. He could lose whole chunks of time staring into the bright forks of red and gold until there were only embers. Since his wife had died many years ago, he found that fire-watching could still the loneliness that threatened to engulf him as darkness fell.

He placed part of the newspaper flat on the floor and started to roll it diagonally across from one corner to the other into a thin tube. Then he folded one end over the other and made a kind of knot. He would do this with sections of newspaper until he had enough to line the bottom of the grate and then he would methodically place kindling criss-crossed on top and then the bigger logs. He didn't read much of the local paper some weeks but it was useful for lighting the fire. As he rolled the second one, he stopped halfway when he glimpsed a picture that looked like – it wasn't, was it? – Rex Glyn.

Slowly, Frank got up from his knees. He sat on the nearest armchair and reached for his reading glasses. With shaking hands, he read the article on Long Acres. How dare they regurgitate that foul stuff about the previous owners of the house!

He and Elizabeth were the ones who had lived there. Their home did *not* smell of dogs, as Rex Glyn had claimed. They did have one dog – an ageing yellow Labrador that barely survived the move. If the house smelled of fried food, then that was because

Elizabeth had made a cooked breakfast on their last day, as a treat, but they had washed down cupboards, skirting boards and windows so that it was immaculate when they left.

It had been a privilege to make Long Acres their home. It had been too much for them by the end and they couldn't really afford to have gardeners and decorators, but Elizabeth never got over what was written in the paper the first time round, and was still talking about it in her last days. He closed his eyes and the images fluttered through his mind like extracts from an old cinefilm. Elizabeth strolling down the paths he had mowed in the long grass by the orchard; Elizabeth in a floppy hat and floral sundress lying in a hammock; Elizabeth picking apples and then in the kitchen creating long curls of peel before making crumbles and pies; Elizabeth sitting up in bed with her glasses perched on her nose as she read the paper in the morning. And Elizabeth without a stitch on lying there, waiting for him at night.

Frank looked at his watch. The estate agent's would still be open. He seized the phone, punching in the numbers.

At Pughes and Palmer, it had been an eventful day. Two sales had fallen through, the first because the buyers had changed their minds. Grace didn't warm to the gentleman who strolled into the office to deliver the news. He had decided that the house was "Too flash. We have more money than them but they have bigger televisions – know what I mean?" The second chain had collapsed because the vendors, a divorcing couple, had decided not to get divorced and to "give love a chance again," as the wife put it, when she called into the estate agent's to announce their decision.

Now, just before closing time, Nancy was reduced to tears, Grace was trying not to sound as angry as she felt and Byron was wondering how long it would take to resolve the problem. He had arranged to see a friend of his, a retired rugby coach, for a quick drink before he went home and didn't want to be late.

"All I asked was for you to include a photograph of Rex Glyn in the spiel about the house," said Grace, trying not to raise her voice.

"I didn't mean to include the horrid stuff. I chopped the article about and I intended to cut that out. I don't know how it happened. I suppose I got distracted. I remember that a young couple came in, new to the neighbourhood, and I gave them a local map and pointed out areas that might suit them. Then that nice old lady who bought the bungalow in town came in with some chocolates for me, not that I'd eat them, mind, but she wanted to spend a bit of time telling me how grateful she was…"

Grace refused to indulge Nancy. "But I asked you to let me check it over before it went to print and you deliberately sent it off without letting me see it."

"Now now, ladies, please," Byron said mildly, looking at his watch.

"You always belittle me!" Nancy exclaimed. "You leave me in the office while you both bugger off out doing your valuations. I hold the fort on my own all the time! I'm perfectly capable of organising my own work." She raked her immaculate hair with both manicured hands, knotting them behind her head, a picture of anguished defiance.

Grace wanted to say, *Clearly you are incapable!* but what would be the point? The damage was done. And it was true, Nancy prided herself on being professional. They did rely on her.

"I think we'd best sleep on it!" Byron announced, retreating to the back room to get his coat.

"I don't mean to do that, Nance," Grace said. "But what are we going to do? The poor man was practically crying on the phone. We'll have to go round to his house to apologise." The women held one another's gaze for a moment. "Perhaps he might have some older pictures of the house that we could publish; we could include his memories but I don't suppose he'd trust us with his photographs." Grace was thinking aloud. Her blue eyes threatened to spill tears. "He was so upset, Nancy. That idiot Rex Glyn shouldn't have said those things about the house and they certainly shouldn't have been published. We said so the first time round. It's awful that we've done it again."

October

Chapter 15

Weak autumn sun shone through the window of the flat and on to the table where Tiffany sat, overlooking the harbour at Tenby. She stared at the signed photograph of her uncle, with the part he had played, written in bold headings: ALGERNON MONCRIEFF, *THE IMPORTANCE OF BEING EARNEST*. He was wearing formal attire from the 1890s and lay sprawled upon a *chaise longue*, the epitome of indolent mischief. The photograph had been packaged with care, with a piece of cardboard behind it so that it wouldn't bend. There was also a note. Rex used an old-fashioned fountain pen, black ink, the words sloping forward in elegant, confident swoops.

My dearest Tiffany,

Thank you so much for the postcard. I have fond memories of visiting you all at the flat. There is nothing more perfect than sitting on your balcony, looking out at the blue yonder, that dear little tourist boat wending its way towards Caldey Island and the monks. The photograph might be described as "vintage" but I thought you would prefer it to a more recent one, given my current state of decrepitude.

Do let me know about any productions you are involved in. I do miss the backstage chatter. I get the occasional missive from my agent but it looks as if I have been cast adrift from most of my acting friends. Perhaps they think that old age is an infectious complaint!

You might be interested to hear that I am updating my last will and testament. My solicitor or myself will keep you informed.

Fondest love,

Uncle Rex

Tiffany laughed out loud. She kissed his photograph as if she were a loyal fan. She must ring her mother to get further instructions.

The only problem was the lack of information that she could give him about her acting career but she could always make it up. She must write to him again. Snail mail worked better than a phone call when it came to her recalcitrant uncle. She wondered if Joshua would be remembered in the Will – but he really was quite brusque when they visited. It wouldn't be her fault if he didn't get a cut. Perhaps she wouldn't tell her brother about the letter. Rex didn't give the impression of being particularly loaded – maybe there wasn't enough to go round. Never mind, as far as she was concerned, the old rogue might deliver after all.

Olivia was seated in her shop, behind the counter with Sarah. She was giving a lesson on how to make a buttonhole. They were watching a video on YouTube on Olivia's iPad, featuring a florist whose voice and manner were soothing, to such a point that Sarah feared she might drop off to sleep. You never saw the woman's face, merely her dextrous fingers with their surprising lilac polish on short, workaday nails. So far Sarah had only been trusted to wire up the leaves, but she was to progress to the wiring of the rose and hopefully to the construction of the whole thing, if she got it right. She was well aware that if she made a mess of it, she would lose Olivia money. Every now and again, Olivia would pause the video and clarify further points, which seemed a little unnecessary as the lilac-nailed narrator couldn't have been more clear. Good God! Sarah was in possession of a host of GCSEs and A levels! She got how to use florist tape, stretching it down the stem of the flower, and how to remove the guard petals of roses and, in spite of the chaos of her bedroom floor, she was a surprisingly careful and dextrous worker. Nevertheless, after barely surviving Freshers' Week, it was soothingly restful in the cosy environment of the shop, wafted with the scent of lilies.

The postman interrupted their tutorial, bringing a clutch of envelopes. He was perfectly capable of posting them through the letterbox but it was one of the highlights of his day to visit the young women in the florist's shop. The dark one, Olivia, had the warmest smile and the blonde one was a new addition, always ready with a quick reply.

"Morning, my ladies!"

"Hello," said Olivia.

"My Lord!" said Sarah, dropping a curtsy.

"Is it *young women* that you'd prefer, then?" He put the letters on the counter, the smile ebbing away from his lips.

"Well, you could always try Olivia and Sarah."

"Right! Got that! Busy, then?"

"Yes," Olivia replied. "We're working on buttonholes today. Wedding tomorrow."

"Nice. I look forward to any freebies. A pretty buttonhole would perk up my uniform and I could think about you for the rest of the day." He liked to think that he was a bit of a cheeky chappy.

Sarah rolled her eyes.

"No freebies, I'm afraid," Olivia responded. "Now when was the last time you bought flowers for your wife?"

Five minutes later he left with the smallest, cheapest bunch of flowers he could get away with, wondering if perhaps he might post the letters through the letterbox in future.

"Oh dear," Olivia said when he was out of sight. "I think we ganged up on him a bit." She sifted through the delivery on the counter. "Bills, fliers, something else." She opened a white envelope, the name and address written in black ink. She was silent a moment as she started reading.

Dear Olivia,

I know this might seem a little unorthodox, given that I see you frequently when you arrive with my beautiful bouquets, but what I have to say might be difficult face to face. I've always felt at home with the written word.

I have admired you for some time now. Forgive an old man. Those who work the hardest aren't always the ones who are rewarded and I imagine that being self-employed is an arduous undertaking. I worked as a delivery driver for a florist once before my acting career took off and it seemed to me to be a highly pressurised environment when the work floods in. The tempestuous nature of a dissatisfied bride can be a wearying proposition, not to mention that of a bullying groom!

I don't wish to pry but it would seem that you have formed an attachment to Stephen Samson. His reputation goes before him. He is something of a local star, I understand, with the Midas touch. I wonder, however, if he might take advantage of you. I want you to know that I am considering leaving you something in my will to allow you a little more financial independence. The legacy should be coming your way in a matter of months as my condition is terminal. Please don't be offended. I mean well.

You will hear from me or my solicitor in the near future.

Yours, most sincerely, an old thespian, who is your biggest fan,

Rex Glyn x

Sarah watched the expression on her employer's face change from bewilderment to something like anger. Olivia rarely frowned but there it was, an unfamiliar crease on her brow. "What's the matter?"

Olivia was uncharacteristically brisk, stuffing the letter back into its envelope. "Nothing to worry about." She was careful to remove it from the counter and thrust it into the depths of her handbag. "I'll deal with it later."

Chapter 16

Byron was glad to shoo away Grace and Nancy during a quiet lunch break. He had had a telephone call from a new player for the Scarlets, looking to find a suitable rental, and he had invited him to come into the office to discuss his options. Byron knew that the sportsman would be better off looking at somewhere within a short drive from the rugby stadium but somewhat secluded so that he wouldn't be bothered by autograph hunters and general busybodies. His excitement at the prospect of meeting and advising the younger man was palpable and he struggled to suppress his irritation with the women as they took their time gathering bags and coats, traipsing in and out of the staffroom. When Nancy popped into the loo to touch up her lipstick it was all he could do to stop himself from running after her and marching her to the door.

The reason why Nancy prolonged their departure was simple. She did not want to sit beside Grace in the car. They had patched up their disagreement but conversation was still strained. She still didn't see that it was necessary to apologise to Mr Whitehead, who had once lived in Long Acres. Grace was her boss. She should take responsibility for smoothing over any unpleasantness. Nancy didn't earn enough to qualify for the unwelcome task of saying she was sorry. Sometimes she resented her employer. One woman's decisiveness could be interpreted by another as bossiness.

The car journey passed largely in silence, Nancy's face a picture of mutinous resentment as Grace endeavoured to hold her breath –

the pungence of the younger woman's perfume in a confined space was overwhelming. She opened her window a little and switched on the radio. "We might as well listen to the news," she said.

"I don't see why. It's always so depressing. Just so you know I'll apologise if I think it's appropriate. I'm not being forced to do something I don't want to do."

Grace, who was equally reluctant to visit Mr Whitehead, would have liked nothing better than to be back in the office having a quiet lunch break. She longed to have a moment to close her eyes and breathe softly but she was buzzing with caffeine and an urgent desire to get the job done. Shooting through an amber traffic light just before it turned to red, the force of Nancy's furious glare was ignored and she kept her eyes pinned on the cars ahead.

Having flicked through the pages of an interior design magazine at the dentist's recently, Grace had been surprised by the return of what was called *maximalism*, crowded objects and frantic designs. Currently too many images and recurrent thoughts fought for her attention. It was like staring at one of those busy wallpapers complete with flora and fauna in clashing colours, while at the same time trying to catch tennis balls. She had always been hopeless at catching and throwing. Her son had phoned and told her that she needed to process her daughter's decision to leave university and try not to be so anxious about her future – at least she thought that was the gist of it. What he had actually said was, "Move on, Mum. It's cool. As long as she's okay now. Forget about it." It was easier said than done; any other concerns layered on top of the ever-present unease threatened to erupt into a migraine.

"*Tensions continue to build in the Middle East*," the newsreader announced. Nancy was right. Grace turned off the radio and wondered if she had any paracetamol in her glove compartment.

At first, it seemed that Mr Whitehead wouldn't let them over the doorstep. A pergola framed the front door, festooned with an assortment of overgrown climbers. They were trapped in a living porch. Liver-spotted leaves from rose and honeysuckle were scattered on the path as the last blooms of the year vied for attention on twisted, straggly stems. Nancy took a step back, distrustful of what might lurk beneath the foliage. "He's not in," she said. "Let's go back to the office."

Grace scrambled in her handbag for a business card. "I'll leave a note. I don't want him to think that we didn't come when we said we would."

As she was about to push it through the letterbox, the door opened, allowing dead leaves to eddy about Mr Whitehead's slippered feet. He wore cords and a clean cotton shirt, the only creases visible were those down the front of his trouser legs. He might live alone but he was clearly accustomed to looking after himself, his clean-shaven face and tidy hair unexpected, contrasting with the neglect outside. Grace wondered if it was a deliberate ploy to keep people away by making the front of the house look so uninviting.

By now Nancy was on the other side of the wall that protected the house from the pavement and busy road. She did little to disguise her dismay as she was obliged to walk back through the gate and up the path.

"Take your shoes off!" Mr Whitehead instructed as he turned his back, returning to the living room.

Nancy and Grace exchanged anxious glances. High heels were part of Nancy's armour but she followed Grace's lead and did what she was told. Grace arranged her own brown boots and Nancy's heels in a neat row beside an umbrella stand. They trod softly on the parquet floor, Grace leading the way.

The first thing that you noticed in the living room was a painting of Long Acres over Mr Whitehead's fireplace, a 1930s construction with green tiles. The view was from the orchard, blue sky streaked with cirrus clouds above the house. Its presence so prominently displayed reaffirmed the old man's affection for his previous dwelling place. There were photographs of relatives on the mantelpiece, comfortable armchairs and a sofa covered in a floral Sanderson design, a newspaper folded on a side table beside a cup and saucer. It was the perfect family home with a household of one.

It was evident that he was agitated. He tried to fold his trembling hands together in his lap as he sat opposite the women. His expression was defiant.

"Mr Whitehead, thank you for agreeing to see us," Grace began. "This is my colleague Nancy. It was me that you spoke to on the phone."

"I know who you are. I looked you up. It was your father who sold me Long Acres."

"Yes, that's right. I remember coming up to the house with my brother. We waited outside on a picnic bench. That's not strictly true. My brother had a rugby ball and we played on the field at the front of the house. I think my father—"

"You should never have printed that piece in the paper!" The words came out louder than he had intended. He seemed to be as surprised as the women at the force of his own words.

"I know," Grace said softly. "I wanted to say I was sorry again."

"But who was responsible?"

Nancy stiffened beside Grace. She was teetering on the edge of the sofa.

"It was entirely my fault," Grace continued. "I should have checked my work. I was interrupted by someone coming into the office. There is no excuse but I wondered if there was anything we could do to make things better."

Nancy looked down at her stockinged feet and noticed that her toes had instinctively curled as she listened to the words of her boss. She consciously uncurled them and focused on the small tattoo of a tiny butterfly on her right foot. If she wiggled her toes it looked as if the butterfly was fluttering its wings. If only she were a butterfly and could fly away, she thought.

But then butterflies didn't live for very long, though, did they? And what if someone used insect spray to kill you? She concluded that it was probably best to be herself, albeit facing her current discomfort. Bringing herself back to the conversation in the room, she watched Mr Whitehead's pale eyes flare in anger.

"You could write a piece about that bastard Rex Glyn. Tell everyone what he was like." He twitched in his seat and started scratching his forehead as if he hoped that he could erase the memories. "He swanned around our home as if he owned it the moment he put a foot in the place. He manufactured things that were wrong with it and beat us down on the price. And then he slandered our name. My wife wasn't well – she died soon after we moved. And it was his fault that it wasn't a peaceful death."

"I'm so very sorry. But you know that we can't do that. But we could perhaps write a piece about your memories. Maybe we could take a photograph of that lovely painting on the wall."

Mr Whitehead was surprisingly agile for an elderly man. He shot out of his seat, with his back to the fireplace, arms stretched wide like a knight defending his castle. "You will not write anything else. You've done enough. And I don't want to give free publicity to that… that actor to help him make the sale." His heart beat so fast and loud that he feared he might collapse. "Just go. I can't think of anything else to say."

The women scurried into the hall. Nancy hadn't uttered a word but Grace could see that she was distressed. Instead of claiming the high-heeled shoes that the older woman tried to hand to her, she retraced her steps to the living room where Mr Whitehead was leaning against the fireplace, a dazed expression immobilising his face. "I just wanted to say sorry too, Mr Whitehead," Nancy blurted, a guilty conscience making her brave.

The old man did not reply. He sank into his armchair, his head rolling to one side, eyes unfocused and mouth open wide.

Chapter 17

Maxine's eyes looked heavenwards as she lifted another postcard of Tenby from the mat by the front door. This one had a picture of Goscar Rock. She remembered Sunday school outings when she was a child, scampering up the striated surface like a monkey in Gibraltar. Although it irritated her that Tiffany kept sending postcards, it was uplifting to remember summer outings and adventures from her youth. She turned it over and read the printed description before gritting her teeth to read Tiffany's effusive prose.

Goscar Rock, North Beach, Tenby.

Once part of the surrounding cliffs centuries ago until sea and wind erosion created the large detached rock that we see today.

"So you're reading my post now, are you?" Rex appeared behind her to see what the postman had delivered. She could tell by the tone of his voice that he was having a good day.

"Tiffany again." Maxine handed over the post. She looked at her employer. "You need a haircut."

Rex raked his hand through the grey mane. "Rubbish. I hate a short back and sides."

"I didn't get the chance to read the postcard, only the description of the picture. Are you going to share the news?" There was more than a trace of sarcasm added to the last two words.

Rex returned to the kitchen and sat down at the head of the table. He gestured for Maxine to sit beside him. He cleared his throat. "*My dearest Uncle,* – Rex raised an eyebrow – *Please send another picture of you. I have framed the one of you performing the Oscar Wilde. I thought it would be fun if I could gather a collection together of important moments from your career—*" Rex broke off. "Do you think she's got enough room in that flat to accommodate all my 'Important Moments'?"

"They might cheer up her loo," was Maxine's response.

He smiled at her, peering over his reading glasses. "How fortunate I am that I've got you to bring me down to earth." He continued reading. "*I have been auditioning for different plays for next year. Pantomime isn't really my thing so I won't be performing before Christmas I don't suppose.*"

"She doesn't know about your Widow Twankey, then?"

"That was quite the little earner. They loved me in Brighton. Now stop interrupting. *I'm so glad that we are back in contact and look forward to hearing from you very soon. I hope the doctors are looking after you. Love, your favourite niece. LOL – I know you only have me! Tiffany xxxxxxxxxx.*"

"Ten kisses. A very affectionate girl."

"Is she really an actress?"

"Actor, my dear Maxine. We're all actors now."

"It's all bull, isn't it?"

Rex laughed. "Of course. I don't suppose the little minx does any more acting than I do now. Zilch. But it's quite fun reading her 'Musings from Tenby', don't you think? Now what further excitement have you got lined up for me today?"

"Auntie's Angels are calling round so that you're not on your own at night."

"What's this? Are you procuring prostitutes for me now?"

Maxine wrinkled her nose in distaste. "You're not living in the seventies any more, you know." She collected up the coffee cups and walked away from him. It was a deliberate ploy to distance herself from the inevitable protests. "No. You're having a nurse staying over in case you're taken poorly in the night and I'm not around to see to you."

"I'm not listening."

Maxine looked over her shoulder to see why he wasn't threatening pillage and murder. He was gazing out of the window as the familiar florist's van rounded the corner of the lane.

"Ah," he said. "Olivia is here."

Olivia had been trying to work out what to do. She really didn't like confrontation and preferred to wait until difficulties were resolved or forgotten rather than tackle them head-on. But she had to talk to Rex Glyn about his letter. Sarah wouldn't have batted an eyelid, but would have told him where to get off. Olivia didn't want to confide in anyone else, not even her parents, whose protective instincts would fan the flames of parental indignation and cause an unholy row here at Long Acres. It was up to her to deal with the problem.

Usually Rex would hang about like a lonely bridesmaid at a wedding, trying to delay the bride's departure. Olivia would have to extricate herself as politely as she could, the bouquet thrust into Rex's hands by way of consolation. She knew he had a massive crush on her, which was a bit sad, considering he was supposed to have been a famous actor pursued by hundreds of beautiful women. That's what her mum had told her, anyway. Where had they all gone?

She parked her van and got the flowers from the back. She had gone for orange gerbera and spray carnations, cream roses and dahlias. She was tempted to throw in a few chrysanthemums, knowing that Rex disliked them, but thought better of it. He meant to be kind, she supposed.

There he was, standing on the doorstep, all eagerness. How on earth was she going to have a proper conversation with him? They needed to sit somewhere quietly on their own when she made it clear that his interference was unwelcome. Lord knows, she wouldn't mind the money but it was none of his business what she got up to with Stephen.

Rex had been looking forward to this moment. He had been rather pleased with the letter he had written, almost moved to tears by its pathos. Olivia would be so grateful to him that they would surely be spending a little more time together. Young people could be so energising. He felt better already just looking at her. Poor love, she seemed quite reticent, uncertain. He took a confident step towards her.

"Mr Glyn," she said. "Can I come in for a moment? We need to talk."

Inwardly Rex rejoiced. She used the pronoun *we*. She had acknowledged the connection between them.

Before he had a chance to reply, Maxine was at the front door, waving her arms about. That woman! She always had to spoil everything.

"Quick!" she shouted. "Come quickly! It's the estate agent's on the phone. You've had an offer on the house!"

With a sorrowful backward glance, Rex dragged himself to the door. "I shan't be long, Olivia. Would you mind waiting?"

It was Grace Palmer on the telephone. The offer from Stephen Samson was, as they expected, quite disappointing. Given that there had been no survey as yet and there was every possibility that the offer could sink lower should there be recommendations for significant repairs, it was judged that it would be best to push back. "I'll tell him that you were expecting a great deal more. It's early days yet, Mr Glyn. Don't despair."

At that moment, Rex couldn't have cared less about how much the house fetched. He threw the phone down and walked as quickly as he could to the front door.

Olivia had gone. The moment had passed.

Chapter 18

Grace Palmer had tried to locate Frank Whitehead. After he had collapsed, she had rung the emergency services and the response was mercifully quick. Frank had regained consciousness just as they were trying to wheel him away to the ambulance. Grace was preparing to go with him but he became so agitated that she had to back off.

Nancy reckoned that she was suffering from flashbacks. "You didn't see him collapse, eyes all glassy and peculiar. I can still hear the noise as he took what I thought was his last breath."

Grace had lost count of the number of times she had tried to ring, first the hospital, where the policy was that news could not be disclosed to someone who wasn't a relative, and then the house. They had sent a Get Well card to his home address in the certain knowledge that it would be ripped up if he was still around. When she was at the market, getting the Welsh cakes for the office, she had bumped into the local undertaker, a jovial man, who assured her that he would be the first to know if Frank Whitehead had died. Grace quickly curtailed the conversation. The family joke had always been that you didn't hang around long with Barry the Box, in case he was sizing you up for your coffin.

Returning to the office, she distributed the Welsh cakes, pausing by Nancy's desk. The younger woman had taken to wearing a two-piece pinstripe jacket and shorts, teamed with an immaculate white T-shirt. It looked very smart when she was sitting behind her desk but eyebrows were raised when she came out from behind it to go to the filing cabinet. It wasn't as bad as if a newsreader had just stood up to reveal that she was only wearing knickers, but what was wrong with a skirt? On balance, Grace decided that it wasn't worth upsetting Nancy by initiating a conversation about work-appropriate clothes. It would get colder soon and the shorts would surely be replaced with trousers.

Nancy was looking at her computer screen with distaste. "You know after that article about Rex Glyn, I don't like to talk about it, but Mr Whitehead wasn't the only one who's come out of the woodwork." She moved her screen round so that Grace could read from it. "It's on Twitter. Lots of chat. There's the usual stuff, fans going into overdrive, but there're loads of people bitching about him."

Grace read a few entries.

He never did anything for the town. I asked him once to talk to our film society and he flatly refused unless we paid a ridiculous sum we didn't have. #notaniceman

He was supposed to be compere for the Pontardeilo brass band concert years ago and he arrived late, steaming drunk, fell down the steps to the stage and swore in front of everyone. #notaniceman

He pinched my girlfriend at the time, right from under my nose. Ancient history but I haven't forgotten. Hope his house goes up in flames. #notaniceman

An anonymous contributor, in Trumpian mould, added,

Burn him up!

"I don't know about '*#notaniceman*', it's really not nice being famous," Grace said. "Never mind. We'll get the best price we can for him. Eat your Welsh cake while it's warm. I'll get the coffees in."

Sarah arrived unannounced. She had taken to popping into her mother's place of work if ever there was an idle moment at the florist's. It often coincided with coffee breaks at the estate agent's. She grabbed a Welsh cake from the paper bag on her mother's desk and shouted to her in the back room. "Mine's a strong tea, no sugar," as if her mother needed to be told.

"Hiya, Nancy. Where's Byron?"

"Doing a probate valuation."

Nancy immediately busied herself at her desk, her childish hope being that Sarah would report back to Grace that she was a diligent worker, ever eager for Brownie points after the temporary falling out of favour. Her pretty fingers moved quickly over the keys as she typed up property details. "I'm afraid I can't talk now, Sarah," she sniffed. "I'm busy at the moment."

"All right, I'll talk. You listen." She sat behind her mother's desk, her Dr. Martens resting on a chair beside her so that she was looking towards Nancy. Her lower half of drainpipe jeans and boots were entirely at odds with the lilac tabard that she wore above. She also wore a badge that said, My name is Sarah. How may I help you?" As Sarah herself had said, "That's an open-ended question. I could get into all sorts of trouble with that. And anyway, do they think I've lost my powers of speech?" Grace had been surprised that her daughter had agreed to wear it.

"Shall I give you a quick update of the latest gossip in Flower Land?"

"Really, Sarah," Nancy replied. "You should know by now that I'm not interested." Sarah watched as Nancy slowed her typing and inclined her head towards the younger woman to indicate that she was willing to pretend that she was working while listening to whatever Sarah had to say.

"So... the word in the florist's is that Olivia is back with Stephen Samson. Now there's a girl who doesn't gossip. Really, I don't know what the score is but he keeps popping in and they're going to the races together at the weekend." She paused. "I wonder what first attracted the penniless florist to the millionaire Stephen Samson?"

Nancy giggled. "That's Caroline Aherne's line about Debbie McGee and Paul Daniels!"

"Yeah! It's a good line, though. I mean, like he's not bad-looking, not a complete minger, but he wouldn't do for me. He's a bit full of himself, dropping into the conversation his particular achievement of the day. There's no need, is there? Either Olivia fancies him or she'll tell him to eff off. I know God loves a trier but I think He'd want to give that Stephen a bit of a slap, trying so hard to play it cool but failing so miserably."

Grace came in with the drinks, her face alight as she saw her pretty daughter lounging at the desk, blonde hair in a plait, tied at the end with garden twine. She was going to be okay, of course she was.

Sarah took a slurp of her tea. "Right, back to the land of the flowers," she said, kissing her mother on the cheek and walking out with the mug. "Seeya, Nance!"

"You'd better bring that back!" Grace called after her.

"Yeah, yeah."

"Honestly, she didn't even wait to have a chat. She uses our office as if it were a cafe. I'm going to have to start charging her." Grace adjusted her chair and tutted but Nancy watched how her boss's face broke into a smile.

Grace knew that she would never see that particular mug again. It wouldn't have mattered had it belonged to her but it was Byron's. She would have to buy another one from the Scarlets rugby stadium after work.

Chapter 19

At Long Acres, a sombre mood enfolded the two occupants every time someone from Pughes and Palmer Estate Agent's rang with an amended but still derisory offer for the purchase of the house. Stephen Samson was bullish about its deficiencies but was still in pursuit of the prize. There had also been some recreational viewers who just wanted to nose round an actor's home and report back to whoever would listen. Maxine had decided to knock some sense into Rex.

She sat on the edge of his bed, lingering after she handed over his mug of tea before breakfast. Her employer eyed her with suspicion. Her jaw was set and she was frowning.

"What is it this time? A pay rise?" Rex asked in between sips. "Not being funny, lovely girl, but isn't it a bit familiar, you sitting on the Welsh blanket like this as if you've been here all night?" He took sharp intakes of breath as he tried to use his inhalers.

She continued to perch beside him, waiting for him to finish. "I've been thinking."

"Don't do that now. It doesn't do you any good." He smiled to himself. "That's what you say, now, isn't it?"

"Is it fair to say that you're getting upset over this proposed house sale? Yes or no?" she persisted.

"Now then, a direct question. If I were a politician, I would say, '*Let me be clear on this. A house sale can be unsettling but a necessary evil in some circumstances.*' Then I would say. '*But our party will facilitate the smoothest and fairest of transactions for vendor and buyer.*' Then I'd give my warmest, most sincere smile and everyone would vote for me." The lengthy speech prompted a series of racking coughs.

"Stop it, Rex. Yes or no?"

Rex glowered into his tea. She was right, of course. He had got into the habit of trying to imagine that there was no end date for his life. He was physically and mentally unable to move. His executor, the solicitor, could sort it out when he had gone. "Yes," he muttered.

"And wouldn't it give you a bit of a boost to disappoint that Mr Samson by sending a message via the estate agent's that you aren't going to sell after all?" Maxine, sensing victory, realised it was essential that she tried to sound neutral in the delicate final negotiations.

Rex lifted his handsome leonine head and proclaimed, "Yes, it would. I don't want him to get his hands on Long Acres, especially not for such an insultingly low price."

"Good. We're agreed." She sprang from the bed and stood above him, trying not to look or sound triumphant.

Rex put his mug on the bedside table and took her hand, squeezing it. "That was nicely done, my friend. You're right. I was wrong. My bad."

Maxine wondered why he insisted using silly slang expressions. She assumed he thought that he was endearing himself to younger people when in fact he was making himself ridiculous. Not to worry. He'd changed his mind, that was the important thing.

"Would you like me to make the call to the estate agent's?"

Rex nodded, stripped of all pretence. "Would you? And I want to finalise my will. I need to speak to the solicitor. Would you ring her too?

"Happy to," Maxine spoke into his ear as she helped to ease him out of bed.

Rex, knowing that he had capitulated on one point, sought to push back, to even the score. "Any chance of upgrading the string of matrons who stay the night as my so-called carers? That woman last night – what a harridan! And she reeked of sweat."

"I hate to break it to you, Rex, but sometimes you smell too. That woman who was kind enough to stay had probably been working long hours already by the time that she came to you – so, sorry, no. It was hard enough to sort out cover for you in the first place." They walked arm in arm to the bathroom. She smiled reassuringly as she left him. "Call me when you're ready to come downstairs." Like a naughty child, he poked his tongue out at her retreating figure.

In the hall, she stooped to pick up the post. She recognised the handwriting from Rex's agent on the front of an envelope. They were beginning to gather like virtual vultures round a virtual corpse, keeping a prudent distance, fearful of appearing in person. A number of acting friends had written recently. One had asked for the return of several LPs that had been borrowed decades ago. You could only suppose he feared that they would be lost forever once Rex took up residence in the heavenly stage above. Jaunty Get Well cards were worse – did they not know that recovery was unlikely? She caught a glimpse of a photograph at the bottom of the pile. Ah, there it was – another postcard from Tenby. Maxine smiled. That would cheer him up.

What was it this time? The view was taken from St Catherine's Island, looking back at the shore and the sweep of grand houses on the clifftop.

Dearest Uncle,

Me again. Did you hear that some poll voted this beach as the best in Britain? Of course it is. We all knew that. I remember when you bought me a bucket and spade – I was made up.

Recent news: I changed my mind about Panto after you wrote and told me about Aladdin in Brighton. I was in Upper Frog Street and there was a sign outside the Pavilion, advertising auditions for Cinderella. Anyway, long story short, I got the part. I'm Cinderella! Hope you're pleased for me. I must have inherited some of your talent! LOL Speak soon,

Much love,

Your loving Tiffany xxx

As if that really happened, thought Maxine. She chuckled at the girl's brazen self-promotion. Hats off to her – she was determined to worm her way into Rex's affections one way or another.

Tiffany couldn't remember when she had laughed so much. It was probably at school, when she had a gaggle of girls around her and they spoke so much nonsense that her sides hurt from all the giggling. It was pure joy to be standing on stage again.

It was only by chance that she had seen the sign for auditions outside the Pavilion, having popped in to have her nails done on the same street and then she remembered that she needed to go to Poundland and had to walk further up the road to get there. A maternal sort of woman was standing at the entrance and tried to persuade her to come in. She prattled on about culture and art, how you could buy all sorts of stuff on the road they stood in but there was nothing like immersing yourself in something that could not be bought. Tiffany was just wondering if she was quite all there, when the woman changed tack. "At one end of the street is a letting agent if you want to move and at this end of the street is the Pavilion, where you can quite simply *be* moved."

Tiffany shook her head, smiled and walked away, but for some unaccountable reason stopped, turned on her heel and was through the doors into the hall before she had processed what she was doing. Uncle Rex had something to do with it. There had been no time to be nervous, it was just a question of reading a few lines and leaving her phone number.

She got a text later that day to say that she was performing in a Christmas-themed variety show, in aid of the lifeboat fund. So much for culture and art.

Tiffany was working in the pub at the time and was so excited that she spilled beer over a customer. But it didn't matter because she apologised and explained that she had got a part in a play and he gave her a hug, congratulating her. He said that his jeans were old, anyway.

The pantomime was based on an extract from Roald Dahl's *Revolting Rhymes*, his version of Cinderella. Consequently the narrator had the most lines and the whole thing only lasted about five minutes. Nevertheless, Tiffany got to dress up and even had a few words to speak. And she got to meet new people and was enjoying flirting with the handsome prince, although in the Roald Dahl version Cinderella rejected him on the basis that he chopped off people's heads. In reality, her prince was an artist who exhibited his work around Pembrokeshire, running *craft fayres* as an extra means of making money. She wondered if Uncle Rex would live long enough to purchase an original painting. That would get her in Zachary's good books.

When she dashed off a postcard to her uncle, it was a peculiarly satisfying feeling knowing that she was telling the truth, even if that truth was embellished a little. There was absolutely no need to mention that it wasn't a full-length pantomime.

November

Chapter 20

In the Palmer household, Grace tentatively asked Sarah's advice about suitable clothes to wear to the races. Sarah could also be relied upon to blend in patchy foundation or smooth recalcitrant hair. One of the advantages of having a daughter was that she was always eager to perform the role of personal stylist. Sadly that role was never reversed, the mother's words cut short with a sardonic laugh, eyes raised heavenwards as if Grace had absolutely no idea about fashion. It was decided that the trusty long camel coat over black trousers and a cream polo neck would work, being smart and warm. Paul opted for a tweed three-piece suit that Sarah shrieked with laughter about, his clothes being so ridiculously old-fashioned that they were on trend. He had just been to the barber's and his trimmed blond hair and clean-shaven face completed the ensemble. A scarlet faux-fur jacket over a silver-grey jumpsuit and wedge shoes were Sarah's choice and she plaited her hair to prevent it flying about her face. Her mother had warned that the site was windy and exposed, the racecourse having been built on derelict land that had once been an open-cast coal mine.

It was a last-minute decision that Sarah should come with Grace and Paul. Olivia's mother was holding the fort at the florist's and the original idea was that Sarah should have a lazy day off, but she had never been to the races. It could be claustrophobic in the shop; the wild outdoors, where she could indulge in a bit of people-watching, appealed. It was a dry, surprisingly bright day for November. And her mother would pay.

Grace watched as Sarah battled her way through the crowds. "Whoa!" she said as she entered the concourse and processed the scale of the event. When she was spotted by a shiny-faced youth who was still at school, Grace held her breath when he shouted, "Aren't you at uni?" Sarah jutted out her chin. "No!" was her cheery reply. On she strode, immediately spotting Olivia with Stephen Samson.

Olivia's dark head was bent over a programme that he held. His right arm draped round her protectively. Grace watched as Sarah barrelled her way into their private space, effectively pushing them apart. The two women looked one another up and down, exchanged smiles and presumably complimentary remarks. They seemed to be admiring one another's outfits. Olivia had opted for pale blue with silver shoes and matching handbag with a silver chain. Sarah's clothes seemed cumbersome by comparison but she looked to be the warmer of the two. Perhaps Olivia had been snuggling into her boyfriend for warmth rather than affection. He smiled at Sarah and then started to frown when he began to speak.

Grace wasn't keen to engage in a conversation with Stephen Samson, given his obvious disappointment when she rang to tell him that Long Acres was being withdrawn from the market. "I could kill him!" he said. "Wasting my time! What was he up to? I'm sorry he's ill but he must have known that he couldn't go through with it." She beckoned Sarah over, watched as she embraced Olivia, nodded to Stephen and returned to her family group.

"He's not happy about Long Acres!" she said cheerfully.

"Neither am I," Grace replied.

It was always an assault on the senses, entering the grounds. Announcements were blasted over the tannoy, music was playing, colourfully dressed punters weaved around one another, shouting to be heard, the smells of fried food emanating from food stands. And then there were the horses.

Paul shepherded his party to the parade ring, explaining that this was where the horses would appear. It gave everyone a chance to decide which horse looked the most likely to win as they were led in front of the assembled crowd. "I didn't know they would be so beautiful," was Sarah's remark as she watched the lean, muscular animals complete the circuit, their manes plaited and sides gleaming. One horse tried to rear up, snorting, before being persuaded to walk round the enclosure compliantly like all the others.

"I'm backing that one!" Sarah announced.

"Ms Palmer!"

Grace turned her back on the horses and tried to remember who the smartly dressed middle-aged woman was before her. She was standing next to someone who looked like a younger version of herself. A sister? It was an occupational hazard. So many people came through the doors of the estate agent's, it was impossible to remember them all, especially out of context. Grace had developed a reasonable technique for bluffing her way through. Smile, be confident and wait for clues.

"Hello," she said warmly. "And how are you?"

"Fine, thanks. I'm sorry that we had to withdraw the house from the market."

Clue number one.

"Sometimes it can't be helped," was Grace's neutral response, awaiting further information.

"It was foolish to think that we could sell it, given the current circumstances."

That wasn't giving much away. *Economic circumstances? Personal circumstances?* Grace nodded as if she knew the answer.

"I can't say I didn't tell Rex. But he was determined. It was upsetting having folk traipse around the house. He's really not well."

Clue number three. Of course. Maxine, Rex Glyn's housekeeper. It had in fact been a blow when Grace realised that there would be no sale. All that work and upset for nothing. Grace considered the woman before her. She scrubbed up well. A bit of make-up, a stylish dress and jacket, topped off with a helmet-like bob that withstood the wind. Grace introduced Paul and Sarah. The sister – it was a sister – shook hands with them all and they were gone, swallowed by the crowd.

“Time to place your bets. Ladies, this way.” Paul was in his element, buoyed up by the bracing weather and rural splendour of green hills around them. Mother and daughter slotted an arm through each of his as he led the way to the betting stands.

After watching six races, Grace was beginning to flag. It had been a good day, though. Paul had studied the form while Sarah had usually chosen each horse on the basis of the most appealing name, but it was Sarah who had made the most money. There had been good-natured teasing that Paul had pretended to be offended by but it pleased Grace to see that both her companions had enjoyed themselves. They were looking at their programmes, trying to decide which horse to choose for the last race when they became aware of a commotion nearer to the parade ring.

Olivia Garland was leaning against the rail with her back to the horses. She was Sunday-magazine material, so exquisitely turned out in high heels and an expensive-looking pale-blue fitted dress, her dark curls piled up so that the contours of her pretty face were more apparent. But she was looking distressed. Stephen Samson stood to her left and appeared to be shielding her from a man and woman whose aggressive gestures and loud voices were attracting attention from those around them.

“It’s Olivia!” announced Sarah unnecessarily. Before Grace had the chance to restrain her, Sarah was off, Paul following closely behind. Reluctantly, Grace trailed after them.

“What’s going on?” Sarah shouted to her friend.

“I don’t know. I think it’s his ex-wife.”

The woman shouting at Stephen Samson was hopelessly drunk. She leaned unsteadily towards him. Her outfit would have been more appropriate for a summer’s outing – strappy, short, low cut and lacy. Grace could only assume that alcohol was keeping her warm. If you removed all the profanities, there were few remaining words but the argument was something to do with money. “You know you can afford more, you bastard!”

The man who accompanied her was a contrast. She was willowy

and undeniably attractive beneath the heavy layers of make-up and thick painted brows, while he was stout, with sagging jowls, reminiscent of a British bulldog. Clumsily he pulled off his jacket and waistcoat, lurching towards Stephen, who was readying himself to dodge blows.

It all seemed to happen in slow motion. One minute Sarah had been at Olivia's side and the next she was in the thick of it. "What's the matter with you?" she shouted at the drunken man, moving into the space between him and Stephen. "Back off!"

Stephen was distracted by the extraordinary spectacle of Olivia's friend launching herself into the fray, yellow plait swinging, red faux fur blazing. He turned towards her and was punched on the side of his face, although Sarah had managed to put her hands up to deflect the blow, with the result that she ended up on the floor. The ex-wife wasted no time in rounding upon Sarah, who was struggling to get up from the ground. She aimed a kick with her stiletto heels. Grace held her breath. If the woman hadn't been so drunk, she might have done some serious damage, but her aim was unsteady. Nevertheless, Sarah's leg was cut. Blood seeped through the material of the jumpsuit.

Grace ran towards her daughter but Paul had got there first, dragging Sarah away from harm. Stephen was furious, his face flushed. He fought back at the troublemaker.

The spectacle was gladiatorial, more exciting than watching horses race. There was something primeval in the delighted roar from spectators as blood was shed. Grace wondered why there were no policemen or even willing officials to intervene. She cradled her daughter in her arms as Paul tried to restrain the square-shaped assailant. She screamed as Paul was elbowed on the chin and staggered backwards to the sounds of cheering.

But alcohol was taking its toll. The fighter was beginning to flag, in spite of Stephen's ex-wife urging him on. Paul's intervention had confused him.

"Rip his head off!" she shouted.

Two men stepped forward from the crowd to restrain Stephen,

their gentlemanly attire at odds with their pumped-up aggression. A woman who had achieved modest success locally in body-building waded in to help Paul, kicking off her heels and stripping off a pastel cardigan to reveal a muscular torso beneath a contoured dress. Grace was impressed by the sleeve of tattoos that adorned the woman's left arm. It wasn't long before the newcomer had the man in a headlock and Paul was no longer required to assist.

"Good on ya, gal!" someone shouted. The woman allowed herself a modest smile. Checking that her opponent's violence was spent, she released her grip and the bulldog slid to the floor, clutching his head. Theatrically, she brushed her hands together, as if she had been contaminated by dirt. The cardigan and heels were replaced and she was reclaimed by friends, delighted at her success in subduing the fighting man.

It was over. There was an audible sigh of disappointment from the crowd, which rapidly dispersed to watch the final horse race. Hostility had relaxed into cheerful laughter that could be heard on the wind as spectators meandered into the distance, this way and that, like a watercourse that had burst its banks.

Stephen sat on the ground, legs splayed, his face bruised and nose bloodied. Olivia hovered above him, like a pale and delicate moth.

Paul gathered up Grace and Sarah. "We're going home," he said.

"But what about Stephen?" Sarah asked.

"He's fine," Paul said flatly. "No arguments. Home."

"Let's go to the St John's ambulance tent first," Grace suggested. "We need someone to check that Sarah is okay. Shouldn't we report all this to someone?"

Paul was grim-faced. "I don't think so. We need to get home as quickly as possible. It's always a nightmare trying to get out of the grounds at the best of times. And anyway, if someone in the crowd took a picture, which is highly likely, it might look as though I was part of it. And what if that idiot gets a second wind and starts throwing punches?" He gestured at Stephen Samson's opponent, who was struggling to get to his feet. There was no sign of the ex-wife. Having started the drama, she had vanished before the end.

"But I made it worse. I ought to say sorry to Stephen," Sarah wailed.

"I don't know why you always have to wade into other people's business," Grace grumbled. She wrapped one of Sarah's arms round her shoulders and Paul did the same the other side, propelling her towards the exit as she limped between them.

Chapter 21

Olivia and Stephen sat side by side on plastic chairs in the Accident and Emergency department at Pontardeilo Hospital, encompassed by a miasma of shame. There were no words to convey how either of them felt. They stared at a wall of posters opposite, warning of a number of ills, from overlooking handwashing to unprotected sex. Olivia tried to avoid making eye contact with other people, aware that their appearance was attracting attention. First of all they were overdressed for Pontardeilo on a Saturday afternoon, and secondly, Stephen looked a frightening mess, his beautiful suit, dusty and ripped, adorned with his own spilled blood, his face bruised and swollen. A woman with a black eye, a victim of her partner's temper the previous night, was sitting across from the couple and you could see that she was trying to make sense of the pairing of immaculate brunette seated beside broken man.

A toddler who had fallen downstairs struggled in her father's arms, hiccupping sobs of despair. "How much longer do we have to wait?" he shouted at a nurse, who was trying to help a pensioner to hobble to his seat.

It transpired that there had been an accident in the garden. "I'm going to have to give up power tools. The wife said we should get someone in."

Olivia looked down at her shoes. It seemed an age since she had fastened the silver buckles and yet it had only been a few short hours previously. If she could wind back the clock she would have refused Stephen's invitation and spent the day in the cool, fragrant environment of her florist's shop. She couldn't live life like this. Passion and excitement were overrated. She had certainly had too much excitement for one day. How on earth had Stephen been married to that dreadful woman? *Thank God,* thought Olivia, *that I refused his engagement ring.*

And what about Sarah? How was she going to face her on Monday morning when Stephen's ex-wife had injured her? Mind you, it was Sarah's own fault. What was she doing, coming between the two fighting men?

"Mr Samson?" A junior doctor hovered apprehensively by the doors leading to the consulting room. When he went to medical school, his ambition was to help sick people, unaware that so much of his time would be taken up dealing with injuries that could have been avoided.

Stephen struggled to his feet. Olivia knew that she should try and help but she didn't want to touch him.

"Do you want me to come with you?" Olivia asked. Even to her own ears, she sounded unenthusiastic. She wasn't surprised by his monosyllabic response.

"No."

"I'll wait here, then, shall I?"

Stephen grimaced in pain. "Just go home. I'm no use to you." There was dignity in his departure. He didn't look back and disappeared through the swing doors.

It was becoming increasingly difficult to ignore the stares of those around her. A teenage boy who had broken his leg by jumping from a monument on the site of the old steelworks, had stopped fiddling with his phone. He had a curious sense that somehow he was playing the part of an extra in an episode of *Casualty.* His mother, who was a fan of the soap opera, reached over and patted Olivia's arm. "It will be all right, love," she said. Neither Olivia nor the woman would have been able to say whether the words were sincere or sprang from an unwritten script, clichéd but appropriate for the assembled audience.

Determined to maintain her composure, Olivia stood up,

managed a polite smile and made for the exit.

Outside the hospital, where a woman wired up to a drip was sitting on a wall and desperately puffing on a cigarette next to the No Smoking sign, Olivia got out her phone.

She dialled and waited, hoping someone would answer. At last she heard the baritone voice which prompted the same response in every crisis. It was like being enfolded by protective arms and held close.

"Dad. Can you pick me up? I'm okay but I'm at the hospital." It was only then that she started to cry.

Chapter 22

Maxine had raked up the dead leaves with the elderly gentleman who helped Rex on an occasional basis in the garden. The gardener had cut back branches overhanging the drive. The wild rhododendron had flourished as it always did after vicious pruning earlier in the year. There was a clearing behind the trees that was the site of a compost heap and regular bonfires, where there was a mountain of debris waiting to be torched. Rex's habit of ordering biographies of his contemporaries was useful in that the discarded cardboard helped to ignite the flames. The books were never read diligently from start to finish, only skimmed in case he was mentioned in passing. There followed grumpy sulks if he wasn't mentioned at all, or excitable behaviour if he was fortunate enough to feature in another actor's story. Sometimes the books joined the cardboard on the fire. Maxine rather dreaded their arrival.

The old gentleman left her to it. She was wearing a particularly unflattering sweatshirt bearing the slogan JUST DO IT! over ancient jeans and wellington boots, her outfit of choice for lighting fires. Maxine always enjoyed this task. It was a purging ritual that was personally satisfying. She liked the challenge of sparking the first tongue of flame and enjoyed raking fallen branches into the middle of the fire when it took hold. It was a cold, crisp day, not too windy for once and soon there was a crackling conflagration before her. She even got a kick out of the gnawing anxiety that she experienced when the flames began to roar and she wondered if the whole forest around her would catch alight. It never did because she knew how to dampen down the bonfire. She took a step back as the heat became stronger and admired her handiwork as sparks flew up to the sky.

Solitude can be remarkably healing when simple tasks become therapeutic, but she wasn't alone for long. The scrunching of gravel and percussive coughing behind her heralded the arrival of her boss.

"*Double, double toil and trouble; Fire burn and caldron bubble. Cool it with a baboon's blood, Then the charm is firm and good.*"

Maxine didn't bother turning round. "I know. *Macbeth.* Song of the Witches. You've told me before, probably the last time we had a bonfire."

Rex's laugh was a bit laboured. "Did you pay the gardener?"

Maxine nodded, staring intently into the fire.

"Do you remember that man we had before, years ago now? Ridiculously handsome. I don't know why but it bothered me last night that I couldn't remember what he was called. Joan and Cleo couldn't take their eyes off him when we were sitting by the pond that long hot summer. There were lots of jokes about *Lady Chatterley's Lover.* Increasingly this happens to me. The lost names keep me awake for hours – girls I was at primary school with, people I performed with."

He might just as well have said, *Women I went to bed with.*

"What was his name?"

"Jamie."

"You remember him, then?" Rex was smiling, his eyes alight with a suggestion of mischief.

Maxine was transported back to 2006 to the same part of the garden where she was currently standing because it was a secluded spot, dappled sunlight on leafy ground, trees intertwined to screen the view from the house. She was dazed, leaning against a willow tree, enjoying a long sweet kiss with Jamie, his hands roaming inside her T-shirt. She would have taken it further but it was he who had backed away. "You're lovely, but I'm married," he whispered. She kissed him one last time, adjusted her clothes and patted her hair before returning to the house to help with the catering. Rex had invited his fancy acting friends for the weekend.

Maxine didn't trust herself to speak and merely nodded.

Rex changed the subject. "Who was that reversing back up the lane?"

Using her rake, Maxine rearranged branches that had fallen out of the centre of the blaze. Absent-mindedly, she replied, "There wasn't anyone. I would have heard them."

"I'm sure it was someone in a silver saloon. And I think they've been up before when you weren't here."

"So what?" Maxine turned to look at Rex's face. His expression was serious. He hadn't got enough to occupy his mind. She would have to think of something to divert him. "Rex, people take a wrong turn all the time. It's banjo country out here. There are all sorts of delivery people these days, using their own cars. Fancy a poke?" she grinned, offering him the rake.

"There was a time when that suggestion would have been readily accepted. It was a different era then and I'm a different man now." He knotted his scarf more tightly round his neck and did up the buttons of his navy cashmere coat.

"Oh yes? Back in the glory days?"

There was no reply and the two stared into the flames. "November the fifth tomorrow. Are you doing anything?"

"I might stroll to the rugby club, see if there are fireworks."

"There's a good view of them from my balcony. We could go all out and light a sparkler together."

"I might have to pass on that offer, tempting as it is." Maxine's sister had given her a good talking-to at the races, pointing out that Rex was taking up too much of her free time. It wasn't just that – he seemed to have taken up residence in her head. All she talked about was "Rex this and Rex that." Maxine had resented her sister's frankness but acknowledged that she was probably right.

"I've not upset you, have I?" Rex asked.

Maxine looked into her employer's face. His concern melted her resolve. That was the trouble with Rex. He drew her in after every episode when she was determined to become more detached. She resisted the urge to touch him, to smooth his cheek or pat his arm but she said, "Don't be daft. I'll see how I'm fixed tomorrow."

"Get you with your busy schedule!" he retorted. He sulked for a moment and then rallied. "So how were the races? Any gossip for me?"

"Not really."

"No drunkenness, female frolicking or debauchery?"

Maxine thought about the fight she'd witnessed. It wasn't a good thing to pass on nasty news but she knew that it would divert her employer. "You know I don't like to gossip, but there was an incident that you'll probably hear about anyway. It concerns your beloved Olivia and that twit Stephen Samson."

Rex seated himself on a tree stump and listened to the sorry tale without interrupting. He must make sure that he spoke to Olivia when she delivered the flowers. She seemed to be altering her delivery times. He used to be able to predict when she might call but now she sometimes arrived when he was still in bed and sometimes after dark when the *carer* intercepted the delivery. Anybody would think that she was deliberately trying to avoid him. He may have overplayed his hand, writing that letter to her, outlining his intention to leave her something in his Will. It looked like she had tried to speak to him that time when Maxine had insisted he answer the call from the estate agent's. Instead she wrote him a terse note, thanking him for his concern but refusing all financial help. It sounded as if she needed his help more than ever. Poor sweet girl, caught up in such a farrago of violence and humiliation. He must make sure that she knew that while he had breath in his body, he would be willing to support her.

Rex had retired to bed. He used to be what his mother called a *night owl*, carousing into the early hours with Maggie and Robert, Judi and Michael. Now going up the "wooden hill to Bedfordshire" was an event to be greeted with relief. He'd made it through another day. He was cheating the Gods, though, by equating bedtime with the end of the day. He was going upstairs earlier and earlier, now it was dark at teatime, and had settled into a routine of eating snacks on a tray and watching downloads of old films. He preferred to be out of the way when the carer arrived. It was too humiliating to be hauled about by someone he didn't wish to know, although it was reassuring to acknowledge that he wasn't alone if he became ill in the night.

His agent had rung, a courtesy call. They had an unspoken agreement that it would be pointless to mention the possibility of any future work. She seemed to be increasingly sycophantic. He enjoyed the meander down memory lane as much as the next person but was suspicious of her motives. He imagined Carrie rolling her eyes to a junior colleague in that fusty old office of hers while extolling his acting abilities. Rex wondered if she was hoping for a legacy in the Will. Just as he was preparing to bring the charade to a conclusion, she surprised him by saying, "Just one other thing. Talking of the glory days, I had an unexpected call from an old friend of yours. You remember Amal?" Rex momentarily lost his powers of speech. *Remember?* He looked at her photograph every day, his beautiful Cecily. She wanted his phone number – would that be okay?

Rex wasn't sure whether it was okay. He wasn't even sure if he wanted to revisit that particular period of time when he was at his glamorous best or possibly worst, depending on your point of view. He hadn't spoken to Amal since they had split up. What on earth would one say? Best to remember the goddess he had made her into rather than the human being she really was. And what if he got one of his coughing fits and was unable to speak. It was one thing to suffer from her fury; quite another thing to be on the receiving end of her pity. Unable to think of a reason why he should disagree with Carrie's suggestion, he tried to sound nonchalant. "Yes, fine. Why not?" He had to admit, he was a terrible actor sometimes. His reply would fool no one. Carrie probed a little, hoping for an emotional response, Rex supposed, that it might be repeated to other friends and colleagues. She reminded him of his desire to act with Amal again after *The Importance of being Earnest* had finished its run – a romantic film, perhaps, or something more meaty. "I seem to remember I got you both the chance of an audition for a film about William Wilberforce."

Amal had been sick of the limits placed on her acting because of the colour of her skin. As she had pointed out at the time, she was cast as the ward in the Oscar Wilde play, but would never have got the part of Gwendolen, an English lady. Even her casting as Cecily had raised a few eyebrows. When the Wilberforce play came up, her response had been "Slavery? You've got to be joking?" But that wasn't why she didn't go for it. Work was work.

Carrie was still talking: "… but for some reason you weren't keen to go for it. Why was that?"

She bloody well knew why. Rex wasn't going to go there. He began to cough. It was a fake cough at first but his wheezy chest did its bidding and he wasn't lying when he said that he couldn't speak any more.

Since that call, Rex had been poised to answer the phone to Amal. He had the receiver on the bedside table and willed it to ring. It was like a watched kettle. Nothing doing. He even tried calling his mobile to check that the line was working. It was.

Chapter 23

The radio was on in the florist's shop as Olivia and Sarah unpacked the delivery of fresh flowers. Simon and Garfunkel's 'Sound of Silence' was playing, an appropriate background because neither of the women were speaking after their initial greeting when they arrived at work. Sarah wanted to know whether Stephen was recovering but Olivia didn't want to talk about him or what had happened at the races. She was surprised that her employer didn't ask whether the injury she had sustained was healing. Not exactly caring.

Olivia was attuned to body language. Sarah managed to turn on the cold tap to fill the flower buckets with a ferocity fuelled by temper. Water was spraying all over the floor. Best to ignore it. *Why had the girl waded into Stephen's fight?* Olivia wondered. She had exacerbated the situation. Stephen had been injured when he was distracted by her involvement and the disagreement had escalated into a brawl.

When Olivia's parents collected her from the hospital, they had been sympathetic but vocal in their united opposition to her continuing to see Stephen. Olivia was not to be bullied or cajoled. She would make up her own mind, thank you very much, but as she lay in the bathtub that night, surrounded by bubbles, their reasoned argument as to why he was unsuitable seemed to make sense. Her father, a man's man who fought fires for a living, had asked "What sort of man gets caught up with a woman like his ex-wife?" She knew that it was contrary to the rules of The Sisterhood to blame the woman. Her mother had once said, "Always be wary of a man who pours scorn on his previous partner. If he says she was hysterical, depressive or downright mad, ask yourself: who made her behave like that?" But still.

She had blown into her cupped hands, scooping bubbles from the tub so that they soared and popped. Olivia had worked hard in her English lessons. She knew all about figurative language. Those popping bubbles would be a good example of a metaphor for her fated relationship with Stephen. *If my mind can go off on such a tangent*, she thought, *I can't be too depressed.*

Sarah's family had also given their opinions about Stephen Samson. Her behaviour at the races had somehow driven a rift between her mother and Paul. Although he was the nearest she had to a stepfather, Sarah had rarely heard him wade into an argument so forcibly. He tended to wander off into another room if there were disagreements. She had renewed respect for the man and could imagine what he was like when someone crossed him in the classroom. Her mother had intervened with a curt, "I'll deal with this." And she had. The argument seemed to go on forever. After Sarah had retreated to her bedroom, she was more upset to hear the two of them arguing downstairs. Memories from her childhood of voices raised as the young Sarah drifted in and out of sleep while her parents bickered, prompted a Pavlovian response and fat tears seeped into her pillow.

Wesley wasn't usually allowed upstairs but the soft thud of his paws on the stairs and the thwack of skull on door to push it open, heralded his arrival. With a heavy sigh, he sank his golden head on to the bed right near her, so that they were face to face, although not looking eye to eye. He tended to avoid it, being hard-wired to think that a direct stare was an unwelcome challenge, so he looked at her left ear instead. He had terrible breath now he was older, but never had a visitor been so well received. Sarah hugged him tightly. Wesley sighed again. He liked to think that he was an empathetic dog but it was a bit of a bore, all this outpouring of emotion.

The women had their backs to the front door of the shop when it opened. They turned in unison to see who had arrived. Olivia stood stock-still and Sarah dropped her bucket, gaping at the man at the door. Without hesitation, she shot towards Stephen Samson. "Are you okay? I'm so, so sorry that I made things worse."

Stephen winced, the unexpected embrace catching him off guard, bruises throbbing as the girl thrashed about. He wanted to speak to Olivia but one look at her startled face told him all that he needed to know. It was over.

Simon and Garfunkel continued to croon.

"But my words like silent raindrops fell
And echoed in the wells of silence."

Chapter 24

Nancy shook her umbrella at the door of Pughes and Palmer, not in the best of tempers as she had stepped in a puddle and her left foot was wet. She was usually the first person to arrive at the estate agent's, but had stopped off on the way to get milk, tea and coffee, as supplies were running low. Grace was at her desk, head bowed over her computer. *She'll have problems with her neck and shoulders if she sits like that all day*, Nancy thought. Byron, resplendent in a recently purchased plaid suit, was laughing loudly into the telephone in a way that he reserved especially for clients.

The receiver was replaced. "What a bore that Mr Thomas can be!" he announced to no one in particular.

"Is Sarah all right?" Nancy's opening gambit was prompted by concern, although she knew that her boss would be unlikely to relish the chance to relive the events at the weekend.

Wearily, Grace raised her head. The joy of living in a close community was tempered by the misery of enduring the spotlight-focus of others. "You weren't at the races, were you?"

"No, but my neighbour told me all about it. 'It can't be true that both Sarah and Paul were involved in a fight,' I said, but she said that they were and that your Sarah, love her, had a terrible wound in her leg and had to be rushed off to hospital, poor dab. I hope she's okay."

"Nancy, we're all fine, thanks for asking." Grace managed a thin smile. "Sarah didn't even need the attention of the St John's ambulance. You talk as if her leg had to be amputated!"

"You don't want to talk about it, then?" Nancy tried to sound sympathetic but there was no disguising her eagerness for further details that would surely be relayed over the garden fence.

"What would really cheer me up would be a nice cup of tea. Would you mind making one?"

Nancy and her colourful waterproof cape disappeared into the interior of the office, with only the merest suggestion of a flounce.

"Actually, I was at the races," Byron admitted. "I was going to ring you but I thought to myself, *Grace is a private soul. If she needs me, she'll ring*. You would do that, wouldn't you?"

Grace ignored the question. "Why didn't you come and say hello? How peculiar of you."

Byron momentarily lost his customary swagger. "I was upstairs, in a box. Hospitality with a friend. A chap from the rugby club. I did wave but you didn't look up."

"Jean didn't go with you, then?" A futile question. Byron and his wife Jean led completely separate lives.

"Oh no. She's too busy reconfiguring the bathroom now. First it was the kitchen. It seems to have sparked a mania for home improvement. Costing a fortune but it seems to make her happy."

Darren, her kitchen bloke, seemed to be round all the time. Byron felt sorry for him, really. It was sweet of him to have a quiet word and check that Byron was okay with the extent of the refurbishment and, in a roundabout way, that he was spending so much time there. Byron suspected that Jean had a bit of a crush on her builder. There was a definite whiff of perfume every weekday morning when Jean emerged from the bathroom.

His thoughts returned to the races. "I heard it was Stephen Samson at the centre of it all. That man! Seems to spoil everything." He was still smarting from not having had the chance to meet Rex Glyn after Long Acres was withdrawn from sale.

Grace knew that Byron would want an eyewitness report of the fight so she tried to precis the order of events as much as possible. Byron would breathe drama into her story, however she told it, but she tried to squeeze the tale into a flat and colourless account. She finished with an upbeat, "Nothing to worry about!" just as Nancy brought in the mugs of tea. *Not entirely truthful*, she acknowledged. Paul had threatened to move back to Suffolk.

Chapter 25

Hello, Uncle Rex!

Sorry I've been silent for a while. Zachary got me working in his gallery. I haven't got a clue about art, to be honest, but I pretend I like all the pictures with strange blobs of paint and bits of paper stuck to them! Zachary's paintings aren't like that. You should see them – great pics of the beaches and town. I don't know how anyone manages to paint waves and stuff. Have you ever thought about investing in art? The play's going well too. Best thing I could have done, going for that audition. Hope you're okay.

Your ever-loving niece, Tiffany xx

On the other side of the postcard was an action shot of Ironman athletes, muscle-bound men and women, running up the path from North Beach, with less fit competitors in the sea behind, stirring up the ocean like steroidal fish. In biro, Tiffany had scrawled a sentence with an arrow pointing to a man changing out of his wetsuit.

That's Joshua at the front. He did the Ironman. Must be mad!

Well, it made a change from the traditional coastal shots. The postcards usually improved Rex's mood. It was odd that he hadn't mentioned it, leaving it, without comment, on the dresser in the kitchen. It was time for Maxine to clock off, having prepared vegetables for Rex's evening meal and wiped down the worktops to make them shine.

"Where are you?" she called to Rex.

"In here."

He was sitting in front of the fire watching *Pointless* on television and looking desolate.

"I'm off, then."

"Enjoy your fireworks at the rugby club." His tone suggested that he hoped she had a thoroughly miserable time without him.

"Thanks. You've got broccoli and carrots to go with your pie. Don't forget to eat. I know you sometimes throw it out. I've seen your meals discarded in the food bin."

"You know I hate broccoli."

"The other *Pointless* answers include..." Richard Osman chirruped.

"Yes, but it's good for you."

"Bit late for that."

Maxine laughed as if he had made a funny remark, making her way out, losing her smile as she turned her back. The door slammed.

In his youth, Rex had rarely been alone. His mother and aunts had fussed, overcompensating for an absent father. When he was older, friends had been as plentiful as flashbulbs popping on the carpet at Cannes. It would have been undignified of him to grab her hand and plead with her to stay, but he regretted not saying something. However, he was sufficiently self-aware to recognise that it was childish of him to sulk because she had the chance to go out with friends. He was nothing more than an anxious fool since speaking to his agent, waiting for Amal's call.

Vegetables were put on to boil and the pie was slotted into the oven. He might as well do what he was told but where was the fun in eating alone?

Just as Rex was about to serve up his meal, the telephone rang. His heart seemed to have acquired an amplifier as he picked up the receiver. "Yes?"

There was a pause. A recorded message, supposedly from his Wi-Fi provider, informed him that his Wi-Fi would be disconnected shortly if he didn't give a few simple details from his bank account. He decided to channel his latent Noel Coward and, in fruity tones, reeled off as many quotations from the playwright as he could remember. That would fox the scammer on the other side of the world, trying to make sense of the recording.

He ended with, "*My importance to the world is relatively small. On the other hand, my importance to myself is tremendous!*" Finishing with a crescendo he slammed down the phone, feeling much better. Maxine usually dealt with nuisance calls. Perhaps he might tackle them in future.

The pie was nearly eaten when the phone went again. Rex snatched it up, registered a pause on the line and launched himself into another quotation.

"*I like long walks, especially when they are taken by people who annoy me!*"

He was about to throw the receiver along the worktop when he heard a voice that wasn't recorded. "Rex, you stupid bugger! It's me."

Amal's voice had lost a little of its Welsh lilt, but was still unmistakably, gloriously her. It summoned up the smell of her perfume as he nuzzled her neck, somewhat at odds with the current smell of boiled broccoli in his kitchen, past and present colluding to stupefy him. Basking in her concern about his health, he rejoiced in her forgiveness.

But she hadn't forgiven him. Words tumbled one after the other, almost the exact same words that she had uttered the morning after he had slept with another member of the cast.

"Miss Prism! For God's sake, *Miss Prism*. The part that demands the plainest of women."

She was right. No beauty was ever cast to play the part of the governess, a censorious individual, uptight and humourless, harbouring a dark secret. It had been a surprise when she knocked on the door of his dressing room, making some spurious excuse about going over lines, especially as she was word-perfect from the beginning at the read-through, and they had just finished the run. She said she was taking on the role again, in Chichester with a different theatre company. Amal had been taken ill. She had only just limped through the last performance. Flu. He was going to meet her back at their hotel.

He had been drunk, of course, but not so drunk that he couldn't do the deed. She seemed so grateful afterwards, as though he had done her a favour. Gazing up at his face, she was transformed. He remembered thinking that she had lovely skin and a radiant smile, but when she started rambling, he assumed that she, too, had been drinking, maybe too many glasses of Babycham. Truth to tell, he had no idea about her tipple of choice. "You're impossibly handsome, Rex. Any children you have will be beautiful people." Then she seemed to sober up, dressed rapidly, ruffled his hair and disappeared. He never saw her again, except on television occasionally. She made quite a convincing Miss Marple in later life.

Rex thought that he had got away with it, but that bastard of a stage manager spotted her leaving his dressing room. It wasn't a wild assumption that they had been at it, but still. Why did he think it was necessary to tell Amal? Rex had given him a bottle of whisky at Christmas. What was that expression? *What goes on tour, stays on tour.*

The pain of discovery for Amal had not been assuaged. Rex wasn't sure but it sounded on the phone that she might be choking back a sob when she said, "I know I was an idiot thinking you might be faithful but I had this ridiculous idea that we would marry and have a family together." Then she pulled herself together and said, "I have been so fortunate to marry my lovely Tony. I suppose you could say that I had a lucky escape."

Tony was a dentist practising in Poole, where they now lived in a light-filled glass construction facing the sea.

"You always said that you would come back to Wales," was Rex's inadequate reply.

"Yes, well. *That was then, this is now* – isn't that what they say?"

"Amal, I'm sorry. It is a constant regret." He paused. "Over the years, I have apologised again and again to your photograph. I still have it. It's in my bedroom. The one of us together. I had it framed." He had run out of steam. "Do you still have yours?"

Amal paused. "God, no! All that memorabilia got thrown out when we moved. Why would I keep a picture that reminded me of you?"

Just then, Rex heard a knock at his door. No one ever called. He would ignore it, but the knocking became more insistent, as unsettling as Macduff and Lennox's arrival, after Macbeth killed Duncan. "Sorry, Amal, can you hang on? There's someone at the door. I'll get rid of them."

Putting down the receiver, he walked to the front door, muttering a line from the Scottish play. "*Wake Duncan with thy knocking!*"

Amal toyed with the idea of putting down the phone, but she hadn't finished with him yet. She strolled over to her Ercol sideboard, pulled open the top drawer and took out the photograph of the two of them dressed in their costumes from *The Importance of Being Earnest.*

The cold air prompted coughing as it always did. Rex doubled up and it was a while before he straightened to see on the doorstep a man about the same age as him, smartly dressed, whose expression was wary. "May I have a word?" he said.

"I'm on the phone," Rex said. "I don't open my door to strangers, particularly after dark." Suspecting that the man was collecting for some worthy cause or another, he finished rather pompously with the announcement, "I support a number of charities, particularly to do with the arts." The door was slammed in the man's face.

God! He missed Maxine. She, of course, was *oohing and aahing* at the firework display, no doubt eyeing up some hunk from the rugby club as the skies above filled with forks of fire. If she had been here, he wouldn't have had to cut off Amal and stagger to the door. Having said that, the long-awaited call was not going the way he would have expected. He could do with a ceasefire, that they might polish some gems from the past and bask in the reflected shine.

"You do the talking, Amal. I'm out of puff. I'll listen," he said and that is what he did.

The carer cancelled. Something to do with a domestic crisis, the details sketchy. Rex was physically and metaphorically spent, clinging to the bannister as he hauled himself upstairs. He tripped and collapsed on a step halfway up, hoping to garner greater strength. His mind rewound to events he thought he had forgotten. He used to sit on the staircase of the two-up two-down, his childhood home, when he was supposed to be playing with toys in his bedroom. He was baffled and intrigued by his mother's stories, when she shared with her friends the horrors of childbirth and sex ("*ych-a-fi!*"). Sometimes she would talk about Rex, rarely his sister. "He's going to be something, I know it!" She didn't have any specific ambitions for her son, although standing him on a chair in front of all the relatives and coaxing him to sing nursery rhymes was one of his earlier memories.

The words of a children's poem came to him. His mind was stuffed with useless snippets from plays and poems but they could be a distraction in moments of despair. A. A. Milne's words were whispered as tears threatened to fall. He was consumed with self-pity, remembering his mother reciting them when it was bedtime.

"I'm not at the bottom, I'm not at the top;
So this is the stair where I always stop."

This would not do. He was an adult, once a glittering star. Another memory resurfaced of him lying prone at the bottom of a fire escape, after being ejected from a nightclub. That had been a good night, although precise memories had been lost in the untidy filing cabinet that served as his brain. He could only remember staggering to his feet and saluting the bouncer who stood above him before tabloid cameras captured his degradation.

Rex crawled further up the stairs and his relief at arriving in the bedroom was as if he had climbed Everest. He just about made it to the bathroom and sat on the toilet. How long he sat there, he did not know, but at last flopped on the bed, too weak to remove his clothing. He found a lozenge in his bedside drawer and hoped that it would suppress the coughing. Eyes closed, he tried to quell rising panic.

He heard the front door open and shut. They must have found a replacement at the agency after all. He heard the brisk tread on the stairs of some no-nonsense carer. Who would it be this time?

"You're a bloody nuisance, Rex. I'm fuming, I am. There I was having a whale of a time, and I get a call from Auntie's Angels saying you're on your own."

Rex opened an eye. Dear Maxine! All dressed up, make-up on, not a hair out of place. She didn't look cross at all. "You keep doing this! Bursting in on me when I'm trying to sleep." He paused. "Please keep doing it. I can't remember when I was so pleased to see anyone. I missed you the moment you stepped out of the room."

She sat beside him on the bed. "I could have got lucky tonight, you know?" It was true. The call had come just after she had been invited in for coffee with a man whose marriage had recently ended. He was a friend of her sister. After the firework display, they had ended up walking home in the same direction until they reached his house. She had been sitting on the stranger's sofa while he put the kettle on, wondering why she had taken up his offer. The speed with which she exited the house, with a cheery, "Tara, then," shouted over her shoulder, did little to boost the poor man's self-esteem.

Rex smiled. "You came to see me instead."

"I did."

He took her hand and kissed it. "Thank you."

Maxine got up. "You're welcome. Now then – nebuliser, hot drink and then I'll help you get undressed."

Rex raised an eyebrow. "The last item on the agenda sounds promising."

"I'll have you for sexual harassment in the workplace." She smiled broadly and Rex discovered that he could breathe more easily.

Chapter 26

Outside in the darkness, the gentleman – who was not collecting money for charity – inspected the contents of Rex's shed. Frank Whitehead had come prepared and shone his torch around the walls that he knew so well. In the days when he lived at Long Acres with his wife, each part of the shed was in order. On the left-hand side, he had a basket of kindling. Outside, he stacked logs in a lean-to structure that he himself had constructed. Rex had instructed that this addition was to be destroyed on the grounds that it looked ugly. Instead, he stacked the logs against the exterior wall of the shed. They spilled untidily near the oil tank at the side of the house. Perhaps Rex mistakenly thought that the effect was more rustic and natural.

In Elizabeth and Frank's era, there was a workbench on the back wall. On the right-hand side was a metal cabinet and each shelf within was arranged so that he could always find what he was looking for. Cans of paint were organised according to colour or type – gloss or matt – on the top of the cabinet. Gardening equipment and a lawn mower were stored in front, along with a bicycle.

The order had been replaced by chaos. A red gas canister was in a corner next to a barbecue, but mostly, the place had become a dumping ground for old furniture and anything on its way to the recycling centre in town. There was an enormous cardboard box that contained empty bottles. Frank Whitehead knew little about wine but the labels looked rather fancy. It was unlikely that Rex would settle for corner-shop plonk. He replaced an empty whisky bottle as quietly as possible, although he really wanted to smash the lot, preferably over that vile man's head.

Frank had been sitting in his car half a mile away after he had been summarily dismissed as if he had been an unwanted tradesman at the door. He had to pull over. He was shaking so much, he feared he might crash. All he wanted was to tell the story of his beloved wife's demise and perhaps extract a grudging apology for the pain that had been caused. His recent stay in hospital had been a salutary experience. In fact, it had prompted him to book a holiday – a month's cruise, entitled *Sydney and Treasures of the South Pacific*. Frank was not an impulsive man, but his *carpe diem* moment led him to the remaining travel agent in Pontardeilo and he was able to take advantage of a last-minute cancellation. He was due to leave the following day. Life was brief and if he intended to accomplish anything, it was necessary to get on with it before his own existence was snuffed out.

It was not the first time he had called, but on every other occasion he had chickened out of confronting the famous actor. However, the explosion of fireworks in the sky seemed a fitting backdrop for their conversation. Frank had gone out of the house to fill up with petrol before setting off on his cruise and instead of going home, had kept driving into the wilds, to Long Acres. Not usually a sentimental man, he felt that Elizabeth was urging him on as every exotic bloom in the sky burst into life, quivered and died.

A taxi had snaked its way to the top of the hill and Frank decided to follow at a distance. If Rex Glyn's reputation was anything to go by, it was probably a woman, summoned after dark. He waited until the driver had re-joined the road, having dropped off his passenger, and cautiously proceeded along the drive leading to Long Acres, parking the car round the corner so that it could not be seen from the house. He wasn't sure what he was going to do, but took out his torch from the glove compartment and walked on the grass in the shadows, avoiding the gravel that might alert the occupants of the house to his presence.

It was typical of the man that he should abandon the greenhouse that had brought Frank such joy, yielding an abundance of flowers, fruit and vegetables. Elizabeth had said that he had green fingers, but that was ridiculous. A successful gardener was someone who was prepared to spend time nurturing the plants, remembering to water and feed them. It was no hardship, devoting time to the seedlings, and his efforts had been richly rewarded.

Where the greenhouse had stood was an ornamental pond, mostly choked with grass and weeds. Any fish that might once have lived there had presumably been devoured by herons. Frank shivered as a gust of wind flapped open his raincoat. He had never minded the wind when he was tucked up in bed, listening to the howls and screeches as it rattled through the rafters at Long Acres, but it wasn't so comfortable battling it outside.

A light was switched on in the kitchen and Frank darted round the far side of the house and took refuge in the shed, hiding like the coward he knew himself to be.

Rex was persuaded to wear pyjamas. He became uncharacteristically coy and demanded that Maxine leave the room when he put them on. "Good God, woman! Let me retain some dignity!" He got into bed, awaiting her return. When she reappeared, she was at a loss as to what she should do, so turned her back on her employer and tidied up discarded clothes until it was suggested that she might like to go and get a bottle of red wine and two glasses.

Maxine poured the wine. She walked round to the other side of the bed, took off her shoes and sat upright beside him, her legs outstretched on the Welsh blanket. They clinked glasses and took the first sip. Rex was uncharacteristically silent.

"So," began Maxine. "Are you going to tell me why you were in such a state when I arrived?"

"I suppose so." He sighed. "I was expecting a call from Amal."

"Who?"

"The woman in the picture." He gestured at the photo frame. "My agent told me she wanted to speak to me. I imagine she had heard that I wasn't well and she wanted to make peace with me."

He could have said, *forgive me*, but chose not to, wanting to ease his way into the story.

Maxine raised an eyebrow. "What did you do?"

"Don't look at me like that, like some censorious teacher. I'll tell you. I'm not proud of what happened. I know it's no use saying that it was a different era then, but it was. I had a chance of making a future with a lovely woman but basically cocked it up." He smiled ironically. "Actually, my choice of words couldn't be more appropriate."

Maxine listened, occasionally frowned, but didn't interrupt when he told her about the actress who played Miss Prism. Rex wouldn't look at her when he spoke about the agony of being found out and of Amal walking away. Maxine gazed into her glass and found that it was empty.

"You deserved to be left," was her conclusion.

"I know. Don't think that I don't know." Rex poured more wine. "I thought that with the passing of the years, her bitterness might have faded, but she was more full of vitriol on the phone just now than at the time."

"That's because she was in shock at first and now she has had plenty of time to think of what she might have said to you, if she'd had time to prepare. She's an actor, after all. She's had many years to prepare her speech. What I'm interested in is the other woman, the Miss Prism character. Were you aware that she fancied you?"

Rex didn't know what to say. He was used to women looking at him in a particular way, when the lights shone brightly and his career was in its ascendancy. "Not especially." He remembered her smile after the sex, the speed with which she got dressed and the ruffling of his hair, almost as if he had been her conquest, rather than the other way round. She hadn't lingered or asked to see him again.

Maxine threaded her fingers through Rex's. "You're such a fool. You could have had a lovely wife and a family, but it's no use. You can't undo the past. Tomorrow will be brighter." Maxine was partial to an inspirational mantra.

Rex gazed at his friend, wondering if he should finish the story. "There's more."

"All right. In spite of what you might think, I've probably heard it all before."

"Amal told me a secret, one that she should have shared with me years ago or kept to herself now that she knows I haven't got much time left. Miss Prism met her years later when they were cast in the same episode of a *Morse* drama. You can imagine the atmosphere on set. Anyway," Rex gulped the remaining wine in his glass. "She says…" he faltered. "She says she thinks that I am the father of Miss Prism's child."

"Oh, Rex!" Maxine suppressed the desire to laugh. It was so ridiculously predictable. "Do you think perhaps we could give this woman her name, instead of referring to her as Miss Prism?"

He put down his glass, eased his hand from Maxine and buried his head in shame. "I would do, I would… but I can't remember her name."

Without a word, Maxine went and got the iPad and looked her up. "Eleanor Smythe Thomas!"

"That's right. Eleanor."

"What are you going to do now? Honestly, Rex. It's too late to have the talk about contraception, but what is it about men in positions of power? Do they not know about these things? Or don't they care? Mind you, you would think that Eleanor might have taken steps to prevent getting pregnant. In all honesty, this particular piece of news is not entirely unexpected, now, is it?"

"I don't want a lecture." He avoided her gaze and stared instead at his toes, peeping out of the blanket at the end of the bed. He remembered one of Eleanor's lines as Miss Prism in the play. "*The good ended happily and the bad unhappily. That is what fiction means.*" What an irony.

Maxine changed the subject. "I know you're upset, but how exactly did you think that the conversation would go with your ex-girlfriend?"

His anguished expression conveyed despair. "I don't know.

I thought perhaps we might acknowledge that we shared happy times. We could have looked wistfully on the past and what might have been. I didn't think her tale would be *Full of sound and fury, Signifying nothing.*"

"Where's that quote from? Shakespeare again, is it?"

"*Macbeth*, after his wife has died and hostile armies are marching towards him."

Maxine smiled indulgently. "You don't need to be so melodramatic. Your situation is not as desperate as all that. Now, what we need is a plan. Tomorrow, we will try and contact this Eleanor, if that's what you want, and you can find out if her child wants to see you. Did she have a boy or girl?"

"A girl."

"Right, I wonder if she looks like you." She held his gaze, trying to imagine what features the girl might have inherited. His ears were a little on the large side, more obvious now that his hair was thinner, but it would be a fortunate person indeed to inherit his soulful eyes and full mouth.

"I'll ring for a taxi. Thanks for the drink. I'll see you in the morning." Briskly, she swivelled her legs off the bed and on to the floor. "You'll be all right? You've said yourself that the carer never really does anything. I can give you one of those sleeping pills, if you like."

The shoes were replaced and Maxine rounded the corner of the bed on the opposite side and towards her employer. She leaned in, intending to kiss the top of his head, but he grasped both her hands and gently pulled her so that she was sitting facing him. Outside, fireworks fizzed and crackled as they maintained eye contact, neither sure of how the sequence of events would unfold. Gently, Rex traced the outline of her lips with a finger. "May I?" he asked.

She was unable to speak and merely nodded. He cupped his hands round her face and she instinctively gasped, the kiss transporting Maxine to the agony and bliss of recollected teenage years. Shutting her eyes, the relief that he at last recognised her as a woman and not just a domestic drudge was too much. To her embarrassment, she felt tears fall. He'd think she was an idiot. She pulled back, trying to brush them away. To her surprise, when she looked at Rex, she saw that he was crying too. It was then that they laughed, happiness bubbling to the surface like effervescence in champagne.

"Do you have those sparklers you promised me?" she asked.

"What?"

"When you asked me to call round, you promised me sparklers."

"So I did."

Resting her head on his chest, she couldn't see his face but could tell by his voice that he was smiling. She jumped off the bed and went to collect the sparklers and matches from the utility room.

Rex protested but was wrapped up in a coat and scarf. "What are you going to wear, then?" he asked. "It sounds as if it's blowing a gale out there."

"This," she said, snatching up his dressing gown.

The door to the balcony was opened and they stepped into the dark from the cosiness of the bedroom. The occasional firework lent colour to a blanket of stars. Their antics lacked glamour or polish, at odds with the manufactured images that fill millions of screens every day. In spite of Rex's distinguished acting credentials, he and Maxine would not have been cast in a perfume advertisement. Young, beautiful onlookers might have laughed at such folly as the pair wrote each other's names with their sparklers, but looking at their faces, anyone could see that they were suffused with joy.

And then the coughing resumed. Asthma pumps were found. Water was drunk. Reality returned. Maxine settled Rex into bed and, without any discussion, she found a nightshirt, changed in the bathroom and got into bed beside him.

"Wait!" he said. "Have you got a hairbrush?"

"What? Yes, in my handbag."

"Go and get it!"

"Bloody hell, Rex! I've been up and down those stairs more times than—"

He interrupted. "Last time, I promise."

She returned. "You're so vain. What do you want to brush your hair for?"

"I don't. Give it to me."

Rex took the hairbrush. "Turn round and sit here." He patted the bed beside him and proceeded to brush Maxine's hair. "I don't know why you wear all that hairspray," he muttered. "I want to hold you in my arms but it would be like nuzzling a Brillo pad."

"You're out of order, you. I'll wear my hair how I like, but it's nice having my hair brushed so I'll overlook your rudeness for once."

She turned to face him when he had finished.

"That's better," he announced, but looked away, embarrassed. "About having sex. I don't think I'm up to it, I'm sorry. Maybe tomorrow if I get a good night's sleep."

"Who said we were having sex?" she asked, her eyes bright with amusement.

"I thought it might be appropriate, given that I realise that I'm in love with you."

"What?"

"I love you, that's all." In his long and varied romantic history, the words had been spoken before, but rarely truthfully.

"What about Amal and Olivia and that solicitor, or the estate agent and God knows how many others?"

"Nope. Just you."

"You're a ridiculous man," she grumbled as she got back into bed. "I'm not going to say any more on the subject, but you couldn't even remember the name of the woman whose child you fathered!"

"Don't start now!" He reached for her and Maxine could not remember a time when she had felt so safe and secure.

"By the way," she whispered in the dark before drifting off to sleep. "I love you too."

She didn't know whether he had heard but he enfolded her in his arms and said sleepily, "Tomorrow, I'll speak to the solicitor about the Will. And, if you'll have me, we'll make arrangements to get married."

"I'll think about it," she said. "But you might not be any good in bed. You can't believe everything you read in the papers."

The sound of muffled laughter reverberated around the bedroom walls.

Frank Whitehead heard the excited voices of Maxine and Rex earlier, when they'd opened the bedroom door on to the balcony. When he and Elizabeth lived at Long Acres, there had been no balcony. It was, to his mind, a *nouveau-riche* addition. Leaving the shed, he battled his way against the wind, hanging on to the door as it was thrown open by the force of the gale. Taking care to stay in the shadows, Frank made his way towards an oval-shaped flowerbed filled with tall shrubs that he could hide behind. His fury boiled within him as he saw the oddest mismatch of a middle-aged woman clad in a gentleman's dressing gown and Rex trussed up in coat and scarf, frolicking about like teenagers, wielding sparklers and taking selfies. They might as well have been playing with swords, ostentatiously displaying weaponry to pierce his weary heart. It was their joy that offended him, their happiness and love. It was disrespectful to Elizabeth's memory.

When they disappeared into the bedroom, he didn't like to imagine what they were doing next. He returned to the shed and sat on a discarded bar stool, nursing impotent rage. He had better go home. What else could he do? There was an old chest of drawers beside him. He tugged open the top drawer and found a packet of cigarettes and a lighter. Rex wasn't the sort of man to be forced into a surreptitious puff in the shed, surely. He was a brazen bastard. He'd do whatever he liked and to hell with the consequences.

Frank hadn't had a cigarette for years. Maybe a smoke would calm his fragile nerves. He opened the packet. It was a bit damp. Perhaps it wouldn't light. He flicked the lighter a couple of times and then amazingly it flared into life. Frank lit the cigarette and inhaled. He had forgotten what it was like and felt giddy when he took a long drag. It would be a miracle if he didn't go down with pneumonia. What was he doing, trespassing on another man's property, having a crafty puff for a nicotine hit? He wanted to seek retribution and had ended up behaving like an underage child. He'd finish the cigarette and then go home.

"I'm sorry, Elizabeth," he said, as if his wife were perched beside him. "There's nothing I can do."

Spitefully, he considered stubbing out the cigarette on top of the chest of drawers to leave a burn mark, but he couldn't do it. Someone had made this piece of furniture. Frank noted that the carpenter had created dovetailed corners. It was sad that it had been thoughtlessly disposed of, to moulder away in the damp. Carefully, he shut the top drawer. And he wouldn't discard the cigarette on the grass, either. It had always irritated him, seeing folk casually throwing away their litter. Once, in the town centre, he had been the recipient of a stream of abuse when he was bold enough to suggest that a teenager put his leftover burger wrapper in a refuse bin. Outside the shed, there were bins, standing next to the kitchen wall beside the oil tank. The cigarette could go in one of those.

The wind tugged again at the shed door when he opened it. Frank put the cigarette between his lips as he heaved with both hands to shut the door and slide the bolts outside. He tiptoed past the house, took a last drag, opened the nearest bin and disposed of the cigarette. It was time to go home and finalise his packing for the voyage ahead.

As he drove away, the sky burned orange behind him. Guy Fawkes Night. *How odd*, he thought, *to celebrate, with such flamboyance, the martyrdom of that political activist every year.*

Chapter 27

Grace Palmer was sitting under the kitchen table with Wesley, her elderly golden retriever. He didn't care for fireworks. In fact he hated them. It was demeaning for a noble dog like himself to admit to such a weakness but he couldn't help himself. He was panting like an explorer, lost and alone in the desert and shaking uncontrollably.

Paul was busy tutoring, in preparation for GCSE and A-level exams. There had been an atmosphere of forced good cheer since their argument following the episode at the races, a temporary truce, but Grace was unsure what might happen next. Betty, her neighbour, had been in earlier, hinting that in her opinion, it was odd for two people not to make a permanent go of things. What was wrong with getting married, after all? She had a very nice hat that she hoped to get some wear out of, as it had been expensive and only worn once. She also suggested that it would be a good idea not to let yourself go when there was a man around, wearing unsightly clothes in the house. Why would anyone do that if they had enough money to wear nice things?

During the tirade, Grace was sitting comfortably in a pair of old jeans and a baggy jumper. She had ignored the last jibe, pursed her lips, taken a deep breath and pointed out that Betty had been fortunate not to have gone through a divorce and it was only natural that Grace should be cautious, second time around.

She chose not to add that the miscarriage she had suffered, unknown to her neighbour, was something that had never been resolved. The absence of that child sometimes felt like a sad, soft echo resounding in the dark. At the time, they had comforted one another. Their mutual loss had brought them closer and prompted Paul to rent a house in town so that they could see one another more often. He hadn't wanted to move into Grace's home because he suspected that she enjoyed her own space, without him.

Grace knew that a late-in-life pregnancy would restrict their lives. There were more risks having a baby and no one wanted to be referred to as a geriatric mother. She had been lucky to have two healthy children, and Paul had Liam, his only child, who lived on a canal boat with his partner in Bath.

"No relationship stands still!" Betty had exclaimed. "You're not getting any younger and there might not be many more opportunities if you let this one go."

Now that Betty had left, Grace was unsettled. Why did her neighbour think it was appropriate to give her opinions so freely? It was none of her business. It would have been the sort of thing her mother might have said. Betty had embraced the role of substitute parent rather too enthusiastically.

Grace tried to draw Wesley towards her for mutual comfort but Wesley was too wound up to be comforted.

Sarah put her head round the door. Her mother noted that she was wearing make-up and a smart top and swirly skirt. Betty would have approved.

"Out on the razzle?" Grace asked. Her question was ignored.

"Mum! What are you doing under there?"

"Fireworks. Wesley's off his head."

Sarah walked into the room and peered under the table at the quivering canine. "Poor old Wes. I know, I'll put some music on so that he can't hear the bangs." She put the radio on and twiddled with the dial. Coldplay's 'A Sky Full of Stars' blasted out.

"Pity that's not all there is in the sky," was Grace's response. "It's the same every year – rockets and explosions."

"Have you tried giving him something to eat? That might distract him." Sarah joined her mother to sit cross-legged under the table.

"Yes, but he only wolfs it down and then starts shaking again."

Paul opened the front door. The sound of a fire engine wailing added to the cacophony of loudly blaring music before he slammed it shut. Some idiot had been messing about with fireworks again, he supposed. Wesley bolted from the room to greet the visitor. Although he was still panting, he made an effort not to shake in front of Paul. He recognised that standing before him was the alpha male, blond, tall, broad-shouldered, and thought it best to do his bidding. Man and dog made their way into the kitchen. It was a curious sight. Mother and daughter were sitting under the table.

"You really are an odd family," he announced. "What's going on?"

Sarah shifted her position and crawled into the centre of the room, where Paul was standing. "Right. I was on my way out before you arrived, Paul. Wesley can't be doing with fireworks. Anyway, better get going." She strode off to the hall. Paul and Grace heard, "Don't know what time I'll be back. I'm meeting up with Steve."

The door slammed.

"Steve?" repeated Paul. "Who's Steve?"

"No idea. I think there might have been a lad from school called Steve." Grace took Paul's proffered hand to emerge from under the table. With the other hand, she hoicked up the baggy jumper as it slid from one of her shoulders. Were her clothes *unsightly*? Was that what Betty said? "Sorry about the music. It disguises the sound of the fireworks. That's why all the blinds are down too."

Wesley slurped noisily from his water bowl, feigning normality by picking his way, on shaky legs, to his basket. He was too scared to lie down and sat up instead, staring glassily around the room, panting all the while.

Paul patted the dog's head. "You'll be all right, old fella." He filled the kettle with water and switched it on. "Can we talk?" he asked. "The thing is, I've got something to say to you. I can't wait for the right moment. There's always something going on, an hysterical dog is the least of it. But for once we have the house to ourselves and if I have to shout over the music, that's what I'll do."

Sarah almost skipped, excitement bubbling to the surface, as she was buffeted by the wind when making her way down the hill that led into town. A holly tree, planted at the front of one of the houses, already bore bright berries, spilling on to the pavement, where they were squashed underfoot. If she had been in possession of a stick, she would have dragged it along the iron railings of one of the smarter rows of terraced houses, something she and her brother had done when they were children. The atmosphere was highly charged, fireworks exploding either side of the road, and an ambulance passed at speed, lights flashing and sirens loud. They had agreed to meet in a pub called the Griffith Arms, where confluent roads joined. It was a busy place, with televisions blaring; it was never quiet, so if the two of them had nothing to say, they could always look about, observe other people or stare at a screen.

He was already standing at the bar with his back to her as she entered the room, sharing a hearty laugh with the proprietor. Momentarily, she wondered if she should turn tail and run back home up the hill. But she didn't have time to take action, even if that was her intention. Stephen Samson turned and smiled. There was a brief moment when the image of a cockerel popped into Sarah's head. It was something to do with his pointy shoes, skinny jeans, tan Puffa jacket and spiked-up hair. But Sarah found that she was smiling too. She might have to work on his wardrobe.

Chapter 28

Maxine had moulded her body to that of Rex as he lay on his side, her right arm fitting under his; entwined in a deep sleep, they were deaf to repeated phone calls from a concerned neighbour. It was Rex's coughing that woke Maxine. She had forgotten where she was when she opened her eyes and it was a shock to discover that Rex was suffering from more than the usual asthma attack. She started coughing too as swirls of smoke appeared from under the bedroom door. The fire alarm was screeching crazily and she was briefly disorientated to find that she was in Rex's bed. Was this some sort of dream that had turned into a nightmare?

"I can't breathe!" Rex was stumbling in the direction of the balcony.

When Maxine had worked as a cleaner for an office block in Swansea, there had been a near-disaster with a discarded match used to light a birthday cake. Afterwards, every employee had been made to watch a video about fire prevention. She had been amazed at how quickly a fire could spread as she watched a mock-up of a living room reduced to ash. She remembered what they were taught and had written it down in her notebook. *Keep fire doors shut. Avoid a draught that will fan the flames.*

When Rex was about to open the outside door, she had stopped him with a fierce cry, "Wait!" Maxine sprang into action, grabbing a towel from the *en suite* and placing it along the bottom of the door leading to the stairs.

"You're such a girl guide," he said before they emerged on to the balcony, arms wrapped round one another.

It was like a scene from a disaster movie. The nearest neighbour, a tenant farmer, had rung the emergency services when he failed to get a response from Long Acres: hoses snaked across the garden and water was being sprayed on the west side of the property, near the kitchen. The shed was destroyed. Roaring flames, fanned by the wind, clawed their way towards the sky. Orange sparks outshone any rockets that punctuated the darkness. An ambulance crew had just arrived and were running from their vehicle in the direction of the spiral staircase that led to the balcony.

Rex whispered, "Come on, baby, light my fire," attempted a laugh, pressed his lips to Maxine's forehead, before his breathing became more frantic and he doubled up on the tiled floor.

She should have grabbed his inhaler before escaping outside but it had only occurred to her to get out as quickly as possible. Dear Rex. It was bloody typical of him that he would heighten the drama by going into a swoon. She would tease him about it when the crisis was over. He could move in with her while the building was repaired. She hoped there wouldn't be too much damage. Maxine slid beside Rex and knotted herself about him, wanting to keep him safe and warm. She put her lips to his.

He wasn't breathing.

Someone came up behind her, dragging her away, at the same time that paramedics rushed in to work upon the actor's lifeless body.

As the oil tank exploded, Maxine registered that someone was screaming before realising that it was her screams that tore through the air. "Rex!" she shouted. "Rex! Don't leave me!"

A fireman, she supposed it was a fireman, although it was difficult to tell the identity of the person beneath the protective clothing and headgear, scooped her up and descended the spiral fire escape, boots clanging with every tread as she struggled against an iron grip. Over the shoulder of her rescuer, she caught a glimpse of the one she had loved being laid out on a stretcher.

"I love him," she hiccupped through her tears. "Please don't let him die."

A deep voice, muffled beneath the helmet, asked, "Was that the actor Rex Glyn?"

Chapter 29

In Funchal, Rex's sister Marilyn stepped out from the bar where she worked to walk upon the marble cobblestones that led to the corner shop. The prices were extortionate but tourists, particularly those who arrived on package tours, knew no better than to shop there before they discovered the bigger supermarkets in the centre of town. Still, it was handy for picking up her copy of the *Daily Mail.* She didn't want to go back to living in Britain, particularly after all the nonsense with Brexit, but she liked to keep in touch. Her British Pub attracted hundreds of compatriots annually and some of the visitors came every year; Marilyn prided herself on remembering their names and where they lived back home. She had an A4 box file kept under the bar that she used to jot down the names of people and significant information about them if she thought they might return. The loyalty of holidaymakers was easily won by a few remembered details, and some rather unimaginative folk rewarded her by coming to the pub every night of their stay.

Naturally, she missed her children, Tiffany and Joshua, although Tiffany rang practically every day, bless her. Having said that, they got on so much better now that they weren't living under the same roof. Marks and Spencer was much missed too and some of the other department stores that she alighted upon when she made her annual pilgrimage to the UK. She wouldn't be going until next February, after the Christmas parties had finished and there was a lull in the holidaymakers' exodus from colder shores.

It would already be cold in Wales now and here she was, living in

Madeira, wearing flip-flops and a sundress, her shoulders covered by a cardigan, for modesty's sake. Some of her neighbours were a bit old-fashioned and she didn't like to offend them. Her shopping bag was made from a popular Madeiran fabric – brightly coloured stripes of red, navy, green, white and yellow – that was used for traditional costume and appeared everywhere. The heat of the sun not only warmed her bones, but lifted her spirits. Looking up at the blue sky, she counted her blessings.

"*Bom Dia!*" she called breezily to the shopkeeper. He responded in kind. She paid for the newspaper and glanced at the headlines as she was about to put it in her bag.

There he was: Rex, her brother, on the front page. She was used to him turning up in the popular press. Journalists found that he was the gift that kept on giving. In his heyday, he was always getting plastered or involved in some unsavoury scuffle with burly bouncers or other men's wives. In his declining years, it was possible to elaborate on the barest bones of a story to titillate the public, about how aged and decrepit he had become, how he had lost his marbles and his money and was living as a recluse in darkest west Wales.

The title of the piece was, THE FINAL INFERNO. In his earlier years, he had been involved in a series of disaster movies, usually with the word *inferno* in the title; a branding exercise, she supposed, somewhat repetitive in theme, involving fires in different locations. Rex played the part of the reluctant hero who usually managed to save the day. She remembered him saying that if he carried on the way he was going, he would have no eyebrows or lashes left. He was permanently singed. That was before they stopped speaking to one another.

He couldn't be that ill if he had got a part in an all-action film. Perhaps he was playing a minor role, a walk-on part for old times' sake. She thrust the paper deeper into the bag and sauntered up the hill, turning right at the top to join a main road, with the casino, resembling a crash-landed spaceship, further along on her right.

As always, she stopped to greet the statue of Empress Elisabeth, supposedly life-sized. She looked a bit like an early Disney heroine with her tiny waist, voluminous skirt and diminutive stature. Married to Emperor Franz Joseph, she was a legendary, tragic figure, fleeing to Madeira after her son committed suicide. Her marriage was a failure but away from the constraints of the Austrian court, she found freedom on the island. Marilyn liked to think that she and Sissi had something in common.

Marilyn's husband, like her mother's before her, had disappointed. Madeira had welcomed the princess and it was fair to say that it had welcomed Rex's sister too, even if Marilyn hadn't been greeted by a naval salute on arrival. Fortunately, it was highly unlikely that they would meet the same fate – Marilyn was unlikely to be fatally stabbed by an anarchist, blessed as she was with anonymity and unburdened by royal status. A flower was snapped from the hibiscus hedge lining the road and carefully placed in the gap between Sissi's skirt and wrist. It was a ritual that Marilyn enjoyed, dressing the princess with a fresh corsage.

On she walked towards the park. Once through the gates, Marilyn admired the huge African tulip tree with its beautiful orange flowers, skirted round the pond and the children's play park to arrive at her favourite bench just above a viewing platform that overlooked the sea and where the cruise ships docked. She'd have a sneaky read alone before returning to work. It was a lovely spot, having a panoramic view and right beside a bright pink oleander bush in full bloom. She always thought it smelled of apricots. The newspaper was retrieved and she started reading.

Rex Glyn, national treasure and one of the last of the acting greats, whose antics on and off the screen have delighted the public for decades, fought his last battle appropriately enough on Bonfire Night, when an inferno tore through his house. He was rescued from the blaze by firefighters, was blue-lighted to the local hospital in Pontardeilo, but was pronounced dead on arrival. It is believed that he was with a female companion, whose identity is unknown.

Marilyn stuffed her fist in her mouth and bit on her knuckles. She shouldn't feel anything about her brother, having found life easier without him in it, and yet here she was trying to blink away unbidden tears, biting on her hand to try and prevent the screaming that threatened to erupt in the early morning sun.

She returned to the front page where there was a blurred picture of a stretcher being loaded into an ambulance, the house behind engulfed in flames. It could have been anyone, really, on the stretcher, but she had to accept that it was her brother.

Marilyn thought that she was prepared for the news but who was ever ready for a life being snuffed out? She dug into her bag and retrieved a tissue and blew her nose. A homeless man, who had been sleeping on another bench further to the left, had woken up, seen her distress and enquired after her. He patted her shoulder before making his way to the public toilets. She tried not to wince at his touch and smiled, remembering to say "*Obrigada*." But she felt too vulnerable sitting outside. Checking her phone, she could see that Tiffany had rung several times. Marilyn often forgot to turn the volume up and had been unaware of her daughter's calls.

It would be better to ring her back from home when she was out of the way of prying eyes.

In Tenby, Tiffany was dealing with a customer in the gallery when her mother eventually rang. She was so close to securing a sale on a watercolour, had surpassed herself by the analysis she had given – courtesy of Google: *How to interpret a painting.* Her reference to colour and light, brushstrokes applied and original interpretation, with a nod to Turner (it was a very ordinary picture of boats in the harbour) was impressive. It was such a shame that she felt the necessity to answer the phone rather than close the deal. The gentleman who had been imprisoned for twenty minutes, took his chance and got through the door as fast as his elderly legs could take him.

"Mum! Why the hell don't you answer your phone?"

"It was on silent. I'm sorry."

"I suppose you've heard the news?"

Marilyn was sitting on her bed, but looked down on the street below, her eyes settling upon the jaunty red poinsettias resplendent in a window box across the way, the view exactly the same as any other day, an affront to the feelings she was trying to process. She supposed it would be raining in Tenby, grey driving rain, which might be more fitting, given the circumstances. "You mean about Rex?" she said softly. "Is it raining with you?"

Exasperated, Tiffany replied, "Yes, it's raining. What's that got to do with it?"

"Nothing. I just wondered."

On the notepad in front of her, Tiffany doodled raindrops falling from the sky. It was the rainy season in Madeira, wasn't it? It was a lush, green island, after all. It wasn't as if there was no rainfall. What was she asking about the weather for? "Are you okay? You sound a bit odd."

Marilyn took an intake of breath, wiped her eyes and sighed.

"Are you crying?" Tiffany sounded annoyed.

"Yes, I'm crying. My brother is dead."

Tiffany tried to work out what to say. For more than a decade her mother had chosen not to contact Rex – he was effectively dead to her already. Why was she crying now that he had really passed away? How was it possible that her mother was unprepared for her brother's death?

Practicalities needed to be addressed. Perhaps that was the way forward. "I'm sorry you're upset. I was wondering if you wanted me to try and sort out the funeral. Apart from you, we're next of kin, aren't we?"

Marilyn lay down and closed her eyes. It was inevitable that she should search for images from the past when she and Rex were children, but the eleven-year gap meant that he seemed like an adult already before memories were stored. Mostly she remembered the starring roles he played in school and chapel, whereas when it was her turn, she only managed to secure a lowly walk-on part. She recalled the way their mother's eyes had sparkled with joy whenever he stood before her, granting only absent-minded smiles for Marilyn, as if there was a finite amount of love to be shared, not really enough to go round. It was only when she had children herself that she realised the division of love didn't have to be so unfair. Joshua and Tiffany were so different but Marilyn liked to think she loved them equally.

"Mum! Are you still there?"

"Yes, love. I am. I'm not sure how it works, being next of kin, if you haven't been in touch. I don't really know whose job it is to arrange the funeral. Knowing Rex, he probably had it all planned with sufficient pomp and ceremony to please his actor's soul."

Tiffany had started doodling an elaborate crucifix beside the fat raindrops. "I've been in touch. You encouraged me, if you remember. I've been sending him different postcards for weeks after meeting up with him. So… will you come back for his funeral?"

"No, Tiffany, I won't. You go, if you want to. I just think it would be a bit hypocritical to play the part of the grieving sister, given that I haven't spoken to him for years." She sniffed. "I didn't know how upset I would be. He was so handsome, you know. Charismatic. That's the word."

Her mother's attitude was really disappointing, especially after her previous encouragement to secure any inheritance that might be up for grabs. "Okay, then. I guess I'll try and track down the housekeeper and maybe his lawyer to see what his wishes were." Given her mother's newly acquired sensitivity towards Rex, she deliberately didn't mention that while she was with the lawyer, she intended to enquire about the contents of the Will.

Mother and daughter talked for a little longer before it was obvious from Marilyn's faltering responses that the conversation had drawn to a close.

When Tiffany replaced her phone on the notepad on the desk, she realised that beside the raindrops and the crucifix, she had doodled pound and dollar signs.

Chapter 30

Rex Glyn's demise was not only covered by the newspapers, but by the news channels on television. Breakfast television showed stills from his era at the National Theatre, clips from the *Inferno* franchise and an interview with his agent, whose sorrowful voice fooled no one. The TV schedules were altered to include a biographical film, covering his rags-to-riches ascension (the director, born in Caerphilly, made much of Glyn's impoverished Welsh roots) and also his humiliating demise. *Rebecca* with Rex in the role of Maxim de Winter, replaced *Die Hard 2* and a rather amateurish filming of a theatrical performance of *The Importance of Being Earnest* bumped out *The Sound of Music*.

In Ipswich, Suffolk, one woman paused in her task of loading the dishwasher, transfixed by the early morning news item about Rex Glyn. The sun shone through the glass box extension at the back of her house. Autumn had wrapped up the garden in shades of gold. A rocket from the previous night's firework display in the park had lodged in one of the branches of a Dawn Redwood, whose deciduous leaves glowed in the morning light. She knew that she would have to retrieve it but lacked the will, sitting down carefully to avoid hitting her head on an overhanging pendant light, at the kitchen island to stare up at her television screen screwed to the wall.

Her husband had already left the house to catch the train to London. He was meeting up with some old friends from when he worked backstage in Theatreland. She was glad that he was out of the house. Although she was an accomplished actor, it would have been a struggle to give the impression of nonchalance when her heart was racing in such a peculiar fashion, especially given her husband's antipathy towards Rex Glyn. He had been the stage manager when she, Amal and Rex had acted together in *The Importance of Being Earnest* and had made his feelings very clear immediately after the discovery that Eleanor had slept with Rex. He wasn't a handsome man, but he was as comfortable as a well-worn dressing gown. Dating him was soothingly uneventful and when Eleanor realised that she was pregnant, she immediately accepted his proposal.

Eleanor Smythe Thomas had retained her maiden name, having made enough money to grant the family a comfortable lifestyle in a Victorian house overlooking Christchurch Park. It was a smart address, allowing Eleanor to wander the extensive grounds beyond her garden wall. If she had time on her hands, she would visit Christchurch Mansion, a largely Tudor construction built on the site of a twelfth-century priory that came to an abrupt end when Henry the Eighth decided to ransack the place and keep the spoils. She also owned a flat in London, not far from Bond Street, that she rented out.

When Eleanor was younger, she longed to be pretty but many of her more attractive contemporaries failed to secure acting parts when their looks faded. It was a bit galling to be typecast but no one was more surprised than Eleanor when her plain face proved to be her fortune. Age had been kind to her. She was slim, an avid gym member, who rarely drank alcohol or ate meat. The frumpy appearances on television contrasted with her trendy, short haircut and dangling earrings, jeans and fitted Boden top.

Eleanor's face flushed when she thought about her amorous exploits backstage with Rex Glyn. She knew that her co-star Amal was completely besotted with him but Eleanor's urge to have a child was more powerful than any pangs of conscience. She was motivated by the thought that any progeny of Rex's would be beautiful.

When Eleanor and Amal were reunited on the set of an episode of *Morse*, Amal heard from one of the make-up girls that there was a daughter, did the maths and completely ruined a take on Broad Street when she started shouting incoherently at her co-star. One of the phrases Amal had screamed was "*sperm bandit*". Eleanor had never heard the expression before. She supposed that in a later era she might have resorted to a sperm bank, fully intending to parent alone.

In fact, when she thought about it now, her behaviour had been reckless, promiscuous, even, until she settled down with Ronnie. Lack of self-belief had led her to think that no one would want to marry her and have children. What an idiot she had been. And anyway, why should she feel guilt when all the men in the cast were at it like rabbits?

She remembered one of her favourite lines as Miss Prism. "*I am not in favour of this modern mania for turning bad people into good people at a moment's notice. As a man sows, so let him reap.*" If ever there was a quotation for describing Rex Glyn, that was it.

Eleanor's mobile phone beeped. There were two messages. One was from Ronnie.

> I see that the bastard has met his demise. Champagne on ice for my return.

It was an attempt at irony. He only drank pints of beer. The other was from her daughter, the longed-for child, a child no longer, who lived in West Hendon in a studio flat that was bursting at the seams with too much stuff. It was getting to the stage where it was almost impossible to get from the front door, past the small double bed (Lulu lived in hope) to the kitchen, without tripping over. She had never married, never had children and still required monetary handouts when funds were low. Currently she worked from home as a sort of dogsbody for a financial adviser specialising in shared-ownership mortgages.

I've just heard that Rex Glyn has died; a fire apparently. I thought I might come home this weekend. Would that be okay? I can just about stretch to the rail fare.

It would be nice to think that Lulu was eager to catch up with her mother but Eleanor suspected that the visit was prompted by lack of money for food and heating. Eleanor had a feeling of dread that somehow she would have to keep working to support her middle-aged child. It was a good thing that learning lines came easily – no sign yet of mental decline. She reached for her latest script and started reading. It was a comic ghost story that prompted the occasional smile. It was good to ring the changes – instead of playing an unattractive old woman, she got to play a dead, unattractive old woman. That was a first.

Chapter 31

Olivia Garland was unnerved by the famous actor's death. It seemed that one minute he had been all over her and the next he was gone. Had she been unkind to distance herself from his attentions? It was a nagging regret that they never had a conversation about his letter. She wondered if he really had left her some money or had heard that she and Stephen were no longer an item and decided not to bother.

There was no denying the fact that Rex's life had been snuffed out now that she had been visited by Barry the Box, the local undertaker. His sober-suited appearance was at odds with a habit of erupting into riotous laughter during their conversation. A kind man, he knew how to respond to grief but had learned long ago that liberal application of black humour enabled him to thrive in the business. Just as a hypochondriac sought solace in multivitamins and supplements, Barry took comfort from jokes. Olivia laughed politely at the story of the man who, having gone to the doctor, was upset when he was told that he had to take a daily tablet for the rest of his life. His wife had offered reassurance, saying that lots of people were in his situation. "I don't mind that," the man replied, "but the doctor has only given me seven tablets!" Barry mimed a drum sting to emphasise the awful jest. "Seven tablets! Only a week to live!" he added unnecessarily.

Olivia started to untie bunches of carnations to give a non-verbal hint that whatever message Barry had to deliver, it would be just as well to get on with it. Barry obliged. Rex Glyn had paid upfront for his funeral, apparently, which, as Barry explained, was a relief, given the time it might take for funds to be released. He doubted that probate would be straightforward. Long Acres had been insured but no doubt the insurers would be looking into how the fire started and whether there had been foul play.

The long and the short of it was that the floral tribute for the coffin was to be the biggest that Olivia had ever created. Rex hadn't gone for tasteful white or even muted tones. An explosion of colour was required – red, orange and yellow predominant, but if Olivia fancied throwing in other colours, that would be just fine.

Olivia's father had been responsible for rescuing Maxine from the flat-roof extension. Although he was sorry about the blaze and a famous actor's demise, he had enjoyed his part in the heroics of the team. It made a change from the hoax calls and false call-outs from automatic fire alarms that took up so much of the brigade's time. The blaze had caused extensive damage to the downstairs, which had subsequently been boarded up, but the upstairs had mostly been saved, smoke-damaged certainly, but it could have been worse.

Olivia had mentioned to her father that she used to deliver flowers to Rex Glyn but had decided to keep quiet about Stephen Samson's interest in the house and the tour she had made with him when he was considering buying it. For a moment, when the fireman had regaled her about his exploits rescuing a woman from a burning building, she had allowed herself to imagine what it would have been like, living at Long Acres. Now, in the ordinary surroundings of her shop when she was chatting to Barry, it seemed to have been a frivolous dream.

Sarah was busy in the back of the florist's, trying to update the software. She had persuaded Olivia that the website for the business was woefully inadequate and was glad to be out of the way working on a legitimate task, without having to chat about her activities outside of work.

She couldn't decide whether her mother and Paul were getting on at home. They kept disappearing on long walks, dragging poor old Wesley around the park, and when they returned their voices seemed hushed. If Sarah walked into the room, the conversation often took an unnatural turn, usually focusing on the dog and whether he needed more food, exercise or new bedding. It was most bizarre.

What a relief to be out in town, meeting up with Stephen! But the excitement was tempered by anxiety that she hadn't spoken to Olivia about the burgeoning relationship with Olivia's ex-boyfriend. There were two options, the first – the one that she was implementing at the moment – was to pretend that nothing was untoward and avoid being in her company as much as possible, thus dodging any awkwardness should Olivia mention Stephen. The second option was more honest and upfront, the sort of approach that Sarah would normally go for. She should admit that she had started to see him. The problem was that the relationship had barely begun and she didn't want to ruin it. What if Olivia contacted Stephen and he decided not to see Sarah again? And what if Olivia was so annoyed that she terminated Sarah's employment?

Christmas was only a few weeks away and she was glad to be earning a wage. Her mother's disappointment about Sarah dropping out of university would only be compounded if she had to ask for money. That morning, when Grace had dropped her daughter in town, she had said, "I just want to say I'm proud of you getting stuck into a job under your own steam."

At the moment, option one would buy Sarah some time and it was a blessing to be away from the cloying scent of lilies that pervaded the shop like a ghostly presence.

Chapter 32

Maxine seemed unable to move from under the covers. The bed and its surroundings had become her world. When she closed her eyes, she could see him and when she opened them he was gone. It had never been a particular ambition of hers to marry. Plenty of unhappy people were testament to the folly of choosing the wrong person. She tried to be sensible. If Rex had lived, they might have married and it could have been an unmitigated disaster.

Drifting in and out of sleep, Maxine found that dreams brought no solace. You didn't need a degree in psychology to interpret them. She dreamed about putting a wedding ring on her finger. It was shiny gold, unscratched and new, but as she inspected it, twisting it around, it snapped in two. Panicking, she looked about for her wedding dress, tried to squeeze into it and couldn't fasten the zip. There were chaotic scenes of being in full wedding regalia, veil tangled like a fisherman's net as she ran through the streets, looking for someone to repair the ring. She awoke in tears, the sheets wrapped round her feverish body, and tried to stay awake for fear of being dragged back to the unconscious world that exacerbated the agony of loss. She missed Rex so badly that she was quite willing to die. Alcohol helped to numb the pain but the dreams became more vivid and surreal.

Sometimes there were flashbacks, the flames licking round the corner of Long Acres as Maxine was dragged away from Rex's lifeless body. She wondered what would become of the house. Would someone bulldoze it and start again? She knew every room just as intimately as Rex himself did. She had cleaned and scrubbed and washed and dried and loved every inch of it.

For a week, the phone went unanswered and she refused to open the door. Her mother and sister had put in a brief appearance early on but Maxine had no use for anyone's company. In the hallway downstairs, mail landed softly on top of neglected letters from the day before. A peculiar mixture of pride and shame eventually prompted Maxine to get out of her bed and take a shower after it occurred to her that someone might batter down the door. She had a horror of being found in such a filthy mess. The usually immaculate hair was plastered to her head; shadows and lines on her face mapped the misery of bereavement. It was an older and more broken woman who stared back from the mirror.

Maxine stood shaking in the shower but water cascading from above brought relief. It was a blessing to smell of soap and feel thoroughly cleansed. Clean clothes were found and sheets were stripped from the bed. The washing machine was switched on. She actually felt hungry and put bread in the toaster, watching it spring to life when it was done. At Long Acres she had to use what she called a tennis bat that served as an Aga toaster, fitting on top of the boiling plate. It seemed to take forever, given that she had to turn the bread in the wire contraption after one side had turned brown. Well, she wouldn't be using one of those again. All the things she found irritating or annoying were of no consequence. She realised that now.

Rex would have had something to say about the shocking state she was in. A small smile morphed into a strangled sob. She would try not to think about him.

When Maxine's mobile phone rang, she stared at it for a while and then forced herself to answer the call.

"Hello?" Her voice was shaky.

"Is that Maxine? I've rung so many times. Didn't you see the missed calls?" Tiffany sounded aggrieved. She pressed on. "The thing is that my mum is next of kin but she's in Madeira, so I thought it was up to me to organise the funeral but the funeral director said that there was no need because Uncle Rex had already written down what he wanted. Is that right?"

Maxine shut her eyes. It was easier for her to concentrate on what was being said when she didn't have to process what she was looking at. She shut out the view from her window. Her flat overlooked a sub-post office, one of the few remaining in Pontardeilo. The place was pretty basic, really, but the rent was reasonable and she could conveniently walk into town.

Politeness kicked in. She might not like the girl but it was her relative who had died, after all. "I'm sorry for your loss," she said.

"What? Oh yes, thank you. I hadn't seen him much, as you know, but he'll be missed. I did send him regular postcards from Tenby, though. I hope he enjoyed them."

Maxine was expected to reply. After a pause, she said, "We both looked forward to them."

Tiffany noted the neutral tone. She chose to ignore it, but wondered why Maxine was looking at her postcards. "I thought I could give a reading or something at the funeral."

"No, that won't be necessary. The thing is, we knew he would die sometime soon. Obviously sooner than we'd anticipated." It seemed unreal that they had planned to marry. No, she wouldn't think about that. Her aim was to speak as little as possible and get off the phone. "He had plenty of time to put his affairs in order. He organised it all. I think one of his acting friends is going to say something."

"I see. Right. Well, I'll see you at the funeral, then."

"Yes. Goodbye."

"Wait!" Tiffany tried to sound nonchalant. "Just one other thing. You wouldn't happen to know which solicitor he was using? He wrote and told me that I…" She chose her words carefully. She didn't want to sound grasping. "… would be kept informed of his wishes."

Maxine found her address book and meekly provided Rex's niece with the relevant contact details. She put the phone down. If she had been feeling stronger, she would have managed a more robust response. Rex would have been astonished by her passive behaviour. It was only later that Maxine thought the very least she could have done would have been to supply the phone number for the local takeaway instead.

For the first time in days, she descended the stairs from her flat. She felt a little giddy and wondered if she were going to succumb to a full-blown panic attack. Maxine breathed in and out slowly and, from her vantage point, spotted her over-fussy neighbour who was in the hall below, busy sorting through the post laid out on a table by the front door. She was probably up to her old tricks, nicking the Farm Foods vouchers. A glimpse of normality helped to calm the nerves. Maxine had no intention of creating a scene, especially not in front of Penelope, and refused to collapse in the stairwell. She imagined herself eye to eye with chipped, magnolia-painted spindles, her feet sliding on the ancient lino. "Not happening," she muttered to herself and picked her way carefully to the floor below.

To give the woman her due, Penelope had taken upon herself the task of cleaning the hall and stairs. She liked to leave things tidy: fliers and advertising material were eventually removed and disposed of.

The sallow face turned to acknowledge Maxine's presence. "Haven't seen you for a while," she said, as if it were an accusation rather than a statement. "And you've lost weight. I suppose you're out of a job now that Rex Glyn has died." Penelope sniffed disapprovingly. It was unclear whether it was the actor or Maxine's unemployment that was being denounced.

Maxine looked at her portly neighbour in front of her. *It's quite easy*, she thought. *The pounds fall off when someone you love dies.* What she said was, "You just follow a Mediterranean diet. Very effective." Spitefully, she added, "You should try it."

December

Chapter 33

On the following Saturday, Paul and Sarah found that they were alone, sitting opposite one another at the breakfast table, Grace having gone to the estate agent's.

"Not working today?" Paul asked.

"No. It's the lull before Christmas. Olivia doesn't need me. Then it's purgatory, apparently; millions of holly wreaths to make." She gazed at her hands, already feeling sorry for them. "You get cut to ribbons."

"Ah." There was a pause. "I'm going to the park. Thought I'd take Wesley for a walk. Fancy coming with me?"

Sarah yawned. "Nah, not really." She glanced out of the kitchen window at the grey skies above the skeletal form of deciduous trees. "It's probably going to rain."

"It's not raining now. It will do you good."

Sarah, ever her mother's daughter, didn't enjoy taking advice from anyone and eyed Paul with suspicion. "Says who?"

"That's a little prickly. Come on, Sarah. I want to talk to you about something."

"Are you going to explain the strange conversations you keep having with Mum? You both must think I'm really thick not to wonder what's going on. Every time I enter the room you change the subject and then start talking about the dog."

Paul laughed. "That's not what I wanted to talk about."

He looked uncomfortable. *Why is that?* Sarah wondered.

Wesley, although a little deaf, had heard his name and the word *walk* and had raised himself from the prone position in his basket. He stretched tentatively, hoping that his legs would still bear his weight and trotted over to Paul, sat down, wagged his tail and with soulful eyes looked up expectantly.

"He does seem to want a walk," Sarah admitted. "Okay, but let's go to the seafront and then you can buy me a hot chocolate." Before she had met Stephen, she had spotted a slim, dark-eyed youth with a man bun, working behind the counter at the seafront cafe. It would be worth finding out if he had the same effect on her now that she was seeing Stephen.

Paul sighed. It always seemed to be a process of negotiation in the Palmer household. "Not enough time. I'm tutoring in an hour. Nice kid, no confidence. Overbearing parents."

Sarah appeared not to be listening, snuggling into Wesley's neck.

Paul accepted defeat, got up, grabbed the lead and walked to the front door, where he picked up his coat from the hat stand in the hall. Wesley's progress along the hall gave the impression that he graciously agreed to accompany Paul for a stroll around the park but it would be just as well to take it at a slow and steady pace. He wagged his tail with enthusiasm while waiting for Paul to button up his coat.

"Wait for me, then!" came the call from the kitchen. "I won't be a minute." Sarah dashed upstairs.

Paul knew from experience that it would be many minutes before she would reappear. He sat on the stairs and scrolled through his phone, looking at messages Grace had sent him. Paul hadn't told her that the previous night he had seen Stephen Samson drop her daughter off further down the road, near the humpback bridge and spend some moments kissing her goodbye. Sarah had looked nervously about when she emerged from the car, but darkness and a neighbour's campervan had hidden Paul from view as he walked back from town. Of all the people to choose! The relationship could only end in tears and what about her employer, Olivia? Paul could only imagine how Sarah's folly could affect their working relationship. Olivia had come to her senses and finished with him but that did not mean she would be comfortable with the idea of him dating her employee.

He hoped to discuss the situation calmly, although was realistic about the outcome of their conversation. If she was determined to keep seeing Stephen Samson, then he wanted Sarah to tell her mother rather than be the messenger himself, who would surely be shot.

Wesley lay down at his feet and closed his eyes, blissfully ignorant of the domestic crisis about to unfold.

In the office of Pughes and Palmer, Rex Glyn's funeral was the main topic of conversation. It was a slow news day. Politics had long been dismissed as being off limits since the three supported differing political parties and many a coffee break had previously been ruined by hostile observations about national governance. It transpired that Byron, Grace and Nancy all wanted to go to the actor's send-off. Byron was hoping to spy other famous actors and people he had seen on television. Nancy fancied a change of scene and Grace declared that as she was the only one who had actually met the man, it made more sense that she should go.

Byron made an executive decision, announcing that they would *all* go, shut up shop and post a note on the door that the estate agent's was closed due to bereavement. Grace argued that this would lead to all sorts of questions to be answered later on and surely it was poor taste to invent a relative or close friend who had died. Nancy agreed and felt that it was tempting fate to kill off an imaginary relation in case a real one really did die. Byron said it would be his imaginary relative who passed on and to hell with the consequences. He would deal with anyone curious to know the backstory, looking forward to saying, "I'm sorry. It's something I don't wish to talk about." He wouldn't lie but would give the impression that he was too distressed to engage in idle conversation.

Grace added, "Or we could just say we went to Rex Glyn's funeral."

Byron frowned. "And ruin my fun?"

There followed a sharing of snippets of news regarding the fire at Long Acres, how it might have started and further speculation as to what would happen to the house and who actually owned it now that Rex Glyn had died. More importantly, who would get the job of marketing the property? Would it be offered to them?

December was a disappointing month for sales. One of their faithful clients had decided to start selling off her rental portfolio, which was a blessing because not much else was happening so close to Christmas. No doubt, next year, as the daffodils pushed their yellow heads above the soil towards the spring sunshine, the punters would make their way towards Pughes and Palmer to offer up their properties for sale. It was always the same. By Easter, there would be far more choice for the prospective buyer.

If it had been left up to Grace, then the office would remain undecorated before Christmas but Nancy was discussing a theme. Blue and a silvery grey were the colours of choice. *What is wrong with the traditional colours of red, green and gold?* Grace wondered, but there was no point in venturing an opinion. Nancy never failed to deliver, after all. With a polite nod, she watched Byron make himself scarce. He was off for a wander in the market, ostensibly to buy mince pies, but really for the banter with those he had known for as long as he could remember.

Nancy could tell by the glazed expression on Grace's face that she wasn't listening. She knew what might get her attention. "You didn't say that Sarah had a new boyfriend." The words were light, but as potent as a spell.

"What?"

So Grace didn't know, then. She was listening now. "I must admit I was a bit surprised to hear that she was dating Stephen Samson, particularly after that nasty business at the races."

Grace wanted to laugh, the idea was so preposterous, but Nancy was no fool. She would have checked her sources. "God! I hope you're wrong but who knows with Sarah?" She made a sharp exit to the loo and texted her daughter.

Just had some alarming news. Tell me you're not going out with Stephen Samson?

A text was immediately returned.

Will talk tonight xxx

Three kisses? It was true, then.

Grace nonchalantly breezed through the office, grabbing her coat as she told Nancy that she had a routine doctor's appointment. Once she was in her car, Grace rang her daughter, unwilling to risk a row within earshot of the office. She expected Sarah to ignore the call but the phone was answered. The voice wore the unmistakable tone of forced good cheer.

"Hi, Mum! How's it going? You okay?"

Grace swallowed. "What do you think? What the hell is this nonsense about Mister Samson?"

"*Mister* Samson? How old does that make him sound? I know there's a bit of an age gap but really, Mother."

"I could call him a lot worse – how about *wide boy* or *charlatan*? Good God, Sarah! You were there when it all kicked off at the races. You saw him… what can I say?" she faltered. "… lashing out; what made you think that he's just the man for you?"

"Punchy, Mam – all those monosyllables."

Grace thought she might explode. "I'll give you *punchy*. Clearly we saw enough punches from him."

"To be fair, that was mostly his ex-wife."

"And you'd better not go and get pregnant." Grace regretted the words as soon as she had uttered them. How could she possibly think that was a wise thing to say? Sarah was the sort of person to view that kind of remark as a challenge. As a child, if she was told not to do something, she'd go right ahead and do it.

"Mother! What sort of bollocks is that?"

It had been a ridiculous thing to say, she knew that. "I'm sorry, Sarah, but you're very young."

"Not far off the age when you had my brother."

"It was different then. But this Stephen, he didn't exactly look like a knight in shining armour, now, did he?"

"Knight?" Sarah sputtered. She took a deep breath. "I think that was what made me like him. He looked so distressed and vulnerable, not at all living up to his reputation."

Grace might have known. Sarah routinely stood up for anyone whom she might consider downtrodden – classmates who were wrongly accused, girls who were ostracised by others in the group. He was one of her pet projects. That was okay. It wouldn't last, would it?

Chapter 34

On the morning of Rex Glyn's funeral, Maxine got up, showered, carefully applied her make-up and arranged her hair. She put on her most expensive dress, a black fitted number, and donned high heels – black velvet with diamante embellishment. Rex would surely have approved. After a while, she drove in the opposite direction to the crematorium and wound her way to Long Acres. Following two days of dreary rain, sunshine was making a surprise appearance in early December, as enlivening as a celebrity performance in a pedestrian pantomime.

Maxine had intended to go to the funeral but found that she couldn't face sitting in a confined space with all those false friends and hangers-on. It was a real concern that she might lose control in front of judgemental eyes. Supposing she was made to feel that she had no right to be there, what would she do then? When she imagined that Rex's coffin would be disappearing behind the curtain at the crematorium, she dashed out of the flat and made for the house on the hill.

It was a shock to see the scorched and burned outline of the building, so much so that tears fell the moment she glimpsed it. The porch, sticking out like a square snout, was on the other side of the property from the source of the fire. Two stained-glass windows remained intact, shining eyes in a careworn face.

Maxine acknowledged that she was mourning for the demise of that other dear friend – Long Acres. It was an additional bereavement. Walking around the outside of somewhere that had been a second home to her, the distress of registering its decline was akin to visiting a terminally ill relative.

Since she had been to the doctor, Maxine seemed more able to manage the bouts of crying. It would take a while for the tablets to work, he told her. She didn't want to take them, but needs must. Today she would allow herself the time and space to grieve.

The shed had been reduced to ash. It was rumoured that a discarded cigarette had caused the damage. Could it really have been Rex who had caused the fire, having a sneaky cigarette out on the balcony before she arrived and accidentally throwing it on to the ground below? Who else could it have been? That's what the investigation had concluded. She had always told the stupid bugger that smoking would be the death of him.

The high heels were a mistake as the ground was muddy underfoot. She changed into a pair of old trainers kept in the boot of the car and made her way to the swing seat situated to the right of the entrance posts. Overhanging branches of sycamore trees had been cut back to create a bright spot in the midday sunshine.

Maxine was glad that she had made the unorthodox decision to dodge the funeral. Rocking herself on the swing seat, she knew that it would be better to howl in the fresh air than try to contain her emotion squashed between strangers, arranged in tidy rows. It was her fervent hope that it would be cathartic to celebrate the place and the memory of the man she had loved. Money was tight now that she wasn't getting a wage from Rex, but she had bought white roses and a bottle of Prosecco from the Co-op, for once rejoicing in the self-service option at the supermarket, with its stupid instructions and queries about shopping bags. She was able to arrive and leave the shop without incurring any human intervention.

"Right," she said out loud. "This is it, Rex. I haven't gone to your funeral. You know why. I didn't want to be crushed at the back with all the other no-hopers while the famous people preened themselves at the front." She popped the cork of her bottle. It sailed up into the air and then nose-dived into the long grass, disturbing an unsuspecting robin that was pecking at the ground. A flicker of red coloured the sky as it flew upwards. With a shaky hand, she poured the fizz into two glasses. Maxine wanted to chink them together as if Rex was there but felt how ludicrous it was for one person to do it alone with a glass in each hand. She did it anyway.

"Here's to you!" A gulp of Prosecco. "And to me!" Another gulp. She would have to watch herself. It would be too far to walk home if she drank too much.

Before she had the chance to unwrap the roses, a taxi arrived, driven past her position by the entrance post to deliver its charge by the front door. A middle-aged woman, dressed entirely in black, emerged from the back of the vehicle, paid the driver and looked in wonder about her. This was someone who had never been here before, it would seem, someone small and rounded in a three-quarter length coat with an extravagant faux-fur collar. She started walking in the opposite direction from where Maxine sat and towards the view of the sea in front of the house.

Maxine instinctively wanted to protect the house and grounds from intruders. Without stopping to think, the Prosecco and glasses were abandoned and she launched herself into an indignant trot after the unknown woman to find out what the hell she was doing there. "Hey!" she called. "You!"

The face that greeted Maxine was unfamiliar. She had wide-spaced dark eyes, a broad nose and thin lips that drew themselves into a sneer. "Who are you and why are you here?"

Maxine was taken aback that the words she was about to utter had been spoken by the stranger. She took a moment before she replied. "My name is Maxine. I was a close friend of Rex Glyn."

"Close friend?" An eyebrow was arched. "I didn't see you at the funeral."

"No." There was a moment before she spoke again. "Perhaps you'd like to tell me your name and what you're doing here." Aggression was barely disguised by a forced smile.

"My name is Louisa." She, too, could use a pause, but this was clearly for dramatic effect. "My father is… I mean was… Rex Glyn. I thought it would be a good idea to see what I had inherited.

You wouldn't happen to know the insurance arrangements for the property? I live in London, you see, and it makes sense to check this place out while I'm here."

Maxine was not in a conciliatory mood. She had been the one who had counselled Rex about getting in contact with his daughter and now here she was, strutting about in expensive-looking boots, as if she owned the place. That was the thing. She probably did. "You will need to find his solicitor. I expect she will know." Unkindly, she noted that the woman had not inherited Rex's good looks.

The robin had returned, singing heartily, either to defend its territory or to attract a mate. Maxine found that it was helpful to stare at the bird rather than at Louisa. The best thing to do would be to make herself scarce. She could place the roses behind the swing seat in memory of Rex, pack up the bottle and glasses and go home. No need to prolong the conversation. She was about to leave when Louisa spoke again.

"Did he speak about me – my father?" The strident voice had dropped to a whisper as she looked down at the toe of her right boot, which played with the gravel underneath.

When Maxine looked at Louisa again, she saw that she was crying. The confident posturing had ceased and a vulnerable adult was revealed. Maxine was known for being direct and honest. She said, "On his last night in this house, we talked a great deal about you and his intention to find you. He didn't know of your existence until that day."

Louisa frowned, unsure if it was good news. Rex hadn't ignored her. He didn't know about her. But this meant that the relationship with her mother could hardly have been a close one. Was she a mistake? But he had talked about her and intended to find her. A small smile flickered across her mouth and Maxine noted the charming gap between the woman's front teeth. Louisa was much more attractive when she smiled.

Long Acres usually enjoyed peace and quiet, benefiting from glorious isolation with occasional visitors and bursts of activity.

To Maxine's surprise, another car arrived outside the house – a white Audi – its smart appearance marred by a smattering of mud on either side of the vehicle. A woman in mourning clothes got out of the passenger seat. She looked familiar to Maxine.

She was Eleanor Smythe Thomas, the actor, the woman behind countless unthreatening female roles but Maxine recognised her as Miss Marple. When she spoke, the voice was as comforting as a friend's. Maxine wondered if it was her voice on the television at night in an advertisement for dishwasher tablets. This was not the time to ask.

Eleanor was keen to coax her daughter into the car. She smiled in Maxine's direction, her public smile, bestowing *bonhomie* as a searchlight scatters its beams, while linking her arm through Louisa's, attempting to hasten her departure. But Louisa was having none of it; like a small child, she broke free, scampering towards the spiral staircase on the undamaged side of the house, which led to the balcony at the back. Up she went, her heels clanging on the metal treads.

Maxine didn't want to abandon Long Acres on this significant day, but maybe she could come back. And if gates were erected to keep her out, the memories would remain. Louisa would inherit everything so Maxine might as well accept that this lovely place had never been hers. It would be sensible to go to the job centre on her way home and focus on getting some money.

Perhaps it would be best to make this her last visit. She could toast Rex Glyn anywhere, even if it was in the confines of her flat. It was never a good idea to get caught up in someone else's family struggles. "Goodbye, Rex," she whispered as she walked away.

Chapter 35

Clothed in funeral attire, a long coat over a black silk top and favourite trousers, Grace Palmer kicked off her patent high heels as she walked through the door, nearly falling over Wesley who was sleeping in the hall. She bent to stroke his head, whereupon he roused himself, pretending that he was still an alert, if old, retainer and to prove a point, started pacing at the bottom of the stairs as if he had been keeping guard as conscientiously as those in bearskin hats at Buckingham Palace. Grace flopped on to the bottom step. She felt exhausted.

The funeral had been reasonably well attended. A niece – Tiffany? – had shaken everyone's hand as they filed out of the crematorium and Barry the Box stood beside her to try and disguise the woeful lack of relatives. A few famous faces enlivened proceedings. She recognised the woman who had played the part of Miss Marple, less plain and elderly-looking in the flesh. There was an address, alluding to Rex's colourful past and a few anecdotes that fell just the right side of tasteful. Rex had organised the proceedings, knowing of his imminent demise and it was suggested that the choice of hymn, 'How great thou art', might have been selected as a reference to the actor, rather than to the Almighty.

Rex's agent, a bohemian-looking woman in a fringed, twenties-style dress, had read '*Fear no more the heat of the sun*,' which was printed along with the hymns on the order of service. Grace didn't know much about Shakespeare's *Cymbeline*, but guessed that, given Rex Glyn's well-documented run-ins with the popular press, the lines '*Fear not slander, censure rash*' resonated with him.

His beautiful youthful face stared unflinchingly from the outside cover on the front and there was a picture of the actors in *The Importance of Being Earnest* on the back, Rex Glyn being centre stage, surrounded by the smiling faces of the rest of the cast.

When the coffin had disappeared behind the curtain, Grace looked away, her eye caught by a shaft of light that pierced the clouds. Blue sky and sunshine in December. Not a bad day for a funeral.

"Sarah! Are you in?" Grace called up the stairs. Paul emerged from the kitchen and watched Grace shrug out of her long black coat, a funeral stalwart. He took it from her and hung it up.

"She's upstairs. How was it?"

"Okay. Don't know why we all clamoured to go. It was all a bit muted, really. I've seen better turnouts for folk who have never left Pontardeilo. Someone said that there might be another service in London, at St Paul's in Covent Garden – you know, the one we visited that has all those memorial plaques for actors."

Paul nodded. He raked his blond hair with his right hand, a gesture Grace recognised as something he did when he was nervous. He motioned with his head in the direction of the upper floor. "We'll call her down now, shall we? Let's tell her today."

Grace knew it was time. "Yes."

Sarah had heard her mother's voice. There was no need to summon her. She padded down the stairs in bare feet and joined the pair in the kitchen.

Sarah looked at the serious faces and wondered who had died. Only some old actor. It couldn't be that. "What's wrong?"

"Sit down, Sarah," her mother instructed. "We've got something to tell you. Paul?" She turned her blue eyes upon him as if she lacked the courage.

They ended up sitting round the kitchen table. "I'm really worried now," Sarah said. "Please don't say that you're splitting up." Irritatingly, her eyes pricked with tears. "I mean, I know you've been having lots of deep discussions but you haven't been arguing much, not since that day at the races. And no, I don't want to talk about that." She didn't want to give them the chance to bang on about Stephen again. "I hate it when you argue, Mam."

Her mother's face was flushed; she looked a little tearful too.

"We're not splitting up," Paul said. "Quite the reverse." He took Grace's hand in his. "We're getting married, Sarah, and we wanted you to be the first to know."

"Wow! I wasn't expecting that." Sarah was laughing. "You'd better tell the rest of us." She wondered how her brother would take it, and Paul's son too. She guessed it wouldn't have such an impact on them as they were living away.

Grace hugged her daughter. "You're okay with it?"

Sarah nodded. She wasn't going to launch into a soppy endorsement of the man she realised would be her stepfather, but she would have missed him if he had left. His even-tempered presence steadied their home, somehow. And he was kind. That was an underrated quality.

"There's more," Grace continued. She was really red in the face now. "I've always taught you to be sensible, Sarah. And I hope you always will be. I'm not sure we're a very good example to you, not really, but we do know what we're doing. The thing is," she gulped. "You're going to have a stepsister."

Sarah couldn't take it in. What was her mother on about?

"I'm pregnant, Sarah. Paul and I are having a baby." She lifted her silk blouse a little, to reveal that the top button of her trousers was undone.

Sarah couldn't help it. She burst out laughing. "But you're way too old!" She saw an opportunity to wind her mother up. "I can't believe you gave *me* that lecture about getting up the duff when you were already pregnant. Tell you what, I'll have a baby as well and we can bring them up together." She almost felt sorry for her mother, whose head hung as if in shame. "Don't be daft, Mam," she nudged her. "It's a bit gross, thinking about you having sex, but hey! Celebrities do it at your age." She giggled. "I'm talking about giving birth, now. I guess they have sex all the time too."

She reached over and stroked her mother's hair, conscious of the role-reversal. "It's okay, we'll get through it."

Paul smiled. "I suppose you could say it's a Christmas miracle."

"Please don't," Sarah responded. "It's all too much of a cheese-fest." She giggled again. "All those talks about contraception, Mam! Was it a mistake, then?"

Grace lifted her head. No child of hers would grow up thinking that she was unwanted. "We want this baby – we do. It's none of your business if we had help with its conception." She looked at Paul and he nodded.

"God knows when we'll retire but we'll give her the best life we can," he said.

"Will you pay me for babysitting?" Sarah asked with a smile, keen to lighten the atmosphere. That was the only thing about Paul – he could get a bit heavy.

"Payment negotiable," he said but he was laughing when he said it.

Sarah fiddled with her phone.

"Don't tell anyone," her mother said. "We've got to tell the rest of the family." She added, "The other thing is that there are more risks having a baby at my age. Something might go wrong, so please don't make a big song and dance about it. We're still in the early stages."

"I'm not telling anyone. I'm just looking it up. I thought you were ancient, in your forties, but someone here had one in their fifties. Who knew?"

Grace smiled. "I can't tell you how relieved I am that you're not cross. I don't think the boys will mind. The next hurdle is telling Byron and Nancy at work."

Chapter 36

Maxine didn't get far with her escape plan from Long Acres.

From the driver's side of the Audi, a man in a black suit and a loosely knotted tie, joined the fray. He acknowledged Maxine with a hasty gap-toothed smile. She could see herself reflected in the man's glasses, perched on his broad nose. His face was so strikingly like that of Louisa that Maxine observed her mouth forming an unattractive 'O'. It was surely obvious to everyone that this man was Louisa's father, nothing to do with Rex Glyn.

He lit a cigarette, inhaled and exhaled languorously. With his free hand, he invited Maxine to shake it. "Pleased to meet you." Unsure whose hand he was shaking, but presuming that anyone on Rex's land must be a relative, he added, "My sympathies." Maxine was hoping not to have to explain who she was but need not have worried as Eleanor's husband was happy to fill the silence. "We've come three hundred miles – from Suffolk. It's a long way for us to travel for a funeral and I didn't want my wife to have to do all the driving." He gazed at the damaged building as if for the first time. "What the hell has happened here?"

Before Maxine had a chance to reply, they were distracted by the sight of Louisa descending the external staircase. Eleanor was audible now. "This has got to stop. I know there hasn't been a DNA test, but this ridiculous fantasy that Rex Glyn is your father must end. Look at your dad. Look at pictures of Rex Glyn. Who do you most look like?"

"But this woman," a gesture was flung towards Maxine. "She

said that Rex was my father."

Three pairs of eyes focused on Maxine. It was tempting to run towards her car to depart in haste, but the agony on Louisa's face was enough to prevent Maxine from disappearing. She took a deep breath and began to tell Rex's story.

When she had finished, Eleanor Smythe Thomas pasted a professional smile on to her careworn face. "I do hope you can be trusted not to sell our story to the press. The fact of the matter is that Amal – that is, the woman who was Rex's girlfriend and who apparently spoke to him the night before he died – got it wrong. He wasn't the father of my daughter."

Louisa made no attempt to suppress a loud sob.

"We should have been more emphatic about it but, years ago, Louisa read an article in a magazine. Amal was getting her revenge. You can't really blame her. She was less than discreet about what happened between Rex and myself."

Anger, jealousy and vengeance presented themselves as the Three Furies, flitting across the face of Eleanor's husband. He remained silent, willing the conversation to stop, puffing furiously on his cigarette.

"It became a bit of a family joke, not to be taken seriously, that the famous Rex Glyn was her father."

"He might have left me something if he thought I was his child," Louisa said.

Finally the man spoke. "This is bloody ridiculous! No more. I knew it would be a bad idea to come to this funeral. Eleanor thought that the press would read too much into it if she didn't attend, but nobody came apart from some writer from the local paper. Let's be clear, as the politicians say, he was an egotistical, self-satisfied, overrated has-been." He turned towards his daughter. "If he really had been your father, then he wouldn't have had anything to do with you anyway."

Maxine winced on behalf of Louisa, Rex and finally herself, who had been stupid enough to love him. She tilted her head towards the winter sun. "That's not fair. You didn't know him as I did."

He turned towards the housekeeper. "I suppose he fucked you too, then, did he?"

It was Eleanor's turn to speak. "That's enough. I can only apologise." She fiddled in her expensive-looking handbag for her purse. With shaking hands, she fished out a bundle of notes and thrust them at Maxine. "For your time. I hope I can rely on your discretion."

Maxine surprised herself at the force of her response. She made a loud noise that she had never heard before, an amalgam of a shout and wail, a sort of battle cry. Gwenllian the Welsh warrior defeated at Kidwelly a few short miles away, would have been proud of her.

The family group took a step back away from the crazy woman before them. She took a deep breath and then threw the notes at Eleanor's feet. "I'm not rich but nobody buys me!"

Louisa stooped to pick them up but her mother dragged her away. The getaway was as fast as a masked raider's. Gravel spat in all directions as the car disappeared down the drive.

Long Acres was exposed to the elements. Maxine was rooted to the spot, watching their retreat, while the banknotes were caught by the wind as if life had been breathed into them. When she came to her senses, she fruitlessly tried to capture the pieces of paper that had flown up into the air and beyond the perimeter hedge. She cursed herself. It was all very well to make a stand when you had money, but it was quite different when you were broke.

Years later, the next occupant of the house and grounds would be surprised to find fragments of a fifty-pound note lining the inside of a robin's nest.

Chapter 37

Tiffany knew that some people might think that it was out of order to visit the solicitor on the same day as Rex's funeral, not that it was anybody else's business. It made sense to avoid travelling to Pontardeilo on a separate occasion just to find out what she had inherited. She knew that a letter would probably be sent to her eventually but she might as well find out while she had the chance.

She felt that she had done her old uncle proud. It was not as boring as she thought it would be. She had forgotten how famous he once was and felt as if a bit of stardust had rubbed off as she accepted condolences on behalf of the family. Someone had to do it, she reasoned, as she darted out of the crematorium to shake everyone's hand.

When Tiffany met Rex's agent, the woman must have been impressed with what Tiffany had to say about inheriting her uncle's acting genes. She now had her business card. Admittedly, she was left alone mid-sentence at the wake in the hotel as the agent spotted someone else she knew, but the card was thrust into Tiffany's hands, nonetheless, as a parting gift.

It was a crash-landing when she was dropped by taxi on the outskirts of the town. Initially, the impression she got of the east end of Pontardeilo was favourable since it had been smartened up. Tiffany stopped for a moment to look at a sculpture of a man and woman working in the tinplate industry. They were facing out, backs to one another, and the sculptor had managed to capture dignity in relentless toil. Thank God she didn't have to do what they were doing. Further on, it was good to see that the theatre and cinema looked shiny and relatively new, but as she kept going, the stores that she remembered had long been closed. She skirted round the centre *en route* to the solicitor and had to dodge someone whose eyes were as vacant as the surrounding shops. Whatever substance he had taken, it might have offered an escape but brought no joy. On she went, past a much-loved department store that had been converted into flats, a bar and a betting shop.

She turned into a road that housed a gallery and a pretty-looking florist's shop, where a dark-haired woman was removing a lilac tabard and reaching for her coat. Tiffany spotted an estate agent's and the solicitor's premises, but further along the street, the ghost of business past had clearly fled.

As Tiffany approached the solicitor's office, she became aware of footsteps behind her. Turning her head, she realised that the woman from the florist's shop was following closely. They arrived at exactly the same time. Tiffany went in first; Olivia Garland shut the door after her.

The receptionist, a plump, middle-aged woman, who was finishing a mouthful of what looked like cream cake, smiled, dabbing the corner of her mouth with a paper napkin. "Well, there's quiet it's been all afternoon and then there's two of you!"

The young women spoke at the same time.

"I've got an appointment at three," said Olivia.

"I've got an appointment at a quarter past three," said Tiffany.

"Ah yes," said the receptionist. "Rex Glyn's estate." Her hands clapped together as if she was remembering past applause. "He was lovely in his day. Those eyes! I think I must have seen all his films. I expect you're too young to remember him."

Olivia responded. "I used to deliver flowers to his house."

"Did you now? Well! I never actually met him but my cousin's wife met him once at the Plaza. I was told he was friends with Roger Moore. You've surely heard of him? He played James Bond back in the day – did you know that? Of course, Rex Glyn lived in London for years. Too busy to visit his hometown very much." She sniffed, eyes narrowing, managing to convey that it was an error of judgement by the film star to stay away from Wales. Recovering, she continued. "I think he had a mansion in London or was it a penthouse flat? He's supposed to have a house here, mind, on the outskirts of town. What's it called? Long Meadow, is it? Something like that."

"Long Acres," said Olivia. "I delivered flowers to the house once a week."

Tiffany cut across what threatened to be an outpouring of tedious and irrelevant information. She tossed back her curls, defiant on her uncle's behalf. What did the receptionist know, anyway? "Actually, I'm his niece." She expected an apology or at least discomfort. What was wrong with living in London if that was where the work was? Too often, Marilyn had cautioned her daughter against *getting above herself*. Perhaps her mother was worried that she might turn out like Rex.

The receptionist viewed her through mischievous eyes. "Well now, practically royalty."

Tiffany wondered if she detected a note of sarcasm as the florist covered her mouth with her hand and avoided eye contact with the older matron.

A dark-haired, slim woman wearing a navy suit appeared and Olivia was spirited away.

Tiffany sat on the seat furthest away from the receptionist and picked up a copy of an interior-design magazine from the previous year. Burying herself in the once-glossy pages, she feigned interest in the merits of freestanding kitchen units as opposed to fixed ones. The clock ticked noisily on the wall above a now-defunct fireplace.

Eventually, the pretty florist emerged from the solicitor's office. Her face was flushed and she seemed in a hurry to leave. With a cursory, "Thank you," over her shoulder to the receptionist, she darted out of the front door. Tiffany watched as she doubled back past the office, eyes bright, face animated, as she spoke to someone on her phone.

It wasn't joy stamped upon her features, more like confusion.

Well, she probably wouldn't have expected a legacy, would she? *That must mean good news*, Tiffany thought. If Rex Glyn had left something to a lowly florist, he would surely be more generous with a relative.

Chapter 38

Frank Whitehead distanced himself from the rest of the organised group when he finally made it to Sydney Opera House. This is where they had planned to come in their retirement after they had moved from Long Acres. Elizabeth fancied the idea of having a cocktail, soaking up the sunshine, before entering the main auditorium to see… what was it she fancied? Was it *Carmen*? He couldn't remember. Putting a fist to his mouth, he gnawed on his knuckle in an attempt to stop himself from crying.

An American widow whom he kept bumping into on board, had joined the theatre trip at the last minute. Previously, she had signed up to go on a walking tour around the harbour. Looking in Frank's direction, pity softened her angular face. "You okay?" she mouthed. He nodded but turned away, walking towards the water's edge.

In truth, when Elizabeth had talked about opera, Frank had been more interested in having a tour of the building. He remembered when it was first opened in 1973. The construction had taken years. It had been a novel idea, reusing the same mould to precast concrete ribs for multiple shells. It was a bit disappointing, close up, as much-celebrated buildings often are. It was built to be appreciated as a landmark, viewed from a distance, a glorious representation of white sails against a blue sky.

As he stood looking up at the building, he appreciated the cleverness of the design, but the experience lacked the sense of wonder that Elizabeth would have supplied. She would have pointed out everything that caught her eye – maybe the tiles fitted in a chevron pattern or even the shapes of the clouds above. Sometimes she had got on his nerves, chattering away when really he just wanted to be still and quiet, but more often than not, she opened his eyes to something he hadn't noticed.

The tour guide was now talking to the American. They were staring at him. There was no escape. Frank couldn't hold up the party. He blew his nose and retraced his steps.

Later that evening, he had recovered his composure. It was an enjoyable experience, being served dinner on board, enlivened by conversation, a welcome change from the soulless process of eating alone. Getting smartened up, sitting beneath an enormous dome-shaped chandelier, with stiff white tablecloths and napkins, and being thoroughly spoiled was what the brochure had promised. The American had found an empty place on Frank's table, opposite him, but he latched on to a friendly pair from Dorset.

What a small world it was! Sitting at a round table for eight, he discovered that the woman on his right, a retired teacher who lived in Dorset, had been born in Wales. They talked about favourite towns and landscapes (Narberth for her, Carmarthen for him; Gower for her, Brecon Beacons for him) and then she talked about Welsh celebrities. She had seen Tom Jones and Shirley Bassey live. He mentioned various Welsh rugby stars, Phil Bennet being a particular favourite, but when he started to talk about his trademark sidestep and swerve, he realised that her eyes were beginning to lose focus. He stopped talking and gave his full attention to a smoked salmon roulade, garnished with lemon and dill.

"Did you say that you were from Pontardeilo originally? Wasn't Rex Glyn from there?" the retired teacher asked.

Frank tried not to grimace. He finished his mouthful and replied. "Yes, that's right."

"I loved his performance in *Rebecca*, although I still prefer the old black and white film with Laurence Olivier, don't you?" She laughed, adding, "Probably not a man's film."

"I saw the original performance but didn't catch Rex Glyn's effort." Oh dear, to his own ears, that sounded negative and sneering.

His dinner companion didn't seem to notice. "Terrible business about the fire."

Frank blotted his mouth with his napkin. The starter had been delicious. "Sorry?"

"The fire at his house."

Was she still talking about the film? "Correct me if I'm wrong. Was it Mrs Danvers who sets Manderley on fire?"

"What?" The woman shook her head so that her sparkly earrings twinkled in the light. "No, I'm not talking about the film. I'm talking about Rex Glyn."

Frank had made a conscious decision to have a break from watching *News at Ten* while he was on holiday. It was all so depressing: politicians squabbling, refugees starving, conflict in the Middle East, Syria and across the globe, racism, sexism, famine, disease, murder and abuse. He had been sleeping a lot better at sea, avoiding horror stories before he went to bed.

It was clear from Frank's facial expression that he had no idea what the woman was talking about. She continued. "There was a fire at Rex Glyn's house and he died. Didn't you know?"

Frank looked stupefied.

"You didn't know him, did you?"

His voice had dropped to a whisper. "He bought our house – the house that my wife and I lived in."

Thinking that it might be a shock that Frank had lost a close acquaintance, the woman apologised that he should hear about the death in such a casual way.

"What happened to the house?" Frank asked.

"No idea, the newspapers didn't say."

Frank excused himself from the table, a master of understatement, "I'm sorry. I don't feel too good."

As he walked away, the wife confided to her husband. "Poor

man. He didn't know that Rex Glyn had died. They both lived in Pontardeilo. He knew him, apparently. Must have come as quite a shock. I just blurted it out. I wasn't to know, though, was I?"

The husband, used to his wife's lack of tact, replied soothingly, "No, dear, of course not."

In his cabin, Frank lay on the bed. The maid had already turned back the covers and it was adorned with a swan made out of two towels. Frank was tempted to kick them on to the floor but he appreciated that someone had gone to a lot of trouble. He didn't want to hurt anyone's feelings so he moved the avian origami on to the dressing table, from where it appeared to fix him with a steady gaze. Frank turned his back on it as he tried to scroll through *BBC News*. The actor's death would surely have made the front page of one of the tabloids, if not a broadsheet. No joy. Frank hadn't paid for Wi-Fi in his cabin.

Two foil-wrapped mint chocolates were within his eyeline on the next pillow. They were quickly dispatched. Frank tried to process how he felt. His dislike of the man had bordered on hatred. But he didn't necessarily want him to die. He wondered when it had happened and how the fire started. Would a film star take his last gasp as a consequence of a chip-pan fire? Not very glamorous. Perhaps a log fell from an open grate. Did he fall asleep with a cigarette dangling from his lips? Perhaps he was drunk and insensible. His reputation for drink preceded him.

What about dear, lovely Long Acres? Frank hoped that it could be rescued. If Rex Glyn was an enemy, then surely Long Acres was a beloved friend and as such, if it were destroyed, then it was another loss to mourn.

Chapter 39

The Christmas wreath bonanza had begun. Olivia was instructing Sarah about how to attach foliage to a metal frame when suddenly the younger woman cut across her and said, "Why don't we get ready-made bases with foam?"

"Because it is more expensive." Sometimes it could be a trial, having to explain. Olivia considered herself to be a patient individual but lately Sarah seemed to be questioning a lot of her methods. She didn't mind when it came to the website. That was much improved with Sarah's input. But now the girl was giving her opinions about floristry, which surely Olivia knew much more about.

"I've been looking on YouTube and they often don't use holly. Have you seen the one – I think it's shot in the grounds of a fancy hotel or country house and there are chickens pecking about in the background? The florist uses all sorts of foliage. Blue spruce looks really classy."

Olivia, who had been making wreaths for some years, didn't take too kindly to innovative ideas. In even tones, she answered, "It's all a question of gathering materials that are freely available."

"I could cut some stuff from our garden. It's got lots of different trees."

"Our customers want something quite simple – a plain holly wreath with a festive ribbon."

Sarah, who eyed the red ribbon on the workshop bench with some distaste, considering its shininess to look cheap and a bit naff, continued. "How do you know that they wouldn't fancy a bit of a change? Something a bit, I don't know, perhaps a bit more sophisticated?" She knew, as soon as the words were spoken that she had overstepped the mark. Maybe the aroma of chrysanthemums had finally got to her. She had caught the end of a programme on BBC Two that had explored the link between *olfactory stimulation* – she remembered the phrase – and alteration of mood and social behaviour. It was all about perfume and the effect it had on people. Would Olivia excuse her if she blamed her rudeness on the smell of flowers? The body language of her employer suggested that it was unlikely.

Olivia looked down at her hands and she appeared to be clenching her fists. With a deep breath, she flexed her fingers. "I'm sorry if you find my products don't suit your sophisticated taste, Sarah. But look, it's like this – we've got hundreds of them to make." She was exaggerating to prove a point. "We haven't got time to arse about. Can we just get on with it?"

There followed a period of silence save for the noise of wire scraping on wire, ribbon being fashioned into bows and the odd swear word when Sarah's hands were pricked by holly.

Her phone pinged. With ferocity, she threw down the wreath she was working on and looked at the text. It was from Stephen.

How's it going?

Glancing at her boss, she had a brief spasm of guilt that she immediately ignored. Her reply was a number of aggressive stabs at her screen.

I hate holly and wreaths and even Christmas.

He supplied an emoji of a laughing face before his message.

I'll pick you up tonight. I'll take you out. 7 p.m. okay?

Sarah typed,

Great. See you then. xxxxxxxxxxxx

"Can you stop looking at your phone?" Olivia asked.

"Sorry," she muttered, taking up the wreath. Sarah was aware that she was behaving childishly but the atmosphere was pretty intense in a tiny shop with an angry employer. Perhaps conversation might be steered towards something different. "So how did you get on at the solicitor's? You never said."

Rex's legacy was already a burden, something to be concealed from others. The whisper of gossip would whirl around the sum, numbers ascending, twister-like, to reach the sky. Her father had counselled her to keep quiet but her mother had already told every living relative. "Okay," she answered.

That was going to be it, then, was it? Try again. "Enough money for a raise?"

"Not at the rate you're working, no."

Sarah stood up slowly and sauntered out to the back of the shop to the loo. She didn't really need the facilities, but she needed to remove herself from a situation that threatened to implode. No wonder it didn't work out with Stephen. Olivia was prissy, stuck-up, judgemental. There were lots of other adjectives that could have been applied, none of them flattering. She was pretty, though. Sarah hated her prettiness. Stephen must have loved that milky complexion, those eyes and luscious lashes. She didn't like to think of them having sex, but it was an annoyingly frequent thought.

"Sarah!" Olivia was calling her now. Was she not even allowed to go to the toilet? She returned to the shop. Olivia had Sarah's phone in her hand.

"What are you doing with my phone?"

"You had a message."

Sarah lunged towards it. "Give me that!"

There was a clumsy tussle across the workbench, Olivia's arm raised high. Holly and moss scattered, secateurs and wire cutters were knocked to the floor. Sarah reclaimed her phone. She had had another text from Stephen.

Have I told you? You make me smile.

"Why is Stephen texting you?" Olivia asked. She looked as if she might cry.

This was the moment Sarah had been dreading. She had a choice – either go on the defensive and make a fuss about her phone being tampered with, or confess. Better to be honest. "I'm going out with him."

"I see." Olivia turned her back. Her voice was muffled. "Can you just go home, Sarah? I'll pay you for today. I'll take it to your mother at the estate agent's. To be honest, I don't really want to see you again, let alone work with you."

"But you finished with him! You didn't want him."

Olivia was resolute; she would not turn to face Sarah, fearful that her expression would betray the anger and distress that would give her employee the upper hand. She would not take part in a shouting match.

Sarah waited for a moment, thinking that there might be a reply. The hunched back was as responsive as the violet-white walls. Her belongings were gathered hastily. She toyed with the idea of apologising or making excuses but for once, her first instinct was for flight rather than fight. The door slammed behind her.

Olivia waited for a moment, to make sure that she was alone, before sitting down, hands shaking as they rested in her lap. She reached for the bag on the counter and took out her own phone. Scrolling through Stephen's messages, she found what she was looking for – a message from early September.

Have I told you? You make me smile.

Sarah ran round the corner to the estate agent's and burst through the door as a couple from Margate were trying to decide whether

Pontardeilo or Carmarthen would be better for their retirement.

"Do you think there is enough in Pontardeilo to keep us interested?" the man asked his wife.

Her mother had her sympathetic face on, one that Sarah instantly recognised. She wanted Grace to push past the time-wasters and transfer that sympathetic gaze to her daughter.

Nancy could see that Sarah was looking anguished, and expertly steered her by the arm to the desk furthest from the potential buyers. "Keep it down, Sarah," she hissed as the younger woman opened her mouth to speak. "Your mother will be with you in a minute. Shall I get you a mug of tea? Two sugars, isn't it?"

Grace tried to focus on the couple in front of her but clearly her daughter was distressed. In moments like this, she wondered why she was having another child. There would be a whole new person to worry about, to love and care for. No matter how old they were, her children would always feel like her responsibility, even when she was an old woman.

Fortunately, the decision was made that the husband and wife would go for a drive around the surrounding area and call back if they fancied any property locally. A business card was pressed into the woman's hand and they were gone.

Grace stood up from behind her desk. "*Enough to keep us interested!*" she muttered. "Give me strength!" She walked over to Sarah. "What on earth is the matter? Shouldn't you be at work?"

"She sacked me."

"What? Why?"

"It's because I was being an idiot, trying to change what she wanted to do."

"No, it can't just be that." Her mother knew her too well.

"It wasn't just that. She discovered that I'm going out with Stephen. And then I shouted at her."

Grace gathered her daughter in her arms and tried not to sigh too heavily. First a failed attempt at university and now this.

"I'm sorry. You've got enough on your plate with the pregnancy. I'm sorry."

Grace hadn't yet delivered the news to her colleagues. Nancy returned with a mug of tea for Sarah just as Byron appeared from town with a bag of Welsh cakes from the market. He'd gone to meet a friend in town, "the chap from the rugby club".

"Who's pregnant?" Byron and Nancy chorused.

Grace rolled her eyes. Sarah clapped her hand to her mouth.

"That would be me," said Grace.

Chapter 40

At night, the seafront hotels in Tenby could be likened to a gaggle of partygoers on the promenade, dressed for an evening out, all glittering and shiny, brightly adorned, attracting the notice of passers-by. Trees twinkled in the windows, lights were festooned round doorways and each establishment competed for attention with its individual colour scheme. Any imperfections of the paintwork or plaster were concealed by darkness, the Christmas lights drawing attention to the hotels' best features, like clever make-up on an aged face.

Tiffany usually looked out to sea but found that she was looking inwards at the Christmas decorations, the people sitting in the windows and the passengers spilling on to the pavement from a coach that had just arrived at its destination. They were joshing with one another and laughing as they gathered suitcases from the driver to make their way within.

How was it that those chubby, elderly, unremarkable folk were so happy? They weren't exactly Instagrammable, unless you were posting something as a bit of a joke. How much of a thrill could it be to have a poxy early Christmas meal at a seaside hotel?

Perhaps they hadn't been thwarted by a thoughtless uncle. Rex Glyn had misled her, suggesting that she would receive a legacy. She had lost her composure in the solicitor's office when the woman explained what was due to her. Joshua had since revealed that he was the recipient of Rex's gold watch and frankly he had barely been civil to the actor when they visited him. Tiffany supposed that she had overdone the shared interest in drama. No monetary gift for her, but (she still couldn't believe the cheek of it after all the effort she had made trying to keep in touch) her prize was one of Rex's film posters instead. It wasn't clear whether this was even suitable for rescuing, given that the house had caught fire. The chances were that the contents of Long Acres were smoke-damaged.

She was so horrified by the disappointing gift that she asked the solicitor if she could contest the Will. The solicitor asked if, to her knowledge, she had been mentioned in a previous Will. She thought it was unlikely, given that her mother and by extension the rest of the family had been estranged. When asked how often she had seen her uncle in recent years, the question made her blush. "Only once," was the truthful answer, but she glossed over the truth and talked about postcards sent and signed photographs received. She could tell by the solicitor's face that it would be a reckless idea to pursue a claim.

On the internet, there were dozens of examples where disgruntled relatives had tried to claw back money when they had been disinherited and nearly all of them had been unlucky, losing more money on solicitors' fees than they might have received if they had been mentioned in a Will.

Why was life so unfair? She might contest the Will anyway. She had yet to speak to her mother on the subject. Surely Marilyn would want her daughter to receive what was her due?

She was a little late for the final rehearsal of the pantomime, having met up with a friend at the south beach café. Tiffany was sufficiently self-aware to notice that, having no famous uncle to speak of, her companion was bored by her list of grievances, distractedly playing with the individually wrapped sugars on the table. It would be a blessing to get up on stage with the rest of the cast and forget about reality for a brief moment. Theatre offered escapism for the audience but it also offered an escape for Tiffany.

Although she hadn't got many lines in the Roald Dahl version, she had a challenging costume-change from waif to belle of the ball. Both costumes emphasised her tiny waist and she didn't mind at all that at one point the dress was pulled off and she had to appear in her smalls.

"As Cindy shouted, 'Let me go!'
The dress was ripped from head to toe.
She ran out in her underwear
And lost one slipper on the stair."

It was all very tasteful, the garment beneath – a flattering fitted white slip that was rather like a summer dress. Zachary had popped into one of the rehearsals and cheered very loudly at the end of the piece. He had been very enthusiastic in bed that night.

Zachary said that some of the original Rex Glyn posters had become collectable items and advised her just to take the thing and they could source a specialist collector of film memorabilia and see what they could flog it for, or, he said, she could hang on to it and see if it became more sought-after. Generally, though, the value of these things tended to peak just after the celebrity had met his demise. There was so much coverage in the press to generate more interest. He hoped that she would get her hands on it as soon as possible.

Chapter 41

Stephen Samson was surprised to get a text from Olivia. It just said,

Sarah? Really?

He was walking along the seafront at Pontardeilo, on the way to the old piano factory, and stopped as he reached the brow of the hill to take out his phone, just as a train entered the tunnel beneath him. He watched as it reappeared on the other side. There followed a confusing mix of titanium, Lycra and shouting because Stephen had distractedly strayed into the cycle path. He responded in kind, relishing the swear words hurled at the retreating figure of the speeding cyclist.

What could he say to Olivia? *Yes, really.* What would be the point of antagonising her? A part of him, probably not the better part of him, was pleased that she seemed to be bothered. He considered replying but thought better of it. He had nothing to say on the subject. His mother, however, had plenty to say, her latest remark being, "Olivia might have stolen your heart, but this Sarah seems to have got under your skin."

It was all rubbish, all of it. He struggled to make sense of his emotions but no one had stolen any part of his anatomy or invaded his body like some alien creature. But he knew what she meant. He wasn't going to let her believe that she knew more about his feelings than he did himself and told her to back off. Earlier in the year, all he wanted was to marry Olivia but now, when he wasn't with Sarah, it was as if he still carried her perfume. Her bravery and loyalty had genuinely moved him. He knew he wasn't very good at expressing himself, using the same tired chat-up lines, but Sarah challenged him if she thought he was talking bullshit.

He listened to her when she said that it was all very well marketing the piano business as an evening venue, but young people were often too lazy to go out at night and they didn't have enough money anyway. "Look at me!" she said. "Never happier than when I'm watching Netflix and sipping cider in my PJs." He needed to capture the grey pound. All those retired folk who fancied a breakfast out or young parents who wanted a cheeky cappuccino – those were the people he should be thinking about. Stephen admired her cleverness, the way she threw herself into their discussions. He was considering what she had to say and was having further discussions with the council.

Long Acres would be up for sale eventually and it appealed to him to live in the famous actor's house. Might some of Rex's *bravura* somehow seep through his pores while he slept, giving him the confidence to nail every challenge of each new day as he awoke, refreshed, to look upon the same view that Rex had done? One thing was certain, Stephen no longer wanted to ricochet from one woman to another any more, like the notorious Rex Glyn had done as breezily as landing the ball in one of the pockets of a snooker table during an all-nighter. The extra confidence would be great; the lifestyle, not so much. He was no longer the playboy that he aspired to be as a teenager.

He still thought it would make a great place to live, if only there wasn't so much mud that seemed to be an inevitable part of living in the country. Most of all he wanted a family of his own, but he knew that he would have to proceed with caution where Sarah was concerned. It must not look as if he was on the rebound and settling for someone who was second choice.

His track record with women was poor. He knew it. Sarah's mother, Grace, eyed him beneath a jagged frown whenever he stepped over the threshold of their home. Sarah was never ready to go out, even if he deliberately arrived later than they had arranged.

He would be stuck with her mother in the hall, really trying to make amends, but the conversation always limped along like a tired horse destined for the knacker's yard. He would eventually be put out of his misery as Sarah charged down the stairs, leaping from the last step and into his arms. It was a relief to learn that he would not be invited to Paul and Grace's wedding.

Stephen couldn't get his head round the shock announcement of Sarah's mother's pregnancy. *Why would she make such a mistake?* Her children were grown. Why would she want to start again? He could only conclude that it was something to do with love.

Chapter 42

It had been a particularly lively meal on board the cruise ship, culminating in all the waiters parading around the dining room, some carrying aloft flaming baked Alaska and heartily singing to celebrate its appearance. Frank was given a nudge by the American widow to join everyone in twirling a white napkin above head level, which appeared to be compulsory behaviour. He did what was expected of him but felt ridiculous.

Earlier in the day, Frank had sought out the library on the cruise ship and looked up newspaper reports about Rex Glyn. He waded through tiresome eulogies, heart in his mouth, fearful that somehow or other the cruel article about Long Acres might be resurrected. He was relieved that he didn't find it but there was a lot of anecdotal evidence to suggest that Glyn was an accomplished actor and an equally accomplished drunk and philanderer. He watched a clip on the computer of Rex staggering on to the set of the *Late Show with David Letterman* and walking past the seat he was supposed to sit on. He then proceeded to light a cigarette, take a sip from a mug that presumably wasn't containing anything so mild as tea, and talk incoherently about a co-star called Amal.

Frank looked up more recent news about the actor, his lips twisting into a contemptuous smile as the link was made between his on-screen persona as a firefighter in the *Inferno* series and the conflagration that prompted his death. There followed a critical assessment of his recent work, which was damning. But Frank wanted to know about the events that led to the actor's death. He decided to look up the *Pontardeilo Star.*

There was a horrifying picture of Frank's beloved Long Acres splashed across the front page as it smoked in the early morning winter sun, after the fire had been put out. He peered more closely at the screen. The house could be rescued. That was a blessing. He scanned the write-up for information about the fire under the headline, *Bonfire Night Tragedy.*

> It is with much sadness that we learn today of the death of local acting legend, Rex Glyn, in a house fire on the outskirts of Pontardeilo. The actor, who had a reputation for living life to the full, was rescued from his balcony in the early hours of yesterday morning with a female companion. Unfortunately, his heart had stopped beating at the scene. Attempts were made to resuscitate him but he was declared dead on arrival at Pontardeilo Hospital twenty minutes later.
>
> The fire was apparently started by a discarded cigarette. Glyn, who had been unwell for some months, had supposedly given up smoking, but he will always be remembered as one of the great Hell Raisers, with a glass in one hand and a cigarette in the other.

Frank stopped reading. He almost stopped breathing too. The remembrance of his activities at Long Acres and the cigarette, supposedly carefully disposed of in an outdoor bin, jolted him into sitting upright, mouth agape and holding his breath.

"Bloody hell!" he wailed. Had he killed Rex Glyn? How could that have happened? He thought back to the night of the storm. He took a few slow breaths in and out and tried to rationalise what had happened. The bin, where he'd thrown his cigarette, must have blown over so that the lid came off. It was possible that the discarded cigarette could have ignited the rubbish beneath, the flames fanned, catching the wooden shed, which would probably have precipitated the oil tank catching light and finally the house would have started to burn. Rex Glyn's damaged lungs would have filled with poisonous smoke so that he could no longer breathe. "I killed Rex Glyn," he whispered slowly, thankful that no one else was around to hear him. He felt physically sick and retired to his cabin for the remainder of the afternoon.

Fast forward to the evening and Frank was beginning to feel hungry. He left his room and the American widow, who had been kind to him on the tour in Sydney, fell into step as they walked along one of the two lengthy corridors that ran practically the length of the ship. They ended up on a table together, this time next to one another. Fortunately she was a good talker and he was able to zone in and out of her monologue, which ranged from a comparable study of the political situation in Britain and America, to the pros and cons of assisted dying, with reference to her late husband and anecdotal evidence regarding her children and grandchildren that life had been more fun when she had been growing up. She talked a lot about the evils of social media but also the benefits of connectivity. Was *connectivity* a new word?

At last the nonsense with the baked Alaska came to an end and Frank was able to excuse himself. He found himself up on deck, hyperventilating, with only the steely stars above to keep him company. The temperature had dropped, the cold air firing up thoughts that froze his soul. Should he go home and confess to the police? Would he have to go to court and would he end up in jail? If he was sent down, what were his chances of surviving prison?

Frank had drunk more wine than he was used to. On the top of the ship, caution and everything else was thrown to the wind. A plastic cup danced along the floor and was taken up into the air before descending to the sea. He could see it, bobbing about in the spray.

Perhaps it would be just as well if he jumped overboard. No one would miss him. He gripped the metal rail and tried to work out the logistics of doing himself in. Was he capable of climbing over? Would the death be instantaneous, the icy water stopping his heart? What if he banged his head on the way down? Would that ensure an even speedier departure?

"Don't do it!" It was the American widow Barbara. She had followed him up, the tone of her voice cheerfully ironic. Turning to face her, he continued to grip the silver rail. The moon illuminated his stricken countenance.

Barbara's light-hearted smile disappeared, her angular face taut with concern. "Honey, why don't you come back inside?"

"Why don't you bugger off?" What was wrong with the woman? Why didn't she leave him alone? He turned back to the outstretched arms of the sea.

"I'm not going anywhere."

Frank did not move, his posture resolute.

She continued. "I'm worried about you. You're so obviously in pain. What you don't realise is I've been there too. Nobody should be alone when darkness falls."

Who did she think she was? Some sort of poet? A desperate situation demanded desperate measures. He called casually over his shoulder, "You don't want to hang around with me. I killed a man." That should do the trick. She'd be scampering down the metal stairs as soon as her lean limbs could take her.

There was no reply. Frank waited to hear the door slam behind her as she left. For a mad moment, he wondered if he could persuade her to give him a push, unsure whether he had the courage to do the deed himself. After a minute or two, light footsteps drew nearer. Barbara came alongside him. Her silver hair, cut short, framed a lined, but intelligent face. She was wearing make-up – pink lipstick that had stained her teeth. He remembered Elizabeth asking him to check her appearance before they left to go out, baring her teeth like a horse so that he could make sure she hadn't made the same mistake. It had made him laugh a long time ago.

"You know? You don't look like a killer." In the manner of a police negotiator approaching a man with a gun, Barbara inched herself towards his nearest hand. He was still holding on tightly to the silver rail. One by one, she peeled back the fingers as if he were suffering from frostbite and she didn't want to damage him. Once the first had been released, she tackled the other so that they were standing opposite one another, holding hands. An onlooker might have thought they were about to launch themselves into a country dance across the deck.

"Why?" he asked. "Why are you still here?"

She continued to hold his gaze. Finally she spoke.

"*Do all the good you can,*
By all the means you can,
In all the ways you can,
In all the places you can,
At all the times you can,
To all the people you can,
As long as ever you can."

Frank had a terrible urge to laugh at the absurdity of the situation, holding hands with an unknown woman as she recited John Wesley's words to him in the dark on top of a cruise ship.

"Those are the words I learned as a child. The founder of the Methodist Church – he said them."

"I know that," he said, irritated to be preached at. "I live in Pontardeilo. Nonconformist chapels outnumber Anglican churches by a long chalk."

"Of course, who can really do what he suggests? That bar is set crazy high." Barbara dropped his right hand and tried to massage the left to warm it up. Then she worked on the other. "I think it's a good sign that we are discussing ethical ideas rather than jumping into the sea. Why don't we go inside and you can tell me all about what's happened to you? That's if you want to. I'm not going in without you but you've gotta realise I'm freezing to death in these cotton pants and summer top out here."

Frank nodded, unable to speak.

The sound of two sets of footsteps walking along the deck was so much more comforting than when he could only hear his own.

Chapter 43

Byron, clad in Prince of Wales check with a festive red tie, sidled up to Grace when they were alone in the office. "Of course, as your closest family friend and in the absence of your late father, I would consider it an honour to give you away."

Grace tried to explain that nobody would be there, only Paul and their children. They might never have bothered getting married if it wasn't for the baby. As she explained, "First time round, as you will recall, I did the whole shebang – full meringue dress, dozens of people I barely knew – and that didn't work out so well, now, did it? Most of the guests were business associates of my father. At least you got a ringside seat on that occasion."

Byron's crestfallen face prompted her to add, "And the thing is, Byron, we're giving ourselves to each other, if you know what I mean. It's not a slight to you. It will just be a tiny service, a formality, really."

Later in the day, Nancy put a mug of tea in front of Grace. "So, who were you thinking of having for bridesmaids?" She looked up coyly, Princess Diana-style, from under a curtain of hair. "Or perhaps a matron of honour?" Recently, Nancy had once again updated her hairstyle, shaving one side and allowing a great quiff to flop over the top. It was tempting to ask her to take on the role, to ensure that their professional relationship flourished after the recent falling-out. But then there would be Stuart, Nancy's husband, to invite and then she would have to ask Byron, after all, and also his wife for formality's sake in spite of the fact that he chose to spend as little time as possible with her.

Betty, her neighbour, was also likely to be miffed if she wasn't included. Perhaps she would agree to help her get ready before the wedding. Would that be an insult, if Betty wasn't invited to the actual event?

Paul and Grace were resolute – only the immediate family would be there. Perhaps a party at the house some time might lift everyone from the doldrums a week or two after the event. It would be a momentous occasion for them both. Paul's first wife had died from breast cancer. Had fortune extended a kinder hand to them both, then they would still be married. Grace, on the other hand, had chosen a husband who had moved to America. The siren call across the Atlantic must have been hard to resist when their children hung about Grace as golden chains, shackling her to a life more lived in the domestic sphere than the romantic. In the words of Billy Ocean, *When the going gets tough, the tough get going.* And Anthony had gone. Unfortunately, as far as Grace was concerned, he had decided to return, but that was another story.

At lunchtime, Paul arrived at the office, announcing that he wanted to take her for a drive. Byron and Nancy were consulted to see if it was convenient, but her colleagues were sinking into individual sulks.

Paul and Grace perfected a synchronised rictus smile as they waved through the window. Paul was parked outside.

"Where are we going?" Grace asked.

"Wait and see."

It soon became apparent that they were heading out of town and up into the hills.

"We're going to look at Rex Glyn's house, aren't we?" Grace announced.

"That's right." Paul smiled, lightly patting her right arm. "Indulge me. I had an idea when you were asleep."

"When was that? I was awake for half the night. Pregnancy doesn't suit me."

"Too late now," he laughed, kissing her hand.

When they turned into the drive at Long Acres, a familiar car was spotted, parked outside the house.

"That's lover boy's car, isn't it? Don't tell me you've arranged to meet Stephen Samson." Aware that her shoulders were beginning to reach up to her ears, Grace took a deep breath and tried to relax. "I must try and like him if Sarah decides to stick with it. I keep thinking she'll get bored or the scales will fall from her eyes."

She realised that she was mostly talking to herself. Paul seemed distracted as he reversed into the space beside Stephen's car.

"What? Don't go biblical on me. What's he doing here, anyway?"

As they emerged from the vehicle, they were greeted with excessive enthusiasm.

"Grace! Paul!" Stephen's heartiness sprang from his business persona, a barking laugh serving as punctuation between the two names. Fleetingly, Grace felt sorry for him. He looked ill at ease in spite of his bravado.

A buzzard swooped over the field next door, its broad wings spread wide as it called for its mate. For a moment, all three watched the bird as it soared high into the grey winter sky. Paul broke the silence.

"So, what's your interest in Long Acres?"

Stephen was evasive. "Just keeping my options open. You know me – always eager to extend my portfolio."

"Ah."

"And you?" Stephen asked.

"I wondered if Grace could imagine living here."

Grace knew that Paul would have preferred to share his thoughts with her alone.

"And can she?" Stephen asked, looking at Grace.

She took in the outline of the solid old house. She smiled. "You know what? I think she, I mean, I could."

Before Stephen made his excuses and left, he said, "Of course, it's quite possible that it won't be up for sale. I heard from someone who was at the funeral that the house has been left to the… what was it? The Equity Charitable Trust. It helps out actors in financial difficulties – I think that's what he said." He stared into the distance. "And I heard that Olivia inherited his fortune." Stephen looked up at the house. "I expect the old place will need a lot of work. Not a project to be taken on lightly." His parting shot was, "May the best man win!"

"I really don't think that Stephen is as awful as he tries to be," Paul remarked. "Back in the day, we'd just say that the man was a prick, but I suppose now we would say that he is tainted with *toxic masculinity.*" Their laughter joined with the buzzard's call as they walked hand in hand to the field that sloped away from the house with a distant view of the sea.

"I never thought I'd want to move or get married again. Not my thing, that's what I always said." Grace sounded wistful.

Paul apologised. "I'm so sorry to have put you on the spot back there. I couldn't think of an answer when Stephen asked me about Long Acres."

Grace smiled. "No apology needed. And Stephen hasn't had any bearing on my answer. You know I wouldn't pretend if I didn't fancy living here." She paused. "And I wouldn't be marrying you, either, if it didn't feel like the right thing to do."

Paul nodded. "Oh, I know that for sure." He gently tucked a lock of blond hair behind her ear as he scanned her face for answers. "I hope I haven't jumped the gun," Paul said. "But I've put the house in Felixstowe on the market. I only rented it out as a temporary measure, just to make sure that I could settle in Wales. Now we're getting married, I thought it would be a good idea to have a new start, especially now that the baby is due. What do you think?"

Grace was annoyed to discover that tears had inexplicably sprung to her eyes and she didn't trust herself to speak. *Bloody hormones*, she thought. It was difficult to put into words how she felt, so she kissed him instead.

"I don't want to get your hopes up. The old man might have left the house to this Actors' Trust with a view to it being used for – I don't know – maybe a retirement home for old thesps. God! Imagine what that would be like of an evening, with them all trying to outdo one another at charades. And what about the name-dropping? Doesn't bear thinking of. But if Long Acres does come on the market, we'll try and go for it, shall we? You should be able to find out about this, shouldn't you?"

Grace considered for a moment. "I might pop round and have a word with the solicitor Rex Glyn was using. I know who it is. I saw her when I was leaving the house after a valuation and she was arriving to talk to him."

Paul surveyed the field stretching before them. "We could grow vegetables!" he said with enthusiasm.

Less enthusiastically, she replied, "Do we have to?"

Paul laughed.

Rex Glyn had gone for a low-maintenance look, favouring trees and shrubs that looked after themselves while he was away living in London. Grace closed her eyes and imagined growing wisteria, roses and lavender hedges. "We're getting ahead of ourselves, aren't we?" she said as she opened them again.

The buzzard had found its mate; circling one another with fanned tails, they flew above the man and woman who stood in front of Long Acres.

Chapter 44

Maxine was worried about money. It was such a relief to be offered a temporary position in the main supermarket in town but she was anxious about whether she would continue to be employed after Christmas. There was no time for brooding about Rex when she sat on the till or stacked up the shelves. She used to like Christmas carols but now that they were piped, jingling into the airways continuously, only interrupted when it was announced that someone was needed at a particular checkout, they were beginning to lose their appeal.

And she was wearied by the excessive spending, particularly on primary-coloured plastic toys, hideous oversized stuffed animals, chocolates encased in gold frippery and enough cans of drink to unman an army for at least a month. Women seemed to age years, blighted by a siege mentality, panic buying. It was a masochistic aspiration to want the impossibly perfect Christmas glimpsed in glossy publications, with thin, beautiful people sporting perfect hair and wearing immaculate clothes. In front of a glittering tree, they gathered round photogenic tables groaning with photogenic food, unwrapping photogenic presents, euphoria captured on every flawless face.

Maxine tried not to think about the previous year when she had helped Rex to decorate a massive Christmas tree. It was so big that it blocked out the winter light that usually filtered through the tall window to the left of the front door. She had climbed up a stepladder to put the star at the top and tie the glass baubles on the upper branches. As ever, he liked to take command of the situation from the comfort of a safe distance, sitting down. "Up a bit, left a bit; there, that's it!" He had a glass of mulled wine in his right hand – *for medicinal purposes* – and a cigar in the other. Music from a CD of the top-Christmas-songs-ever variety played in the background.

When she had finished, Rex stubbed out his cigar as Maxine climbed down the stepladder and took his outstretched hand. They stepped back a couple of paces to admire her handiwork and in a strangled falsetto, he repeated Tiny Tim's words from *A Christmas Carol*, "God bless us, everyone!" Of course he said it with heavy irony, as was his way, but they laughed as one and it was a few seconds before they stepped apart. "We've done a good job, there, haven't we?" he said, gesturing at the tree.

"We? You haven't lifted a finger, Rex!" she replied. Such episodes recalled now were agony and yet, in the knowledge that they were fleeting, had a profound significance.

Her memories could not be spoiled by disappointment. It was, however, like a further bereavement when she realised that she had been overlooked in his Will. It wasn't so much about the money, although Lord knows she could have done with it, it was the fact that others might think she meant so little to him that bothered her. Her sister had been sympathetic but also furious on her behalf. "All that time you worked for him! The shit! I told you not to spend so much time up there. I told you!"

Maxine hadn't received a legal letter as his niece had done. She wondered if she might ring the solicitor to check if there had been an oversight but couldn't face the humiliation of hearing from a stranger that there had been no provision made for her. Worse, she might learn that he had left her one of those dreadful film posters as he had Tiffany. The young woman had called her and ranted for a bit until Maxine had put down the telephone.

When she heard on the grapevine that Olivia had inherited Rex's money, the news had floored her. The pretty florist hadn't loved him. In fact, you could see that she was irritated by his silliness when he bowed and scraped before her. You would think that a man of his age would no longer be susceptible to a teenage crush.

Maxine felt that she and Rex had been like a long-married, bickering couple; they were kin, yet he had left her with nothing. That was the difficult truth. In spite of all those years of Maxine looking after him, it was Olivia who received the money, even though she did her best to restrict any interaction with the man to the briefest chat.

"Speed up, Maxine!" It was her manager, a jovial middle-aged man, whose girth challenged the elasticity of the supermarket uniform. Maxine looked along the line of shoppers. It stretched halfway down the store and not one of the faces before her wore a smile.

"I'm doing my best," she replied. "Isn't it time I got a break?"

He looked at his watch. "Not yet. Maybe in another half an hour." As he squeezed in front of her to stack up the carrier bags, a waft of aftershave and chewing gum enclosed her. It wasn't an unpleasant smell but instinctively she recoiled. When he emerged, he was perspiring, red in the face and smiling. He patted her on the shoulder as he walked away.

It was always the same in work as in life – never the right time to get a break.

Chapter 45

Barbara knocked on Frank's door. She had got into the habit of collecting him on the way to dinner, since their cabins were on the same corridor and she passed his room on the way to the lift.

Several days had passed since his confession. Barbara had sat in Frank's cabin, uncomfortably perched on the dressing-table stool as he settled himself on the edge of the bed before telling his tale. His speech was halting and there were innumerable interruptions from Barbara, who insisted he spoke in the third person as if he were describing a friend. "He went into the garden shed and found cigarettes in a drawer." Barbara's thinking was that should she be questioned, then she could truthfully answer that he had never admitted to anything. She told him that no one would question her anyway because she lived thousands of miles away from South Wales, UK. But still.

Frank kept reverting to the first person. "I didn't mean to set the house alight, I was just disposing of the cigarette."

"Your friend – shall we call him Jim? – didn't mean to set the house alight. He was just disposing of the cigarette."

When eventually Frank had said all that needed to be said and was sprawled out, exhausted, on the bed, Barbara did a summing-up.

"Now let's see. Jim had a grudge against the famous actor Rex Glyn. It was understandable, given the thoughtlessness of the actor, beating Jim down when it came to buying Jim's house and also being a heel in an article in the paper about Jim and his wife.

"Jim felt that after his wife's death, he should get an apology from the actor. Jim had reacted badly to the republishing of the newspaper article, when Rex had put the house on the market himself. Jim had ended up in hospital but had recovered and booked a holiday, thinking that he needed to get away, but on impulse drove up to Rex Glyn's house to get a long-overdue apology.

"Rex Glyn had answered the door but dismissed Jim, thinking he was begging for money for a charity or something. Jim didn't know what to do. He ended up sheltering in the shed and found a cigarette and lit it to calm his nerves.

"Jim did the right thing and didn't stub the cigarette out in the shed. He put it in the outside bin and drove off home."

Barbara was standing as she did the summing-up. Her husband had been a lawyer and wondered if she was channelling his ability to put together the main points of the story. She used a softer voice now as she sat back on the dressing-table stool.

"Jim might be done for trespass, but he could never be prosecuted for murder."

Frank sat up. "But I, sorry, Jim had means, motive and opportunity. He was angry and wanted to kill the bastard Rex Glyn."

Barbara said, "Honey, whose side are you on? The point is, Jim didn't kill the actor Rex Glyn. His death was an accident." She got up. "Now I want you to be honest. Can I safely leave you, only I'm God-awful tired? You must make sure that if I come and knock on your door before breakfast tomorrow, you will be alive and well. I'm an old lady and deserve some respect. If you rush out and throw yourself off this ship, it will totally ruin my vacation."

Frank apologised. "I've burdened you with my, sorry, Jim's story. Forgive me."

"Don't go all stiff and British on me. What time do you get breakfast?"

"Between eight and eight thirty. Why?"

"Jeez! That early? I usually go at nine. Okay, I'll pick you up at eight thirty tomorrow."

Frank straightened his back as he repositioned himself on the bed. "I'm not asking you to take care of me."

"Who says I'm gonna do that?" She got up again and walked into the shower room.

"Hey! What are you doing? Surely a man is entitled to some privacy."

"Just checking the contents of your sponge bag. Don't want you to have the means to top yourself." She emerged triumphant, having had a rummage through his toiletries. "You're gonna be just fine. We might have a chat sometime about your digestive tract. Pills for constipation *and* diarrhoea? Something's not right there."

In spite of himself, Frank laughed.

"See you tomorrow – eight thirty." She turned and waved at the door. "See ya, Frank." And then she was gone.

They had spent most of their days together since then. But now there was no reply when she knocked on the door of his cabin.

Barbara felt herself breathing fast. Was there anything to suggest that Frank has decided to kill himself after all? She cast her mind back to the conversation they had had in the lounge bar the previous night as the resident pianist played Gershwin's 'Rhapsody in Blue' in the background. Frank had requested it for Barbara. Gershwin was the only American composer that he could think of.

"Have you ever thought that there's no point in going on, now that your husband has gone?" That's what he had said as he sipped his rum and Coke.

And she had said, "Maybe I did at first, but I had the children and the grandchildren to think about. That's what has saved me." She thought for a moment and then continued. "My husband and I loved one another but we weren't joined at the hip."

Perhaps she shouldn't have talked about other family members, given that she knew that he had no children or grandchildren of his own. But he was perfectly okay at the end of the evening when she left him at his cabin. He'd even made a joke about it being a novelty, being walked home by a woman.

No, surely he wouldn't kill himself? But what if he were actually dead behind the door, from natural causes? All of the big boats were fitted out with an impressive range of facilities – swimming pools, spa facilities, theatres and casinos – but the brochures tended not to boast about a ship having an on-board morgue. It was an unsettling fact that it was frequently occupied by the end of the holiday.

"Frank!" she shouted as she banged louder on the door. "Frank! Answer the door!"

January

Chapter 46

As weddings go, it was an unremarkable affair. The dress the bride wore was something that Grace had found in the back of the wardrobe, unworn, complete with tags from a Monsoon sale, purchased when Sarah used to work there. It had been a bit big for Grace when she had bought it but was perfect now that she was pregnant. It was cream and sparkly, an impulse purchase and an absolute steal. She had been unsure when she might have the occasion for wearing it. Mid-length and with an empire waist, it skimmed over her emerging bump and she teamed it with a pair of cream court shoes last worn at Nancy's wedding some years ago. Sarah pinned up her mother's hair with a silver slide. The groom wore his best suit and fanciest tie.

Their children dressed up but would not have graced the pages of *Hello* magazine, choosing not to wear colour-coordinated outfits. Sarah had bought some flowers at the market, not brave enough to return to the florist's shop and face Olivia. With her newly acquired floristry skills, she had made buttonholes to match her mother's flowers, which were cream and white roses and carnations, secured in a slightly wonky posy, also Sarah's handiwork.

Grace and Paul sang out their vows, which echoed in the largely uninhabited chapel. Nobody dropped the rings or stumbled over their words.

The boys were responsible for the music. They had thought it was a great joke when, at the end of the ceremony, Etta James's '*At Last*' blasted out.

"You smiled, you smiled,
Oh and then the smile was cast.
And here we are in heaven
For you are mine
At last."

Back at the house, they opened bottles of champagne and beer. The kitchen table had been covered in a white cloth, usually reserved for Christmas. Sarah had picked some holly from the garden and put it in a vase with trailing ivy.

Wesley wore his smartest collar, a bright red number, and thumped his tail wholeheartedly on the kitchen floor. Always a sensitive dog, he picked up on the general good cheer.

The groom disappeared for half an hour and no one questioned his absence, but his was an enthusiastic reception when he returned with parcels of fish and chips. There was minimal screen time at the table. The only squabbling during the meal was, as usual, over the varying size of the portions, nature not having yet perfected the production of equal-sized fish.

After they had eaten, everyone managed to suppress a groan when Paul said that he wanted to say a few words.

The family were less restrained when he began with, "My wife and I…" But he persevered.

"My wife and I want to thank you for being here. Without you, the day would have been a bit flat."

"Charming!" Grace exclaimed as she removed the silver slide from her hair. "Not the words a bride wants to hear on her wedding day!"

He took her hand. "You know what I mean, Grace. We wanted to get married but by joining together, we recognise that our families are officially joined too. Thank God you seem to get on."

There was a cacophony of cheering and banging on the table from the small gathering.

"I want to say that we are fortunate to have this new start. We are fortunate to have met and fallen in love. We are so fortunate to be looking forward to the birth of our new baby." Tears glittered in his eyes. "I'll stop now. Just to say, thank you, Grace, for everything. And now I want to toast everyone here today!" He raised his glass. "To our family!"

"To our family!" was repeated.

Betty, next door, had given herself an excuse to go out into the garden. The bird feeder was almost full but she topped it up anyway, scaring away the blue tits that were happily pecking away before her unwelcome arrival. She made her way to the fence between the two houses, where she stood shivering, head tilted, like an elderly spaniel. She smiled when she picked up the three simple words shouted by her neighbours and went inside to tell her husband what she had heard.

Chapter 47

Maxine had no work after Christmas. She could cover her rental costs for January, but was uncertain about the future. Enough rain fell to swell the rivers and saturate the land. She made herself go out every morning and walk around the town for half an hour as water from the sky mingled with her tears. She sheltered in the covered shopping centre, walking past the supermarket where she had worked and further to the indoor market, where she did a brisk circuit without buying anything. Then she would retrace her steps.

One morning, she made the mistake of stopping momentarily outside a jeweller and caught a glimpse of the selection of engagement rings. Who knew there was such a choice? White gold and traditional coloured bands with all sorts of gems tempted, but diamonds dominated, sitting on fat white velvet pads. They came in different shapes and sizes. There were square-cut, round-cut, diamonds cut in pear shapes or even in the shape of a heart. She allowed herself to choose what she might have had – a square solitaire; not the biggest gem but sparkling merrily in the centre of the display. Shaking her head, she continued walking back to the flat, trying not to cry. *What would Rex say*, she thought, *of this counterfeit person, so mired in misery?*

Maxine was worried about heating costs and, after shaking her coat out in the hall at the bottom of the stairs, she draped it over the cold radiator in her sitting room. She put on another jumper and switched on the television. With the odds stacked against ever owning her own property, Maxine quickly dismissed *Homes Under the Hammer.*

She muted the television when a yelp was heard from downstairs. What was her neighbour up to now? Maxine looked down from her landing to see Penelope sitting on the bottom step, legs akimbo as she rubbed at her right knee. Quickly, she rushed to the woman's aid.

"What happened?"

"I tripped on the stairs when I was dusting!" She glared at Maxine. It was implied that the accident was her neighbour's fault. It was a definite possibility that the backless slippers Penelope wore might have contributed to the accident, but sensibly Maxine remained tight-lipped. She managed to help her up and they staggered together to Penelope's front door, which was opened, and they picked their way to the sofa.

Maxine had never crossed the threshold of her neighbour's place before and it was something of a revelation. The woman was a collector of a myriad things. China elephants were herded together on one shelf; unicorns clustered below. There was a wall covered in wooden Welsh love spoons; painted jugs were crammed on a dresser; brass objects were balancing on the window ledge; china dogs of varying sizes dwelled in a silent pack on a side table.

"Goodness!" Maxine exclaimed. She straightened up. "You do have a lot of things!"

"What of it?" snarled Penelope. "They keep me company."

"Sorry, I didn't mean… I just meant you have some lovely trinkets." Maxine knew that her lie was unconvincing but she mustn't be rude.

"You do know that if you turned your hand to doing the job once in a while, then I wouldn't have banged my knee. It's all right for some, having a fancy job in a big house with a film star, but we can't all be so lucky."

Maxine looked at the injured woman before her, oozing resentment from every pore. How dare she mention Rex to her in this way? Maxine was tempted to leave without saying a word but had sufficient empathy to realise that her neighbour was unhappy and her way of dealing with sadness was to lash out.

The only thing to do was to apologise and make an effort to help out in future. She offered to ring the doctor's surgery for advice but Penelope wanted to be left alone. The rotund knee appeared visibly swollen. Maxine suggested she get some ice cubes from the fridge and wrap them in a tea towel to act as a cold compress.

Grudgingly, as if Penelope were doing Maxine a favour rather than the other way round, she pointed her in the direction of the kitchen, not that Maxine needed directions; the flat was identical to her own.

The kitchen was similarly stuffed with unnecessary objects. Maxine had never seen anyone visit Penelope, and yet there were dozens of mugs – mugs decorated with every animal and flower you could imagine.

At first sight, she glimpsed dogs, cats, rabbits, horses, sheep, meerkats, lions, tigers, roses, camellias, daffodils and tulips. Multi-coloured tea towels and tea cosies were pinned to a wall. Daniel Craig, bare-chested, oiled and muscular in swimming shorts opposite, had the misfortune to stare at them forever more from an astonishingly large black and white photograph.

The kitchen table was obscured by magazines with screeching headlines of the *My Mother Slept with my Boyfriend* variety. Post and a collection of coupons and vouchers were stacked beside them, with multiple books of stamps.

Maxine bent down to the freezer compartment and looked around for a tea towel that she could actually use. She opened a couple of drawers, finding the cutlery first and then another containing old envelopes. Third time lucky, she found one, folded and neatly ironed, emblazoned with pictures of a Rottweiler insufficiently pretty, she supposed, to merit a position in the tea towel gallery above. She wrapped up the ice cubes and was on her way back to the living room, when something prompted her to open the second drawer again. Was she imagining it or had she just read her name on the envelope on top of the pile? She was sleep-deprived and wearied from grief. Was she losing her mind as well?

When Maxine opened the drawer a second time, she saw it: an official-looking envelope, and she was right – it was addressed to her. The envelope was removed and underneath was a postcard from her sister who had holidayed in Turkey the previous summer. Underneath that were birthday and Christmas cards. Maxine scooped up her post but didn't know what to do with it. Had she the energy for an argument?

"What are you doing in there?" called Penelope.

"Coming," replied Maxine. Holding her post in one hand and the cold compress in the other, she returned and knelt beside her neighbour to apply the pack to her swollen knee. Penelope flinched when she felt the ice melting through the cotton towel.

"Can I do anything else for you?" Maxine asked with studied politeness as she stood up. Penelope shook her head. "I had to get a new tea towel out of the drawer and came across my post."

Penelope flushed an angry red. Before the woman had a chance to speak, Maxine continued. "Thanks for looking after it for me." She spoke as if it were a routine habit to pick up letters from her neighbour. Maxine glimpsed silver fillings as Penelope's mouth fell open. "But in future, just leave them on the table, would you?" It was a small triumph but Maxine felt surprisingly energised when she closed her neighbour's door, the sound of Penelope's feeble, "I never touched the bills or anything like that," following her out into the hall.

Chapter 48

The cruise was over. *Sydney and Treasures of the South Pacific* had been explored and the passengers were all disembarking, apart from the elderly man who was stored in the ship's morgue. He had what the doctors referred to as *existing health conditions*, but his death came as a shock to the other guests who were used to him sitting at their table at meal times. No one liked to ask about the circumstances of his death. Black humour countered depression, but those in poorer health were on heightened alert, expecting the grim reaper to put in another surprise appearance.

Barbara felt as though she had morphed into a different woman from the one who had walked up the gangplank in November. For one thing, she had met Frank. She would miss him. As she disembarked the ship, she had a ridiculous desire to run back. If only she could relive the last few weeks.

She didn't want to go home. The previous year, her best friend, Tammy, suggested that they both went on the holiday together, but she backed out when they had to pay the balance owing on the trip. For a while, Tammy had been flirting with the idea of online dating and soon she was actually flirting. Having met a silver fox from New Orleans, she had no interest in being Barbara's companion on the cruise. Barbara had considered abandoning her holiday plans but she was damned if she was going to lose her deposit and she was no quitter.

For a while, it was awkward joining tables of couples; perhaps she was over-sensitive but it seemed that every time someone spoke to her, they were doing her a favour. Glass flutes chinked and eye contact was maintained as everyone shouted, "Cheers!" at the beginning of the meal and, by the time that coffee was served, those either side of Barbara were generally engaged in lively conversation, but sadly not with her. She met a few single folk. A very jolly British spinster was keen to tie her down to being a regular friend but Barbara found that they had nothing in common. Having endured a very detailed description of how a crocheted shawl had been made for a neighbour's baby grandson and the rapturous reception when it was received, Barbara knew that she had to concoct an escape plan.

She had spotted Frank from afar. He was always smartly dressed, not cut out for casual wear and usually to be found in the lounge, where he read by a window. She observed his habits, worked out the times he ate and was fortunate to catch the stranger in reception, booking up a trip. She stood behind him, listened to what he told the receptionist and when he had gone, altered her booking so that they would be on the same tour. When she saw how emotional he became, standing below the Sydney Opera House, she was intrigued. Barbara, a compassionate woman, recognised that he needed help. Could she cheer him up?

Frank was no piece of cake, that was for sure, but they had bonded over mutual interests and shared secrets. Barbara had admitted to him that, although she missed her late husband, when they were constantly in one another's company, she found him to be critical and demanding. The marriage had succeeded because he worked long hours and was a fan of racquet sports. When he retired, the desire to transform the garden drove him on. He could be very boring indeed about begonias.

For all the drama about so-called murdering the actor guy, Frank was a decent man. And despite the heartache, her holiday had certainly turned out to be more exciting than if she had spent it swapping crochet patterns with the British spinster.

As she descended the stairs, she began to smile. Her luggage was clearly visible, stacked up on a trolley. She had treated herself to a brand-new set of cases in a bright red colour.

And there he was – Frank, waving to her, his luggage on one side of him, Barbara's on the other. He turned away for a moment to reposition a suitcase that threatened to fall from another woman's trolley. The sagging posture and air of bewilderment marked the lady as the widow of the poor man who was awaiting repatriation, having had a heart attack a week or so ago.

Barbara flushed, still embarrassed, reflecting on her behaviour that morning, banging on Frank's door when she couldn't get an answer. Frank was a stickler for timekeeping and, when she had been a little late that particular day, he had strode off to the dining room without her. She had insisted that an announcement was made to try and locate him and, just as she had managed to persuade a steward to open the cabin, Frank appeared, frowning and understandably irritated that he had been forced to abandon his fried breakfast. "Barbara, why are you trying to break down my door?"

It was a reasonable question but she avoided answering it by linking his arm with hers and walking with him, following the busily patterned carpet that took them to the dining room.

"I'm not going to top myself!" he announced rather loudly as they got into the lift. A woman in a pink kaftan turned her head to see who was speaking as she walked past. The doors shut and Frank continued, "Don't you worry about that. I've felt much better since I told you all about my worries."

And now here they were, about to be parted. They wheeled their trolleys from the holding place into the world outside. Neither spoke. As they stepped into the sunshine, they were confronted with an endless row of coaches to spirit the passengers away. The holiday had ended.

The smell of diesel fumes engulfed Frank and Barbara as they stood rooted to the pavement. Wheelchairs and luggage were swiftly manoeuvred around them as they remained there, unwilling to move, although clearly in the way of others.

It was as if an unknown deity had taken up remote control. The action was no longer suspended and the volume was cranked up. Frank shouted over the din.

"Well, this is it. Thank you for your company." He stuck out his hand. "I enjoyed the cruise."

Barbara might have shaken the proffered hand, turned and walked away, given the stiffness and formality of Frank's words, but the tone was uncertain and his face was suffused with sadness.

"You foolish man!" Barbara exclaimed. "I'm not going to let you go like that."

Frank's facial expression turned to alarm.

Barbara laughed. "Don't look so scared. I'm not after romance. But I'd like to stay in touch." She scrabbled in her purse for a piece of paper. "My details – email, phone number, address."

"But we live so far apart," Frank said.

Barbara withdrew the note.

"Would you mind getting out of the way?" The voice belonged to a man dressed in cream linen slacks and a panama hat.

Frank and Barbara pushed their trolleys out of his path and watched as the holidaymaker proceeded, dragging his matching, expensive-looking luggage behind him.

"The last of the bloody Raj," Frank muttered.

Barbara's name was called.

"I've got to go, Frank." She turned from him. It was her turn to look distressed.

"No, wait! Give me the note!"

"But you don't see the point of it." She started to move away.

"I do, I do." Frank fiddled with the bags on his trolley before looking up at Barbara's retreating figure." We'll be holiday companions," he shouted.

"What's that?"

"Ever been to Cuba?"

"Hell, no."

"That's where we'll go next, or maybe, I don't know, the Caribbean?"

Barbara suddenly understood. "Vacation buddies!"

Her name was called again.

"Vacation buddies!" Frank repeated. Then, abandoning his trolley, he ran after her and took the note, crushed in Barbara's hand.

"Frank Whitehead!" shouted a bus driver, whose vehicle was situated in a nearby bay. There was only time for the briefest of hugs before they went their separate ways.

As Frank settled on to the bus, he took out his phone and entered Barbara's details in case he lost the piece of paper. He was determined to back it both ways, folding the paper until it was small enough to store in his wallet. He patted it shut with a smile. "Vacation buddies," he said to himself once more.

Chapter 49

Maxine, energised by her altercation with her neighbour Penelope, put on the kettle and made a pot of tea. It was a soothing ritual and one that she had shared with Rex. Then she turned her attention to her post. Some of the Christmas cards weren't even addressed to Maxine but belonged to the previous tenant. The writer couldn't have been in contact with the intended recipient for a very long time. The message was intriguing too.

Hope that trouble you had with the neighbour got sorted and you got the boiler fixed. The landlord sounds like a right piece of work.

All the best for the New Year.

Jay xx

Perhaps Penelope had pinched the post from other people too. That was quite comforting, if the theft wasn't driven by personal dislike. Maxine got on all right with the landlord; he was obsessed about condensation and the need to open windows, but he seemed straightforward. Having said that, Maxine had always paid the rent on time. Anxiety gnawed at her insides as she imagined broaching the topic of lack of funds.

The postcard from Turkey revealed a deserted sandy bay with a wooden boardwalk stretching to the sea. What looked like four-poster beds, draped with white linen curtains, were positioned in rows, facing the ocean. The photographer must have got up at sunrise to take the shot. Presumably the beach was normally crammed with holidaymakers.

Maxine turned it over. Her sister's handwriting was as familiar as her own.

Dear Sis,

Having a great time. The sun shines all day, the food is great, glad I went for the all-inclusive. Haven't spent any money because all the entertainment is free.

Wish you had come with me. Honestly! You're so stupid about Rex bloody Glyn! As soon as he decides to visit Wales, you drop everything! Sorry – we've had this conversation.

It's lovely here, really relaxing. Nothing is too much trouble for the staff. One of the waiters is lush. I'll tell you all about it when I get home.

Maxine found that she was smiling. Good God! Her sister was as good as her word. No detail was spared of the romantic adventures she had with Aydin. One of those four-poster beds on the beach had featured in their first sexual encounter – after dark, following a naked swim in the sea. He was half her sister's age, but Maxine wondered how he had the stamina, given the long hours he worked. After the holiday, money had been sent from Pontardeilo to Bodrum every month for nearly a year, until he sent an email to the wrong woman. It turned out that there was another generous benefactor called Judith. Who was the stupid one, then?

Penelope had been telling the truth. No bill had been taken from Maxine's correspondence as far as she could see. She binned the Christmas cards and the postcard. She didn't want her sister being reminded of Aydin if she popped round.

She turned her attention to the envelope. Penelope had sliced at it with a knife. Maxine was surprised that she didn't steam it open like they did on all the murder mysteries. The letter inside was written on headed notepaper. It was from Rex Glyn's solicitor.

Maxine read it twice, in case she had misunderstood something. It did not reveal what Rex had left her. Gazing round the flat, she tried to imagine one of the film posters staring at her from the wall. The swashbuckling hero was at odds with her Rex, the man she knew. If she did get a poster, it would keep her company, she supposed, but then she made a connection with the woman living downstairs, gazing up at the photograph of Daniel Craig as darkness fell. Were she and Penelope exactly the same, lusting after glamorous film stars? It made Maxine want to weep again.

Ever practical, Maxine focused on the financial implications of the legal letter. Maybe there was some jewellery coming her way, but it was unlikely. She'd never seen any. Rex's mother was not a wealthy woman and anything she might have had would surely have been left to Rex's sister, Marilyn. Rex's watch didn't just reveal the time – it was flashy, the movements of selected planets as they orbit the sun, replicated in semi-precious stones. It might be worth a bit. There would be no qualms about selling it. Only the wealthy could afford to be sentimental and if she wanted to learn about astronomy, she could look up at the sky at night. There was an urgent need for ready cash. Maxine did not allow herself to imagine that there would be a large sum of money awaiting collection but rang the solicitor immediately to arrange an appointment.

As Maxine approached the solicitor's office, she nearly bumped into Grace Palmer, who was walking towards her while looking at messages on her phone. Maxine was surprised to see that in spite of wearing a loose-fitting coat, the woman looked pregnant; she had learned a long time ago that if there was any chance of being mistaken, it would be best not to mention it.

Grace looked up. "Hello," she said, blue eyes conveying sympathy and concern. "How are you? I was so sorry to hear that you had lost your employer and friend, Rex Glyn."

It was kindness that prompted tears. Penelope's nastiness had failed to wound, but the fact that the estate agent acknowledged her friendship with the film star, left Maxine blinking away tears. She wasn't being dismissed as an irrelevance, a footnote on a payroll. At some point, surely, the tears must dry up.

Maxine flushed, remembering that she had been abrupt, bordering on rude, when the woman had called to value Long Acres. It had been a difficult time, Rex defying the rules of life and especially death by flinging himself at any woman who entered his realm. Grace Palmer looked away as Maxine scrabbled for a tissue from her jeans pocket and blew her nose.

"Thank you." Maxine's reply was muted. She was fearful that she might howl in the street if she elaborated on how she had felt about him. "I'm sorry if I wasn't very friendly when you called at the house. The thing is that I knew how ill he was and could see that it wasn't the right time to embark on selling Long Acres." She changed the subject. "Were you just coming out of the solicitor's office?"

It was Grace's turn to look uncomfortable. "Ah, yes. Sometimes there are hiccups with house sales," she said vaguely. There had been no joy, finding out about Long Acres. She quickly moved on to another topic of conversation. "I could tell that you were finding the situation difficult, as anybody would. No need to apologise."

She excused herself, but added, “From my own experience, I would say that you cannot predict how long it will take to feel better, but you will recover, honestly.”

As she turned to go, Grace unconsciously cradled her unborn child as she remembered the baby she had lost. Maxine noticed the movement. Grace Palmer *was* pregnant, then.

Chapter 50

The estate agent hurried back to the office. Nancy was experimenting with ear cuffs for January and wore them with panache. Faux diamonds glinted as she threw back her head to laugh. She and Byron were busily engaged in polishing the desks, duster in one hand, a can of Pledge in the other. Byron was breaking into a bit of a sweat, red-faced, as he embraced the task, jacket abandoned and waistcoat undone. Grace caught the end of what Byron was saying, haltingly, as he caught his breath. "As I said to Nigel, Jean's renovations are costing more than the house did when we originally bought it. And now, God help us, we're revamping the cloakroom and utility room."

Recently, Nigel had been identified by name. He was no longer referred to as "my friend from the rugby club". Now, most of Byron's conversation was stippled with bright splashes of colour; whatever the topic, Nigel's character, interests and abilities, appeared to be relevant.

Grace was reminded of the weather houses she had seen in Austria, Alpine miniature chalets that revealed whether it was wet or dry. Two doors nestled beneath the roof; when the weather was rainy, the man appeared from the right and when it was sunny, the woman appeared from the left. In Byron's case, the genders were reversed: whenever Nigel was referenced, Byron was bathed in sunshine and whenever Jean got a mention, he seemed to have a metaphorical cloud above his head.

Nancy turned her attention to Grace, putting down her

can of polish. "Before we started talking about Byron's home improvements, we were talking about what happens when you go on maternity leave."

Grace took her coat off and hung it up. She was feeling self-conscious in a loose-fitting navy smock and maternity trousers and was glad to hide behind her newly polished desk. "Oh yes?" she replied cautiously.

"Well, you won't be able to go out and do valuations, will you?"

"No, I don't suppose I will."

"I thought perhaps I could do it. I've been wanting to for ages."

"That doesn't seem to be a problem, does it, Byron?"

Byron shook his head as he blotted his face with an immaculately folded handkerchief.

"I've also been thinking," Grace continued. "Do you think you could work with Sarah?" Grace's daughter had made sprawling on the sofa into an art form, one arm dangling on the floor, her hand occasionally dipping into a bowl of giant chocolate buttons. Grace had said rather testily, "If you're going to stay still in the same place, you might as well volunteer to be an artist's model at the college. At least then, you'll be paid for lounging about."

It was Sarah's belief that she was unemployable, having dropped out of university and been fired by Olivia. Floristry wasn't going to be her forever job but at least it gave her a purpose. Stephen had suggested that she should work in one of his hotels. Grace had almost said, "For God's sake, don't do that," when Sarah confided in her. But Sarah had continued, "The thing is, Mum, what if we split up? That would be another dodgy mark on my CV."

In the estate agent's, Nancy played dumb. "Sarah?"

"My Sarah."

Nancy started to play with the buttons of her zebra-print shirt that matched the pattern on her boots. "You're not going to make me answer to Sarah?" While smoothing the contours of her black trousers, she looked up, her expression defiant.

Grace understood. Nancy had felt undervalued for too long. "Of course not," she said. "I rather thought she could learn from you."

Sarah was unaware of her mother's efforts to secure her employment. Some of her friends had the future all mapped out. As far as Sarah was concerned, there was no map. What was she going to do with her life? A girl she had met during Freshers' Week sent her pictures of scenes that struck her as remote as a posting from Peru. Peru was one of the places she fancied visiting but she wouldn't want to live there. It was like that with university – worth a look but essentially strange and unfamiliar. Even so, although she would never admit it, sometimes Sarah wondered if she had been too hasty, running away from college. Life viewed from the comfort of your own sofa was reassuringly familiar but the monotony of it sapped the spark within her soul.

But if she hadn't come home, then she wouldn't have met Stephen. Of course, her mother would have been glad of that. It didn't help that he was determined to press on and buy Long Acres if it came on to the market, even though she pointed out that Grace and Paul wanted it.

"Why do you want to piss them off?" she asked. "Can't you just step away?"

His answer was defensive. "They hate me. It makes no difference what I do, so I might as well please myself."

"But what about me? Don't you care that it makes it so difficult for me at home?"

The intensity of his gaze disturbed her. "You don't get it, do you? I want the house for both of us, to live together and raise a family."

"But Mum's the one having a baby!" How childish she had sounded. He had tried to kiss her and she had pushed him away. The door slammed as he let himself out.

Chapter 51

There was no need to wait at the solicitor's office. Maxine was ushered straight in, to be seated in a modest-sized room, dominated by a battered-looking, leather-topped desk and three chairs, two upright ones on Maxine's side and a more comfortable swivel one on the other. There was a trailing spider plant in a macramé holder that hung from the ceiling behind the solicitor, a rather hopeless gesture to breathe life into the cold and gloom. Maxine sat in one of the upright seats, keeping her padded jacket on. She noted the single-glazed window behind the solicitor, who sat with her back to it, in the North-facing room. It occurred to Maxine that there would be howling draughts when the wind blew.

The young woman seated in front of Maxine seemed impervious to the cold, wearing a white cotton, crisply ironed shirt above a businesslike skirt. Maxine thought that she looked a little like Kate Middleton, with well-behaved hair that fell prettily on to her slim shoulders. Pleasantries were exchanged. It had been a pleasure to meet Rex; likewise, it had been a pleasure to work for him. That wasn't strictly true, but there was no need for clarification. Maxine explained that her neighbour had *accidentally* picked up the letter that had been sent and apologised for any delay in contacting the office. By now, Maxine's hands had become clammy and her heart thundered inside her chest.

She jumped when the telephone rang on the mighty desk. It was answered; a broad smile illuminated the woman's face before a brief response and explanation that she couldn't talk as she was with a client.

Am I a client? Maxine wondered. For a brief moment, she felt important.

"Sorry about that. It was my husband."

Pretty, professional and presumably happily married. A winner in life's cruel carousel. Rex had kissed that young woman's hand when she arrived at Long Acres, as if she were Maid Marian and he was bloody Robin Hood or a sodding knight at a jousting tournament. Why, oh why, hadn't Maxine paid more attention at school? And why had she wasted so much time at Long Acres?

Maxine could bear it no longer. "Can you just tell me if Rex left me anything? Please tell me it's not one of those film posters!" She regretted the outburst because she could see that the solicitor's hand flew to her mouth, presumably to conceal the suggestion of a sardonic smile, or worse, to stifle a laugh. Maxine rose to her feet. "I shouldn't have said that, I feel silly now. I'll go. Send me a letter." Remembering Penelope's pilfering of her post, she quickly corrected herself. "No, don't do that. I'd better sit down." She was mortified by her undignified performance.

The solicitor looked distressed, mirroring the expression on Maxine's face. "I didn't mean to offend," she said. "I wasn't sure how to respond. The thing is, he asked me to give you a letter in person. He wanted to tell you himself what provision he had made for you, rather than me telling you."

That was typical of Rex – controlling, even from beyond the grave.

A drawer in the mighty desk was unlocked and an envelope was produced. For a weird moment, Maxine had a curious feeling of *déjà vu*. Then she realised that she had never been in this position before but a recent drama on TV had featured such a scene. That's probably where Rex got his idea from, not being possessed of too many original thoughts. As she recalled, it didn't end well, the recipient of the envelope being poisoned with strychnine.

No point in making a fuss; she knew what was required of

her. Dignity partially restored, she reached across the desk, took the letter, thanked the solicitor, shook her hand and walked with her head held high until she emerged on to the pavement outside. Once there, she nearly doubled over as a wave of nausea took hold. She breathed in slowly and exhaled.

The occasion felt unequalled. She didn't wish to rip the letter open under the curious gaze of the receptionist, who appeared to be standing up and craning her neck to get a better view through the solicitor's window. It was hastily stowed away in the zipped pocket of her jacket. A few steps were taken and she found that she was outside the florist's shop. Olivia raised her hand to wave. Maxine responded in kind but without enthusiasm. She couldn't blame Olivia for being the beneficiary of a large legacy but it was a challenge to be polite. This also would not be the place for discovering what she had been bequeathed.

It wasn't raining. That was a mercy. Maxine was wrapped up against the cold. She would drive to the seafront and read the letter there, unwilling to risk another encounter with Penelope on the stairs.

Every step she took from the car park, towards the sand dunes, felt as if she were following in Rex's footsteps. In springtime, they would stand close together, holding their breath as they listened to the larks singing and tried to pinpoint where they were. It amazed her, how such a small brown bird, reduced to a dot in the sky, could create such a noise.

In January, the sky was slashed with varying tints of grey; the abandoned cast-iron lighthouse stood alone in an equally grey sea. Maxine had craved solitude and was pleased to find a quiet spot on the dunes, where she dangled her legs over the edge. Immersing herself in the sounds of the waves and gulls, she shut her eyes, breathing in and out slowly, to steady her nerves.

Rex's voice could not possibly have been audible. The man was dead and buried, after all. But Maxine could hear his voice so clearly that she opened her eyes with a start. *Get on with it! Open the bloody letter!*

So that is what she did.

Rex's handwriting sloped forward in confident strokes.

Long Acres,
November

Dear Maxine,

I wanted to write you a letter. I know you didn't approve of me writing to Tiffany and Olivia but it amused me to do so.

This is different. I'm not playing the part of a benevolent uncle or would-be patron. It's you I'm writing to. It turns out that you are my best friend, the only constant in my life. We should have got married. We argued enough! Shame we didn't have sex but I might have lost you if we'd fallen out. Sex does tend to complicate a relationship. By the way, I knew about the gardener and your secret trysts by the bonfire. I remember being first amused and then, to my surprise, jealous.

Sometimes you and I have talked and sometimes there was no need to speak as we sat in companionable silence. You raged against me and we quarrelled and often we just laughed. You knew me at my worst and yet you stayed. Maybe it was selfish of me to hang on to you. The truth is, I couldn't bear to let you go.

I wanted to say thank you. Thank you for putting up with me, my quixotic nature, (look it up) my temper tantrums and recurring crushes on unsuitable women. You have always been my dearest companion and soulmate.

Because I am a sentimental sort of chap, I'm shedding a tear as I write the following. I apologise that I was never able to say it in person.

I love you.

There, I've said it. And because I love you, I have made provision for you to have some money. I don't want you getting into debt because I left you penniless. I've left you ten thousand pounds.

Maxine broke off from reading. She blew her nose. He was trying to educate her, even from the grave – *Look it up!* He was so infuriating! She checked the date. November, not long before he died. And he did get to tell her that he loved her. That was something.

She looked out at the abandoned lighthouse, its top crowned by what looked like an empty birdcage, its outline blurred, glimpsed through tears. How relieved she was to have tangible proof that she had meant something to him, not that she would ever let anyone else see the letter. It made perfect sense that Rex had insisted on telling her any news himself – it was a typically theatrical flourish. It wasn't so much that he was controlling, more like he wanted to direct the unfolding scene.

It would be silly to pretend that it didn't matter that she had been left something in the Will. The money would tide her over until she got further employment. What a relief. She continued reading.

Look after yourself, my dear.

Your friend, Rex.

PS I've left you Long Acres too. You might get a bank loan and run it as a bed and breakfast, perhaps, but if you don't fancy rattling around in the house on your own, then sell it. And for goodness' sake, spend the money, all of it.

Epilogue

April, two years later

Long Acres had been bought and renovated. Stephen Samson had put in the highest bid, but Maxine had rejected his offer simply because she knew that Rex Glyn didn't want to sell the house to him. She had bought a brand-new property for herself on an estate built on the site of the original rugby ground in the town. Maxine sold Long Acres to the next highest bidders, Paul Ransome and Grace Palmer.

The Ransome-Palmer household had settled in; Sarah was studying part-time, following a computer science course and was surprised to find that she enjoyed working for the family firm, proud to call herself the "third generation estate agent". She was only occasionally wistful about losing Stephen to a woman he met online called Tiffany, who hailed from Tenby. He had been attracted to her profile, standing in front of Rex Glyn's poster and an explanation that she was related to the famous actor. She was taken with the description that he was *a successful property developer and hotelier.*

The only lasting sadness was that Wesley had taken his last faltering steps on the grass at the back of the house. He had been buried behind the swing seat, near the orchard, and afforded more reverence than many a poor human soul.

One morning in spring, as the azaleas unfurled to reveal orange and purple and pink, a blonde, chubby infant tottered across the lawn that stretched out towards the sea. She was wearing a red pinafore dress and giggling at the joy of running barefoot. Behind her, Grace Palmer followed, ready to catch her if she fell.